WHAT
WILD
WOMEN
DO

WHAT WILD WOMEN DO

A NOVEL

KARMA BROWN

VIKING

VIKING
an imprint of Penguin Canada,
a division of Penguin Random House Canada Limited

Canada • USA • UK • Ireland • Australia •
New Zealand • India • South Africa • China

Published in Viking paperback by Penguin Canada, 2023
Simultaneously published in the United States by Dutton,
an imprint of Penguin Random House LLC

www.penguinrandomhouse.ca

*Publisher's note: This book is a work of fiction. Names, characters, places and incidents
either are the product of the author's imagination or are used fictitiously, and any
resemblance to actual persons living or dead, events, or locales is entirely coincidental.*

LIBRARY AND ARCHIVES CANADA CATALOGUING IN PUBLICATION

Title: What wild women do : a novel / Karma Brown.
Names: Brown, Karma, author.
Identifiers: Canadiana (print) 20230145086 | Canadiana (ebook) 20230145116 |
ISBN 9780735236264 (softcover) | ISBN 9780735236271 (EPUB)
Classification: LCC PS8603.R68435 W53 2023 | DDC C813/.6—dc23

Book design by Ashley Tucker
Title page photograph © adehoidar / Shutterstock
Cover design by Brianna Da Costa
Cover images: (woman) © Mattia / Stocksy; (texture) © scottsweb / Unsplash

Printed in Canada

10 9 8 7 6 5 4 3 2 1

Penguin
Random House
VIKING CANADA

To Judy and Bob (Mom and Dad), for gifting me, amongst many other wonderful things, a free-range, wilderness-filled childhood. Thanks to you, I learned to explore inside and out. I am a "wild woman" because of you.

AUTHOR CIRCA 1978

When women's lives are in stasis, or filled with ennui,
it is always time for the wildish woman to emerge . . .

—Clarissa Pinkola Estés, *Women Who Run with the Wolves:
Myths and Stories of the Wild Woman Archetype*

ROWAN, 2021.

WE CAME TO THE WOODS CARRYING BOTH types of secrets: some self-protective and potentially destructive, others magnificent and transformative. Only time would tell what happened when those secrets were released, and what became of us afterward.

The price we pay for an external life not matching an internal one is steep, and for that lack of honesty there are consequences—though often they aren't felt until later, and sometimes only after it's too late to change anything.

It's fair to say things didn't turn out how we hoped; none of us is immune to catastrophe.

However, there can be great beauty in what's left behind, if you're willing to riffle through the shards.

MARCH.

I T'S PRETTY SMALL," I SAY, BEFORE WHISPER-
ing, "What *is* that smell?"

Seth takes a dramatic sniff of the air. "Eau de boiled broccoli and something pine-like? Are you getting the same notes?"

I pull back the bedroom window drapes and look into a parking lot.

"I miss California. And the ocean," I say. And I do—enough that it's almost a physical pain. Wrapping my arms around my-self, I hold on tight. Try to keep it together, because there are far worse things than having to move back home and put your plans on hold.

"There are worse things, Rowan," I whisper, tracing the frost patterns on the windowpane.

"What's that?" Seth asks. He's on the other side of the bed-room, opening the side table drawer, being nosy.

I shake my head. "I think it's cabbage."

When Seth gives me a confused look, I add, "The smell. It's cooked cabbage."

It's still cold here, and a recent light dusting of snow has left patches of white on the black asphalt of the complex's parking lot. Our old place in LA didn't exactly have a stellar view—it was mostly other buildings and side streets—but if you pressed yourself in just the right way against the wall and looked to the far right, you could catch a blue sliver of water. Technically it *was* an ocean view.

Seth sits on the bed, bouncing a few times, and waggles his eyebrows at me as the mattress squeaks and the headboard hits the wall behind it. "Plenty of give. This could be fun, right?"

"I wonder how many other people have had 'fun' on that bed?"

"Good point," Seth says. "Probably want to get a new mattress." But we won't, because we can't afford it.

He comes behind me and wraps an arm around my waist. With his other hand he points out the window at a small cluster of trees edging the parking lot. "At least we have a hint of nature?"

I lean my head against his chest and hold back tears.

"Hey, hey," Seth says, turning me toward him and tucking a finger under my chin. He kisses the tip of my nose. "This is *temporary*. A few months. Tops."

I nod. "Temporary. I know."

Seth pulls the drapes back farther, letting a wider swath of sunlight into the room. "And the light in here is good. Great, actually." He grins at me. "That'll make filming easier."

I tense, as filming is the last thing I want to think about right now.

"True," I reply quietly. Without enthusiasm. But he doesn't seem to notice—has conveniently never noticed, or at least paid much attention to, my animosity toward his burgeoning YouTube channel, which has occupied much of his time and focus of late. Or maybe it's that I haven't explicitly told him how I feel, so he's innocently clueless versus purposefully ignorant. Either way, it's a sore spot between us, at least from my perspective.

SETH WRIGHT AND I met in 2017 in LA (he was doing his MFA; I was finishing film school), and we moved in together after our third date, which remains one of the most spontaneous things I have ever done. While I eschew the love-at-first-sight trope, it's hard for me to explain what happened with Seth any other way.

We met at a party hosted by one of my classmates, Tate Alton, whose mother was a moderately famous actor and had a stunner of a beach house. Tate introduced us, and as I shook Seth's hand, I looked into his dark eyes, framed by the most incredible lashes I had ever seen, and my world flipped upside down. We drank too much sangria and sat on the beach in the dark, alternating between making out and testing each other on ridiculous feats of strength and endurance, like who could hold the longest handstand (me) and who could skip a rock the farthest into the ocean (Seth, though we really couldn't see well enough to be sure). Our second date was more traditional, with dinner at a restaurant and then a long beach walk where I held Seth's hand in one of mine and my sandals in the other. He was bright and refreshing—different from the other guys I'd met in LA—like a big squeeze of lemon juice in a glass of water.

I was already smitten, but when he invited me to an escape room for our third date, all the clues leading to a key to his apartment and an earnest love letter written by hand, I couldn't imagine saying anything other than "yes" to his offer of moving in. Sure, my lease was up and it made good financial sense to have a roommate, but it was much simpler than any of that: I was head over heels in love.

Times weren't easy for two creatives without secure jobs, but we hustled and limped along all right until the pandemic hit. Then I lost my server job and Seth his personal trainer one, and sooner than either of us expected we ran out of money and prospects. With Hollywood shut down and no one looking at scripts—particularly from a writer with zero credits—I could no longer borrow against hope. Going "home" to Ann Arbor, where I grew up, seemed the best (or only) option.

Despite the setback, we promised to continue chasing our dreams—me with my screenplay, Seth with his novel. But since leaving LA a few weeks ago, I've been stagnant, while Seth's motivation has grown . . . just not for his manuscript, which remains unopened. He's become single-minded about his nearly two-year-old YouTube channel, TheWrightStory, which started as a place to capture the daily struggles of an author trying to write the next great American novel. He read some article about how much money could be made on YouTube and became fixated on this solving our pandemic-induced financial woes.

Initially, I didn't mind his shift in focus from author to YouTube content creator. I even did the odd video with him because, as he maintained, I *was* a big part of his story. Plus, between the grinding hustle to pay our bills and his frustrations with his unfinished book, it was nice to see him enthusiastic and excited about something again. No one was in a "good" mood in those days, as the pandemic raged on and life felt like one struggle after another, but Seth was particularly darkminded. I'd call it more of a deep apathy than a depression, but it scared the hell out of me. My carefree, creative, and ambitious boyfriend—who had golden-retriever-level positivity—became sullen and disconnected. At least until TheWrightStory took hold of him.

I personally didn't get the appeal, either for creators or their audiences, but figured it was merely a happy distraction for Seth. A hobby until he got his feet back under him. I was wrong.

As his growing number of subscribers asked for more couple-themed content, and our videos together performed better than his alone, I was soon participating in near-daily videos. We did day-in-the-life shoots of our morning routine (curated, naturally)—journaling and stretching, followed by a breakfast of matcha lattes and poached eggs, all before nine a.m. and the start of the "workday." There were craft-related videos, with Seth showing off his color-coded manuscript system (embellished, as he only ever used yellow tabs, and even then not consistently), and me sharing tips for a screenplay's three-act structure.

Sometimes we'd take the camera with us to the grocery store (the grocery store!) for a healthy-dinner video, or to the park to show how a bench and some monkey bars are all you need for a great workout. And very occasionally there would be a prank video, the most ridiculous trend, in my view. Like on Thanksgiving, while carving the giant turkey I'd bought with our bloated credit card, Seth pretended to slice open his hand on camera. I ran into the room at the gruesome sight of fake blood everywhere and a wailing Seth, and played the part of panicked girlfriend to a tee . . . despite the fact that the entire thing was scripted for viewers' enjoyment.

So while I don't fully understand YouTube's allure for Seth after he worked his ass off for his MFA, it turns out he wasn't wrong: The channel *did* get traction, and it started to replenish our bank account. In a sea of content, TheWrightStory found a loyal audience, perhaps more quickly than he might have under different circumstances, as many were housebound and bored. Seth became effervescent and cheerful again. Much-coveted advertising revenue became more of a stream than a trickle, though still not enough to fully support us. When the channel breezed past 100,000 subscribers after its first six months, Seth put his novel aside "temporarily" to focus on the goal of acquiring 500,000 subscribers by year-end.

"Think of the money we'll be able to generate, Rowan. It will be worth it. I promise."

I wanted to believe him. I chose to believe in him.

In the end, even with nearly 600,000 subscribers, our mountain of debt won, and though we left our futon and single house plant behind, YouTube came with us to Ann Arbor.

SETH TUGS ME away from the window and pushes me gently onto the bed, crawling on top of me. I laugh and half-heartedly push him away.

"Seth! Diane is, like, *right outside,*" I hiss as he bounces us on the bed, the springs squeaking loudly.

"Diane did tell us to take our time. Get a 'feel' for the place before we commit." Seth nuzzles into my neck just as there's a knock on the bedroom door.

Realtor Diane—my parents' friend, and so doing them (and me) a favor—opens the bedroom door. She looks the part—a navy skirt and blazer, crisp white shirt underneath, with a folder in her French-manicured hands and a bright smile on her face—and is somewhere between the ages of forty and sixty. She's effortlessly professional. Confident. I want to ask if she loves her work, if this is her "dream" career.

Diane is unfazed finding us in such a position. "So? What do you think?" she asks, glancing around the bedroom with its "great light" and squeaky queen bed, with two small nightstands that look like they've been put together with an Allen key, and a cheaply framed print of Gustav Klimt's *The Kiss* above the headboard. Everything feels muted and dated, but it's within our budget and offers month-to-month rental terms. My parents offered for us stay with them, but that would have kicked the last shred of fighting spirit out of me.

Seth gives me a questioning look, and I nod.

"We'll take it," he says.

"Fantastic," Diane replies. "I'll get my office to start the paperwork." She puts her hand on the doorknob, then turns back to us. "And I'll give you two a minute. No rush."

"Thanks, Diane!" Seth shouts out, to the now-closed bedroom door. He kisses me deeply.

"Just a few months, until we can get back on our feet. It's going to be okay, Rowan."

"And if it's not, and I have to live in the same city as my parents, in an apartment that smells like boiled cabbage until the day I die, at least we'll be together, right?"

Seth nods, gently sweeping a stray hair from my cheek before kissing it. "Always."

I wrap my arms around his neck and pull him tighter to me. It's hard to breathe with him on top of me, but I don't care. I used to say I wanted to unzip his chest and crawl inside to be as close to him as possible. I don't say it out loud now, but I feel it nonetheless.

APRIL.

"YOUR DAD AND I NEED YOUR LIST, HONEY."

"Mom, I already told you. I don't need anything." I know my parents will likely slip money into a card, for something "extra" like they always do, no matter what I put on a birthday list.

Tomorrow is my thirtieth, and while everyone keeps trying to make it a big deal, my main wish is for it to pass quietly. I'm dreading it, actually. Because this is the birthday for having either representation for my work, or my script in the hands of someone who has the ability to change my life. And here I am, on my last day of being twenty-nine, no closer than I was when I set the goal two years ago.

I agreed to a dinner at a local Italian restaurant with my parents and sisters—who are married, with two children each—but that's it as far as celebrations go. My sisters and I aren't particularly close, the way it sometimes happens when you're the baby of the family and there's a stretch of five years between you and your next oldest sibling (Rachel). Eight between me and the eldest (Lily). When Lily left for college, I hadn't even hit puberty. Knobby knees and a flat chest and still putting lost teeth under my pillow for my parents to play the tooth fairy, even though I knew by then it was a hoax.

My mom sighs, and I hear my dad shout out, "If she doesn't tell us what she wants, I'll just have to wear the T-shirt to dinner."

Despite my melancholy, I laugh. It's one of my family's running jokes, the T-shirt that started a birthday trend. When Lily turned thirteen, she told my parents in no uncertain terms that they were not welcome at her sleepover party . . . which was taking place at our house. When it was time for cake, my dad unzipped his sweater and revealed a T-shirt underneath that read "Lily's Dad & Best Friend" in purple-glitter block letters on the front. He made Lily take photos with him in front of the cake, her friends giggling and clearly grateful this wasn't their party, or their dad. Lily never demanded my parents disappear again, nor did Rachel or I when our birthday parties came around. My dad also had shirts made with my name and Rachel's, and on every birthday celebrated since he has pulled out the appropriately named shirt for pictures.

"Tell him the T-shirt is the only gift I need," I say.

THE NEXT MORNING there's a breakfast tray with a gorgeous bouquet of tulips beside me, thanks to Seth, who usually sleeps later than me but must have set an alarm. He's lying next to me fully dressed, a grin on his face. Seth already celebrated this milestone birthday eight months ago, when we still lived in LA. Before reality set in that we had no choice but to leave.

Seth gives me a quick kiss, which is awkward because I'm in the middle of yawning, then jumps up to turn on one of the ring lights beside the bed. He takes the video camera from the side table.

"Just a quick birthday vid, okay, babe?" he says, seeing the look on my face.

I glance at the beautiful breakfast and tulips, and sigh.

"I literally just woke up." I run my hands over my hair, taming the strands that have come loose from my messy bun. "Can we do this later? It is *my* birthday after all."

"This is just for us. Promise. And you look beautiful," Seth replies, turning the camera on. Once he's certain it's recording, he starts singing "Happy Birthday"—softly, sweetly—and I think maybe today won't be so bad, after all. I smile for the camera, hoping he means it when he says this video won't become content.

BY 5:05 P.M. we still haven't left for the restaurant—Seth is mucking about with one of the videos he recorded earlier in the week—and I'm agitated and impatient. Dinner with my family is always early (our reservation is for five p.m.) and always punctual, because of the kids—my nephews—who are on quite strict meal schedules. My sisters and I were raised with less structure, especially around dinnertime, as our parents taxied us to our dance lessons and soccer games and art classes, necessitating what my mom called "car picnics": peanut butter, banana, and honey sandwiches wrapped in waxed paper and sliced apples sprinkled with cinnamon, eaten on our laps. But times have changed. These days families, at least my sisters', seem only to run efficiently thanks to elaborate spreadsheets.

Seth and I are having a mild argument about punctuality—in hushed tones—as we walk into the restaurant, and so even as the chorus of "Surprise!" rings out, the reality of what's happening doesn't immediately register. The restaurant is packed with my family—my dad in my birthday T-shirt, of course—but also with a half dozen or so friends who still live in Ann Arbor. Seth is beaming, and has the camera ready to catch my reaction.

"Oh my . . . What did you do?" I turn to him, smiling even though inside I'm dying.

Seth leads me to the table in the middle of the room, where he has me sit in a chair with a ridiculous number of golden-hued "Happy Birthday!" balloons tied to it. He then asks for everyone to be quiet for a moment and hands the camera to my sister Rachel.

"Happy birthday, babe." He leans in to kiss me, and I kiss him back. I'm waiting for whatever's next. A boisterous round of "Happy Birthday!" Maybe a short and moving speech (Seth is a fan of poignant speeches) or a wrapped gift in my lap. But then Seth drops to one knee and my mind goes blank. He has a small box nestled in his hand. There's a collective gasp in the room, and I realize this is as much a surprise to the guests as it is to me.

Sure, Seth and I have discussed marriage, and it's something I've always imagined in our future. But seeing him on one knee makes my hands and feet tingle with the shock. I'm also suddenly, severely light-headed.

"You are the best thing that has ever happened to me. I am in awe of you. Your commitment, your determination, your *fucking unbelievable talent*." Laughter ripples through the rapt crowd. I hear a cork pop, and see waitstaff pouring champagne for the upcoming toast. For a moment I worry about how much this is costing, but then I force my eyes back to Seth.

"I'm so proud of you, Rowan, and everything you've already accomplished. And I can't wait for what's to come. I even have a tracksuit in the back of our closet—it says 'Rowan's Husband' on the back. I had it custom made"—more chuckling around the room—"so I'm ready for my retirement when one of your films hits the screen."

The room fills with cheers, a "Right on!" from my dad, and the pop-pop-pop of champagne corks. I tear up and reach for Seth, and he grasps my hand.

His voice softens then, and he, too, has tears in his eyes. "You, Rowan Claire Fairfax, are amazing, and I can't wait to be a part of your forever, babe. Partners for life, right? So, now I have an important question for you . . ."

I hold my breath as Seth opens the box, revealing a beautiful solitaire inside deep blue satin. I no longer see the champagne flutes ready to be passed out to the guests. Or my parents to my left, my mom with one hand on her cane and my dad with his arm tight around her shoulders, wiping at his eyes. I barely notice the video camera zooming in on our faces.

I only see Seth.

"Rowan, my partner in crime and love of my life, will you marry me?"

Yes.

MAY.

I TAKE MY HAND OUT OF SETH'S AND RING THE
doorbell of my childhood home. He chuckles. "Why can't
we ever just go in? This used to be your house, too."

"Because my mother believes in decorum," I reply. "Same
reason I'm in a dress for dinner."

The door soon opens, and there stands my mother, dressed
impeccably in a crisp, unwrinkled cream linen tunic, acces-
sorized with a gold-bead necklace. She sets her cane against
the wall and reaches out to hug us—me first, then Seth.

When I was a child, my mom was the more carefree one of
my parents, always ready for an adventure, seemingly afraid of
nothing. As a conference event manager, she often traveled
and on occasion would take us with her. Wherever we went,
she would find us some touristy and often thrill-seeking thing
to try: whale watching in Seattle; dinner at the CN Tower's ro-
tating restaurant in Toronto; zip-lining in Whistler; visiting a
dude ranch in Colorado; a crack-of-dawn bike ride down the

Haleakala volcano in Maui. Her linen clothes were full of wrinkles back then.

But after our accident when I was sixteen—which left me with a long scar on my forearm, but took Mom's right leg below the knee—she left her career and went through a middle-aged metamorphosis that brought with it an unfamiliar cautiousness. I still haven't fully warmed to this new version of my mother, even though it has been years.

"Come in, kids. Right on time." My mom picks up her cane and moves to the side. Seth hands her the wine.

"Thank you!" she says. "Here are your house shoes. Then come to the kitchen. Your dad is puttering away in there."

Seth and I switch our street shoes for the "house shoes" (slippers), even though it's too warm now for woolen slippers.

"Smells great, Lauren." Despite the formality of Sunday night dinner and her wrinkle-free linen, my mom still likes to be called by her first name.

"Oh, I can't take the credit, Seth. It's John's famous garlic-roasted chicken."

"*Again*," I whisper to Seth as we walk toward the kitchen.

He whispers back, "I like your dad's chicken."

"Let's see how you feel in another five years."

Seth hides his laugh behind his hand, clearing his throat. We walk into the kitchen, which is bright and spacious, a big island in its center where my two older sisters and I used to eat most of our meals. My dad stands by the stove, stirring something that simmers inside the stainless steel pot, steam rising in swirls. He was an epidemiologist, working for the public health department up until four years ago—fortuitous timing. During the pandemic he was at home applying his scientific knowledge and precision to concocting the "perfect" chicken gravy versus being in the lab.

"Look, John, the kids brought us a lovely bottle of wine." My mom sets it on the countertop beside six identical bottles.

"Hi, Dad." I give him a side hug, and he kisses me atop the head like I'm ten instead of thirty. "Smells great." A heady combination of sweet roasted garlic and the mouthwatering scent of browned butter fills my nose.

"Thanks, sweetie. Hiya, Seth. Hope you're both hungry?"

"Always!" Seth says. The man is a bottomless pit.

I realize then how quiet it is, that it's just the four of us. "Where are Lil and Rach?" I check my watch. We're five minutes early, and my sisters are usually here before us. I prefer it that way—I like walking into a full, busy house. It means less time being peppered with questions about what's "new" in my life, in the past week. I also adore my nephews, who are boisterous and loud and always make Sunday family dinners more entertaining.

"Rachel's whole crew is down with fevers," Mom says, "and Lily and Jason and the kids are visiting the other grandparents this weekend." Right. Lily had mentioned that last week.

"It's just the four of us tonight," Dad says cheerfully.

THIRTY MINUTES LATER Dad refills my wineglass, then asks, "So, how was work today, honey?"

"Good," I reply. My parents are not fans of one-word answers (when I was a child, an answer like that would have elicited a "Good in what way, Rowan?" response), but today my dad simply says, "Glad to hear it."

"That reminds me," my mom says. "June Davidson's daughter just got engaged. Sloan Davidson, remember her?" She turns to Seth, sitting at the end of the table to her right. "Rowan used to babysit Sloan."

"Isn't she, like, barely twenty?" I ask.

"She's twenty-two. Marrying some sort of professional athlete. Baseball, I think."

"Hockey," Dad says, holding up his knife like a composer's baton.

My mom waves away the correction. "Anyway, June's quite excited about it all. You know how she loves her pomp and circumstance."

I nod, wiping the garlic-mushroom-butter sauce up with a hunk of baguette. I know precisely where this is going.

"I offered your services. To do her engagement photos." Mom looks delighted with herself, enthusiastically tapping her nails against her wineglass.

"Mom, I'm, uh, pretty slammed right now. I can't really work for free."

"*Obviously* she'll pay you, Rowan." She frowns slightly. "I thought you'd be happy?"

My dad glances between us, then wipes his mouth with his napkin and clears his throat. He prefers controlled environments, and that extends to our family dynamics as well. Dad is a skilled peacekeeper—he's a pro at changing the subject. "How's the novel coming along, Seth?"

"Slow, but I can't complain." Seth is writing a dystopian man-against-the-elements novel, inspired by his all-time favorite tome, *The Road*. It's set in the isolation of the woods after a virus wipes out most of civilization. I'm not entirely convinced that this is what people want to read these days, but Seth tells me I'm overthinking things.

Seth is cagey about his writing (he won't let me read even one page of the manuscript), but as a fellow creative, I understand his hesitation. Sometimes you have to keep an idea close to your chest for a time, because it's like a crystal water glass—perfectly transparent and pristine, until someone picks it up, leaving layers of grimy fingerprints behind.

"I'm sure it's fantastic," my dad replies, now smiling at Seth. My dad holds great belief in others' abilities, even when they don't see it in themselves. I know later, over coffee, he'll invite Seth to the living room to offer further words of encouragement, including his favorite saying, "The tallest oak in the forest was once just a little nut that held its ground," while Mom and I clean up dinner. My mom offers encouragement as well, just in a different way. She believes in having a plan and harnessing the power of forward momentum.

"By the way, Seth, any interest in teaching a writing class this summer?" Mom asks. Her best friend runs the summer programs at the University of Michigan.

Seth glances my way. "Oh, thanks, Lauren. I . . . uh . . ."

"Mom, I told you Seth and I already have plans," I finish for him. "We'll be in the Adirondacks end of July. We rented a cabin for a month, remember?" It's the least expensive rental we could find on Airbnb, but it's still more than I'd hoped to spend.

I've been staunchly supportive, if not gently pushy (isn't that what a good partner does?), these past few months about Seth finding time to finish his novel. He's talented, though he suffers from the affliction of believing he can only write when the muse is present. From my own screenwriting I understand that creativity doesn't always show up on schedule; you have to make space for it. So when Seth said he needed to "get lost in the woods" for his novel research, I latched on. Suggested the Adirondacks, because of its mountainous, wild setting, and relative affordability. While Seth wrote, I'd use the time to work on my next script idea.

"Yes, I remember." Mom sips her wine. "But I don't see why

you can't do all that from here? Plus, it's such a long drive. Didn't you say your car needed a new muffler? How will you pay for that if you're both not working?"

I clench my fists into my napkin on my lap, then quickly relax them. While I understand what underpins her comment (worry, not only about the money but also about my well-being), I'm frustrated by her needling. However, she's not wrong. How *can* we afford to rent a vacation property for a month? My fingers clench again, as I think about our near-empty bank account.

My sisters never come to my parents with empty pockets. Rachel's a physiotherapist, Lily works in finance, and their significant others are both gainfully employed—Rachel's husband, Steve, is a lawyer, and Jason, Lily's partner, runs a printing business. They both moved effortlessly from one stage of life to the next, doing things in order, on a respectable timeline. I want to remind my mom about the struggles of creative work. Its meandering, muddled path to success . . . if you can even find it. A conversation I've tried to have before.

But all I say is "Yes, we need a new muffler."

I BALANCE TWO large Tupperware containers on my lap as I reach for my seat belt, latching it with some difficulty. I sigh.

"What's up?" Seth asks.

I open the lid of the top container, pulling out a plastic baggie, which is slick with grease. Inside is a stack of twenty-dollar bills. The smell of garlic wafts out, quickly filling the car, and I feel queasy.

"It's like they think I can't take care of myself." Despite the tinge of irritation in my tone, I am quietly relieved to see the money, which I suspected would be there because that's what happened last week, and the week before that. My dad has been surreptitiously giving me money for years. When I was in film school, a hundred dollars would arrive every couple of weeks, nestled into a greeting card—I don't think Mom knew, as she would not approve of sending cash in the mail—and the baggie of cash tucked in Sunday leftovers seems to be his new routine.

Seth barely glances at the baggie before starting the car. The muffler is impossibly, embarrassingly loud. He pulls out into road a little more quickly than is necessary. The only light in the car comes from the passing streetlamps of my parents' suburban neighborhood. Seth keeps his eyes on the road.

"You're lucky to have them. *I'm* lucky to have them. We don't all have parents who give a shit, Rowan," he says.

Growing up, I wanted for next to nothing; Seth, in his own words, "wanted for almost everything." Raised by his mom, he never met his father because the elder Wright died when Seth was a baby. He and his mom lived in a small apartment over a garage that belonged to the elderly couple his mother provided in-home nursing care to. He rarely brought up his childhood, though when he saw my parents' home for the first time, he said that his entire apartment could have fit into my bedroom. I said he had to be joking; he assured me he was not.

A latchkey kid, Seth often made his own dinner and ate it alone. One of things he loves most about my family, he says, is how loud things get at the dinner table when everyone is home. And it's true—with my two sisters, their families, my parents, and a juicy topic for discussion, at times you can barely hear yourself think. I will never fully comprehend what Seth's childhood was like, but he's shared enough that I know my complaining about my parents lovingly trying to help us get a new muffler is downright thoughtless.

I shift closer to him, straining my seat belt, and rest my head on his shoulder. "I'm sorry."

He kisses the side of my head. "I don't love taking handouts either, babe. But the truth is . . . we need their help right now. And they're happy and able to give it."

The muffler backfires, as though reinforcing that we're in no position to turn down generous offerings.

JUNE.

G UYS, I *LOOOOVE* YOU. *ALL OF YOU.* LIKE, I
don't know any of you, but still . . . *I love you s'much!*"
I laugh. Harder than is called for, and for far too
long. I'm mortified by how sloppy I am when I watch it back
later. My head rolling into my hand as I try to hold it upright. I
point into the laptop's camera lens, adding, "Yes, *even you.*
Looove you the *most.*"

I tip back my glass of tequila—my fifth or sixth, I've lost
count (it was supposed to be one, to accompany my writing,
which I seem to only find time for late in the evening due to
the photography gigs occupying most daylight hours)—and ask
viewers to hold on. I need a top-up and then will be "right back"
to tell them the secret I came on here to share. Off camera
there's banging and clanging as I refill my glass, finally swaying
back to my chair and the laptop. I'm not sure how Seth doesn't
wake up, because I'm recording at our tiny kitchen table, and
he's asleep a few feet away in the bedroom. But he has always
been a heavy sleeper.

Sitting down clumsily, I nearly topple off one side of the

chair but catch myself on the table's edge. I take a large gulp of the clear alcohol—I'm unaffected by the taste at this point, guzzling it as though it's water—and lean heavily onto my elbows so my face is mere inches from the screen. My eyelids droop heavily and my lips glisten wet. My face looks fuzzy on the screen, but I don't know if it's my boozy brain or the camera trying to focus.

Before I sat down and started this spontaneous live broadcast, TheWrightStory had 700,000 subscribers. How it had grown to that, I couldn't tell you. Nothing we posted was terribly interesting, most of it the trendy and (in my view) tiresome content that was somehow still eagerly and voraciously consumed by viewers.

To be fair, Seth *is* terrific on camera—vibrant, warm, funny, endearing—and viewers respond to that, along with his obvious passion for and commitment to content creation. Sometimes, admittedly, I feel jealous, as it can feel like he saves this best version of himself for the channel. It's hard to put my finger on exactly how he's different when it's just the two of us these days, post–leaving LA, and I can only explain it like this: Seth, for an audience (even one he can't see), is like a blazing sun on a bluebird-sky day; off camera, things are a touch cloudier, dimming the sun's rays.

"Okay, so because I love you—yes, even you, and you, and you, all the millions of you!" I slur into the camera, but not so badly you can't understand my words . . . unfortunately.

"I have to tell you a secret." I put a finger to my lips and make a shushing noise, but I'm too wasted to be exact and my finger lands at the corner of my mouth. My blinks grow longer. Closing my eyes for a few moments, I raise the glass for one more sip, then wipe my arm across my mouth and open my eyes.

"Listen up, my friends . . . It's all fake. All of it!" I gesture with my arms, as though waving away a swarm of pesky bugs from the air in front of me. "Everything we do here. Every video we put up. Every prank. Every argument. *Everything.*" I point into the camera again, punching my finger to reinforce each time I repeat, "Fake. Fake. Fake. Fake. Fake. And I am *over* it. I quit.

"Oh, also?" I hold up my left hand and point to my engagement ring. The diamond Seth told me came from his grandmother's ring sparkles with the illumination from the nearby tripod light. "*Fake.*"

This is unfair—actually downright cruel and untrue—because the diamond isn't fake, nor is Seth's love for me or our desire to be married. But there is a part of me that can't escape the truth that Seth's proposal plan made for great content for the channel—uploaded only a few hours after we got home from the restaurant—and that it probably wasn't a happy coincidence. Recently I've begun to resent having my life mined for YouTube content, even though, from Seth's perspective, I have been a mostly willing participant. Why would he think otherwise?

For ten more minutes I blabber on, about how Seth and I have been faking out our viewers most of the past year, just like every other YouTube couple out there (stupidly, I even name names). How even spontaneous-looking events we filmed were well orchestrated.

"Why else would he ask to redo the post-proposal kiss I gave him, because he didn't think we caught the 'best'"—I attempt to make air quotes, but my fingers move at different times, which diminishes the effect—"angle for the channel and for you guys, our subscribers?"

I laughed when he asked because I thought he was joking. He wasn't. So Rachel reshot the moment—our guests good-naturedly sipped their champagne and played along, either well aware of our channel or simply indulging the birthday girl's request. I quietly endured three more takes until Seth had the shot he wanted; then we filmed the thumbnail for the video, all the while I tried not to let it tarnish what was supposed to be one of the most exciting moments of my life.

"So that's it," I say now. I sit back, pump my arms up in a celebratory way once, twice, three times. All my movements are uncoordinated; I'm a mess. "Wow, that felt *ah-mazing!*"

I am buoyed by my truth-telling. Feeling lighter, yet oddly more anchored at the same time, I tip back the remnants in my glass.

"Nighty-night," I add, before waving with both hands (the way one does to small children through a window, animated and cutesy). Then I stumble to bed and fall into a dreamless, drunken sleep while the live recording continues, capturing nothing more than an empty chair in a dark room.

THE NEXT MORNING I feel as awful as I ever have. Furry tongue, pounding head, acid from my stomach ready to breach my throat. At first I think I'm sick, but then I remember the tequila.

It's still early, the room so dark I can't make out much. I shimmy my body toward Seth, but his side of the bed is empty.

"Seth?" My voice cracks. There's no answer.

A faint sliver of light bleeds into the dark from under the closed bedroom door. The white noise of voices not loud enough to form recognizable words comes from somewhere beyond. I rise gingerly, taking the bed's quilt with me to wrap it around myself. The living room is mostly dark except for the brightness of Seth's laptop screen. He's seated at the kitchen table in front of his computer, his back to me. I'm about to ask what time it is when I hear a voice I recognize. My own.

"Everything we do here. Every video . . ." My voice emanates from Seth's laptop. Stepping closer, I see my face, which keeps moving in and out of focus because of my on-camera swaying. My stomach drops; the tequila rises.

"Fake. Fake. Fake. Fake. Fake . . ." I watch myself gesticulate into the camera with my pointer finger, enumerating each "fake."

"Oh my god," I whisper, realization dawning as I listen to myself rant. I want to spread my hands over the screen. Or put my fingers into Seth's ears. To block him from hearing and seeing any more.

Seth, his back still to me, doesn't turn around. He slowly closes the laptop's lid, setting his hand on its top. "Five hundred thousand views already," he says. He lets out a laugh, but I hear the irony in it. "That's the most we've ever had, I think. On one video, anyway."

"Seth, I didn't . . ." I stop. The quilt drops. I press my fingers deep into my temples. "I'm sorry. I was drunk. I've been . . . frustrated."

"You're '*frustrated*'?" Seth shakes his head, then gets up from the chair. He's much taller than me, and I'm lost in his shadow. "We just bled out hundreds of subscribers, Rowan. Like, *thousands* actually."

I look away. Twirl my ring around a few times, at a loss for how to properly apologize for this.

"But you know the worst part? You calling that 'fake.'" He points to my ring, and even in the dimness I see how much I've hurt him. "Is that really how little you think of me?" He doesn't give me a chance to answer. "Don't you see how this channel is connected to our future, Rowan? We can make good money—really good money. And after the past few years, don't you want life to just be fucking easier?"

I nod. Easier sounds spectacular.

"So, why would you try to sabotage that? Sabotage *us*?"

"I am so sorry. Seth, I . . . I didn't mean any—" I clap a hand over my mouth, barely making it to the washroom before I'm violently ill. The guilt is as sickening as the tequila, none of it leaving me fast enough even as I retch over and over.

Seth stays in the living room, which I suppose I deserve.

"IT'S A MEANS to an end, babe." Seth sits on the washroom's vinyl countertop, watching as I delicately sip from the glass of water he's brought me. I've been sitting in front of the toilet for twenty minutes; he joined me about five minutes ago, in time to rub my back and hold my hair while I was sick for a second time. He doesn't seem angry anymore, just disappointed—which is worse.

"We can still do this and win filmmaking awards and hit bestseller lists, okay? Our success can be multifaceted. *It will be*. You just need a bit more faith."

I apologize profusely. Explain weakly that I've been upset and impatient waiting for feedback on my most recently pitched script—the one I've pinned all my hopes on, which is foolish, I know. "Always be writing" was the most consistent advice I got in film school. That and "You're only as good as your last sold script." I can only assume both statements are true, not having sold a script yet. But between handling the logistics of my event photography (the driving, the setups, the editing, the screwups—like the time the balloons released the wrong color for the gender reveal and everything had to be reshot) and filming content for TheWrightStory, I feel creatively empty most days. Writing has taken a back seat to life, and I can't see how to remedy it. So I uncharacteristically drank too much in an attempt to blur the sharp edges of my disappointment, even if for just one day. Things clearly got out of hand. *Forgive me?*

It's all true, but not the whole truth. Which is this: Along with the time pressures of my current hustle, I can't erase the disquieting feeling that being a "YouTuber"—even a half-committed one—is obliterating my creative instincts, and will ultimately diminish my skills as a writer. "Use it or lose it," my dad likes to say about nearly everything, from our brains to a container of soon-to-be expired yogurt in the fridge.

I'm not as driven by the potential income as Seth is, so there's even less upside for me. Part of my confessional video was likely an unconscious attempt to blow the whole thing up, so I no longer felt at odds with my ambitions. However, when you love someone—and I love Seth, wholeheartedly—you make concessions for their needs, too. Coming back to Ann Arbor was my idea, and while Seth believed we could tough it out in LA (he wanted us to ask my parents for a loan, which I refused to do), he pivoted effortlessly, never once complaining. I need to remember that.

"We are a team," he reminds me now. "And teams succeed together or fail apart."

I smile weakly, wondering if he picked this gem up from my dad. Then I promise I'll post another video, taking back all my accusations.

So that's what we do later in the day. My face puffy and pale, which I do not fix with makeup; Seth sitting beside me rubbing my back and looking grim. Casting me concerned glances as I explain everything to our subscribers, including a subtle suggestion I may have a real problem with alcohol (I do not) because Seth feels people may be more understanding that way.

Amazingly, our subscriber numbers start to climb after that, slowly at first and then with dizzying speed. Soon there are dozens of messages of support ("You got this, Rowan!" —@girrrrl34; "AA is hard, but it works"—@soberliving999;

"God is good!"—@JCBeliever). By the next morning The-WrightStory has almost 900,000 subscribers, and Seth is elated. I wonder why people are so drawn to tragedy, what comment they might leave instead if they knew this was just another scripted video. Or if that even matters.

I can't see it yet, but my tequila-drenched monologue put something into motion whose course I won't be able to change.

JULY.

"ARE YOU SURE THIS IS THE RIGHT WAY?" Seth asks.

I glance up at the road we're on—gravel, bumpy, claustrophobic with leafy tree branches pressing past its edges—then back at my phone, trying to follow the directions in the email.

"I think so?" I reread the directions, wishing to be more certain. I'm down to one bar on my phone, and the map won't load.

Seth sighs, his fingers tightening against the steering wheel. We are irritated with each other these days. Too often, too easily. Partly it's money, of which there is never enough. At least we have a new muffler, thanks mostly to money Dad has sent home with Sunday dinner leftovers. But the other part has to do with what happened a month ago, though we haven't explicitly discussed the incident since. Still, it hovers cloyingly above us, like smoke in a ventless room.

I'm trying to get my bearings, to determine if we are in fact going the right way, when Seth slows the car. "What's this?" He turns the music down before coming to a complete stop. In front of us a brood of chickens—I count eight—peck about the dirt, not the least bit concerned about a car careering toward them.

"Chickens."

Seth gives me a wry glance. "I know what they are, Rowan."

He opens the door and I grab hold of his arm. "What are you doing?"

"What, do you think they're going to peck me to death?" He laughs again, and I let go of his arm and open my own door. Together we come around the front of the car, and then look at each other.

"So . . . do we just, like, shoo them away?" I am not scared of animals, but I had a particularly traumatic chicken experience as a child. I tried to take an egg out from under a hen at my uncle's backyard coop, which did not go well. She violently pecked at my hand, drawing blood, and forced me to go back to the house tearful and empty-handed. "You know I don't trust chickens."

"For a kid who grew up all outdoorsy, you've sure softened."

I scoff (though it's not an entirely false observation), and Seth walks toward the group of hens, a couple of roosters in their midst. I follow a half step behind, both of us clapping and shouting at the fowl to get off the road. They move out of our way as we get closer, but then circle back around us to the center of the road to continue pecking at the dirt.

"Now what?" I wonder where in the hell these chickens even came from. We're in the middle of nowhere.

"Fancy some roasted chicken for dinner? We could always call your dad for his recipe." Seth laughs, and at the sound of it I feel better.

I'm about to suggest walking in front of the car and shooing as I go, Seth driving slowly behind me in an attempt to clear a path, when a shrill whistle fills the air.

We turn toward the sound, which comes from a woman who has mysteriously apparated onto the road from between the trees. She whistles again, and Seth and I watch as all the chickens run to her. The woman—older than we are, maybe late thirties, with two long plaits hanging over her shoulders—tosses a few handfuls of grain from a canvas bag into the undergrowth. The chickens busy themselves pecking for the grain between the moss and forest mulch, and then the woman comes toward us, hand outstretched. She smiles, and I'm struck by how beautiful she is—her face makeup-free but sun-kissed.

"Hi, I'm Jess."

"I'm Seth, and this is Rowan," Seth says, shaking Jess's hand. I do the same, and smile back at her. I take in her outfit: the slouchy, well-worn jeans that brands would refer to as "boyfriend style" with cuffs rolled halfway up her shins; the thick socks inside well-scuffed hiking boots; the fact that she's braless under her thin T-shirt.

"Where are you visiting from?" Jess shifts the canvas bag to her hip.

I guess it's obvious we aren't locals. "LA, by way of Ann Arbor," I start, adding, "We've rented a cabin for a month to—" I am only about to say "enjoy a much-needed vacation," but Seth quickly interrupts me. He is superstitious about his novel and doesn't like to tell people what he's working on, or even that he's an author.

"To get a break from city life," he says, finishing my sentence. His tone is easy, friendly. "But we seem to be lost."

Jess nods, glancing between us. I look at my feet, my white canvas runners now covered with fine gravel dust, and swallow around the discomfort of Seth's interruption. Feeling small and like I've made a mistake, which is ridiculous.

"So, are these all yours?" I ask. The chickens continue milling about, pecking at the grain and other treasures that are buried just beneath the soil's surface. It's then I see—or rather hear, as they're quacking quite loudly—two ducks that have joined the flock. Though the ducks seem to stick closer to Jess than the chickens.

"Sure are," Jess replies. "We like to let them roam. It's good for their egg laying." Now she looks down at the pair of ducks, one with brown speckled feathers and the other with a glistening emerald green head. The all-brown one has Jess's boot lace in its beak and is tugging at it.

"This sweet menace is Quackers—females have mostly brown feathers—and our male duck, with his gorgeous green head, is Cheese. Sometimes they think my laces are worms, which are a favorite treat."

I chuckle. "That's funny, Quackers and Cheese." The ducks quack in alternating harmonies as if to acknowledge my amusement.

"You know, I heard that if you play hens classical music, they lay bigger eggs," Seth says, his voice animated, as though this will be the most fascinating piece of new information Jess has heard in a while. Seth is dynamic and charismatic, and he always seems to have a random fact to drop into a conversation, no matter the topic or his expertise on it. But Jess simply nods again and says, "Hmm, is that right?" in a mild tone. I'm surprised and a little embarrassed for him, used to people reacting with more enthusiasm and interest when Seth turns on the charm.

I pull up the directions on my phone. "Can you tell me if we're going the right way?"

Jess gingerly steps around Quackers, who is still tugging at the shoelace, and looks at my phone's screen, reading the directions. She then points down the road. "About five minutes that way. When you get to the fork, take a right. It's only another minute or so after that."

"Thanks," I say. "Well, nice to meet you, Jess."

"Same." Jess smiles again, then walks back to the edge of the road. The ducks quickly scurry to stay at her heels, quacking boisterously as they do.

"I'm sure we'll see you around," Seth says.

"I wouldn't be too sure," Jess replies. "But I hope you enjoy your stay." Then she waves a hand as Seth and I get back into the car.

"That was weird," Seth murmurs, putting the car into drive and slowly starting back down the road, gravel crunching under our tires.

"You know, I wasn't going to say anything. About your book." I don't keep the testiness out of my voice.

Seth tenses his jaw—so briefly I almost miss it—and then lays a hand on my thigh and squeezes gently. "Sorry, babe. I shouldn't have interrupted."

With a sigh I glance in my side mirror, but Jess and her flock of chickens have disappeared back into the woods.

I CAN TELL Seth has never built a fire. I suppose that should be something I already know about him, but up to this point in our relationship Seth has never needed to build a fire.

As for me, I could build that fire with my eyes closed. My sisters and I spent many summer holidays visiting our uncle's farm, where we learned to trim trees with a chain saw, chop wood, build campfires, change flat tires, fix leaky taps, catch and clean a fish, and shoot a hunting rifle. While much of my outdoorsiness has faded, I'm sure I could still work a chain saw or clean a fish if pressed. So no doubt, I'm the fire-building expert of the two of us. That much is clear as I watch Seth fumble about, shifting wood from one pile to another. Stalling.

"Anything I can help with?" I ask.

Seth sweeps a piece of kindling across the soot pile inside the fireplace to flatten it. The ash needs to be shoveled out, but we can do that later. It was a pleasantly warm day, but now it's chilly inside the tiny log cabin. I can't wait for the flames' heat, even though I know by midday tomorrow I'll be sticky warm in only my shorts and tank top.

"All good," Seth replies, his head half inside the fireplace. I wonder if he opened the damper, and if I should remind him about that. Deciding to let him sort it out for himself, I go back to my notebook and snuggle under a scratchy wool blanket that smells of woodsmoke and mothballs. A mosquito buzzes nearby.

I'm feeling better than I have for weeks. Maybe it's the fresh air, or the distance from Ann Arbor. Or maybe it's that we had a good, cleansing laugh when we arrived at the cabin and saw how far our meager budget could stretch (not far). The one-room cabin is built of round logs, the bathroom the only indoor space with a door that closes. Except it doesn't quite, because the floor isn't level, and so the door sits slightly askew. There's a corded, old-school telephone anchored to the wall by the refrigerator, and a small television with rabbit ears on a side table in the corner of the living room.

With few distractions, no distance between us inside and nothing but privacy outside—the trees are our only neighbors for miles—I hope this might be the place where my creativity thrives again. Where Seth and I get firmly back on track with each other.

I planned to spend the evening with my notebook by the fire. But I'm sluggish and achy after the long drive. I sip a vodka cooler—from the can, as there were only small juice glasses in the cupboards—and click my pen a half dozen times, frowning at the page on my lap. I smack a mosquito, and it leaves a speck of blood on the paper.

"You going to write?" Seth clears his throat as the ash kicks up dust.

"Maybe," I reply. "Maybe not. I'm tired." I doodle a flower around the spot of blood, then close my notebook. The script can wait until tomorrow. Seth murmurs something, but with his head inside the stone fireplace I can't hear him.

"Want me to film this?" I ask, watching him break kindling across his thigh. *Crack! Crack!* The wood is nice and dry, procured from a sheltered lean-to behind the cabin. There's nothing worse than trying to burn wood that's anything but bone dry. It's unlike me to suggest filming for TheWrightStory, but I'm trying to keep my promises. One of which is to view You-Tube as the opportunity Seth swears it is. Besides, this sort of rural-life aesthetic—or "cottage core," as it's known—is wildly popular, so something worth taking advantage of.

"Nah," he replies. "Nothing to see here." Seth typically wants to film everything, which reinforces my guess that he has no clue what he's doing. I watch as he makes a teepee of the snapped kindling in the fireplace's center, resting it on top of the balled-up newspaper, and again consider mentioning the damper. He scratches a spot on the back of his neck, and I see a large welt forming.

I decide to stay quiet about the damper. Like my dad always says, "The best way to learn something is to screw it up at least once."

A few moments later black smoke billows out of the fireplace and I jump up and shift the lever to the open position. I fan the air with my notebook.

"The damper." I stifle a cough. I want to open the front door, but know that if I do we'll be eaten alive by mosquitoes. "It needs to be opened or the smoke has nowhere to go."

He mumbles that he thought it *was* open. The kindling finally catches, and I see the change in his posture with the quiet pride of it. His first fire. That is something. I probably should have filmed it.

After Seth sets a sturdy log onto the flaming kindling teepee, he closes the chain-link screen so stray embers won't escape but the heat will. Then he stands and faces the fire, and I press into him from behind. I rest my head in the space between his shoulder blades and breathe him in—laundry soap and fast food—the scent of today's long road trip.

"That's a gorgeous fire, babe."

"Hmm. You're gorgeous," he says, turning so we're face-to-face. "I almost want to grab the camera to show you just how fucking gorgeous you are."

"So . . . why don't you?" This wouldn't be the first time, and I have to admit it's something I like, the way I look in those moments . . . but even more, I like how Seth looks *at me* in those moments. The video camera was expensive, and initially Seth was finicky about its use. But "set the good china for take-out pizza" was a lesson I picked up from my mother, and so one night after a rough workday for both of us, I suggested the camera become multipurpose—it captures our lives for subscribers, but why not also for our own enjoyment? Truth is, it's not the filming I loathe . . . That can be fun. It's the disingenuousness of its end game.

"I'm trying to respect the boundaries." He smiles at me. We

agreed on a YouTube filming schedule for the month: It won't interrupt Seth's research or our writing time, and once the sun goes down, the camera goes away. I reply that maybe we can make an exception, as it is our first night after all, but then Seth is at my neck, with soft lips and warm breath. My body responds with a jolt, and he whispers that I smell like marshmallows on a campfire (my vanilla-scented body lotion mixing with the smoke) as I tug him down onto the rag rug in front of the fireplace.

Seth is all muscle and sharp lines, thanks to his genes and a propensity for exercise that keeps him toned even with his love of fast food and sugary snacks. His face glows warm in the light, the small licks of flames growing as the kindling teepee works to catch fire to the log. The muscles in his arms bulge as he holds himself atop me, his dark hair falling slightly over one eye.

I want to tell him how amazing he looks, but then his lips are on mine and he shifts his body slightly to take his phone out of his pocket. He sets it beside us on the rug, which is made with what appears to be dozens of multicolored rags. Against the otherwise neutral cabin decor—everything some shade of "wood"—it's a tapestry of brightness in the small room.

Opening my legs so Seth can settle between them, I turn my head toward the fireplace as he returns to kissing my neck, tugging impatiently on my shirt as he does. He works to pull it over my head, and I twist slightly to accommodate.

It's then I see his phone, still illuminated beside us. On the lit-up screen is a wiki site—"How to build a fire (with pictures)"—with a photo of a kindling teepee. He must have taken screenshots ahead of time because we have no Wi-Fi in the cabin and cell service is spotty at best.

I smile and close my eyes, turning away from his phone,

giving all my attention to what his hands and lips are doing. The heat of the crackling fire warms my face and bare skin as the log relents to the flames.

I'M UP EARLIER than Seth, before dawn, and am careful not to wake him—not easy in a one-room cabin. Hovering over the kettle, I yank it off the stove the moment before it whistles and pour steaming water into my mug. I find half a jar of instant coffee in the cupboard, and some powdered creamer. Not ideal, but good enough to give me the boost I need until we can get into town for groceries.

The carefully packed bag of dry goods—into which I put ground and instant coffee, a jar of peanut butter, dried apricots and almonds, two boxes of granola bars, a package of beef jerky, a few cans of tuna—was accidentally left behind in Ann Arbor. Seth, in charge of packing the car, said it wasn't there with the other bags, so it never made it into the trunk. This wasn't true (it was right beside the small cooler of road-trip snacks), but arguing about it after the fact seems futile.

Seth must have awoken at some point during the night to put another log on the fire, so the cabin is warm, if not a touch stuffy. I settle onto the firm sofa, a patchwork of dull brown and green leaf motifs, and open my notebook.

Chewing the end of my pen, I consider my opening scene for my current script. The idea is new and loose—its connective tissue not yet visible. After being entrenched in one story for so long, I've found writing this somewhat awkward. Nonetheless, it's a good start, and I know I have to do better. The morning is typically productive writing time for me, but I'm feeling off; I never sleep well the first few nights in a new place. I pick up my phone and out of habit refresh my email. But nothing new pops up, which is when I remember I have no service out here.

Scrolling through old emails, I find the one I'm searching for in my sent folder. It's titled "Pitch," and it outlines a story about a woman who, while on a solo hiking trip in the Appalachian Mountains, gets struck by lightning and develops curious prophetic abilities. That email represents not only my work of the past two years but also everything I hope for in the future.

The pitch was sent to a friend in LA, Clara Cottingham, almost two months before Seth and I left for the Adirondacks—June 3, to be exact. We met when we were both working as waitstaff, chasing bigger dreams. Now Clara is a development executive for a hotshot Hollywood producer, and we've stayed in touch since I left California. When Clara emailed, asking to see what I was working on, I thought maybe the tides were turning—a lucky break right around the corner. I sent the pitch within the hour.

After I hit send on that email, I was a ball of nerves waiting to hear back. But as the days—then weeks—passed without word from Clara, I became less sure about both the idea and its execution. Nearly a month later I was losing hope. No matter how ambitious I was, or how hard I worked, I didn't feel as though I could move the needle. It all came to a head the last day of June, when, after a tedious day of taking headshots for a local insurance company, my email to Clara still unanswered, I poured three fingers of tequila into a glass and sat dejectedly in front of my notebook. I only intended to have that one drink as I brainstormed other screenplay ideas, and then new career options. Instead, I ended up drunk, after which I recorded that mortifying confessional video.

Seth shifts in the double bed that's too snug for the two of us, but he doesn't wake up. Good. I'm not ready to have company. We had a great evening, and I want that feeling to linger. I turn back to my notebook and reread the first few beats for the new scene.

It's not there yet, missing that buzz of energy that comes when I'm enamored of an idea. Maybe I'm just tired; maybe the story doesn't have the legs I think it does.

With a sigh I put my work down and pad softly to the cabin's front door. It creaks, so I quickly step outside onto the porch, carefully closing the door behind me. There's dew on the wooden slats, and the soles of my feet are soon wet and chilled.

Sitting in one of the Adirondack chairs, which is also covered in light dew, I'm glad for my sweatshirt and sweatpants. Looking out into in the forest of trees surrounding the cabin, I breathe in the morning air as deeply as my lungs allow, the heavy scent of so many green things filling my nostrils.

Just then I hear a squawk—so close by I jump—and in front of me on the porch's rail is a bird. Its feathered body a glistening black. It looks at me with round onyx eyes and proceeds to caw a few more times, the tone harsh and urgent-sounding, as though it has a critical message to relay.

"Hey there," I whisper. "What brings you by this morning?"

The crow tilts its head this way and that, then caws again. I see one stark white feather in its left wing, standing out against the glossy blackness. I wonder how a snow-white feather ends up in an otherwise all-black-feathered canvas.

The bird caws again, sounding more irritated now. And then, before I can ask again what it needs—which of course is ridiculous because what do I think this bird is going to say?—it flies off into the trees, continuing its "caw-caw" calls long after I can no longer see it.

It takes me a moment to realize how fast my heart is beating. Out of step with the relative calmness of the rest of my body and the serenity of the woods surrounding me. Then, left slightly uneasy by the interaction with the bird, though I'm not sure why, I retreat into the cabin and slide into bed beside Seth, curling my body against his warm, sleepy form, my feet the last part of me to lose the chill.

LATER THAT AFTERNOON I suggest we go on a hike. Explore the surrounding area and get a start on Seth's research.

"Why don't you go ahead?" he says, stirring the last of the powdered creamer into another cup of coffee. Maybe I should go to town instead, do the full grocery shop today instead of the next day, as planned.

"I'm going to do some writing," he adds. Seth has his laptop open in front of him on the small kitchen table, but as I walk by to grab one of our water bottles, I see video thumbnails on the screen from stuff we filmed before leaving Ann Arbor.

"I thought this was why we were here? For you to get lost in a 'hostile natural environment.'" I use air quotes, for there is nothing hostile about the forest today. The sun shines brightly, and the air is warm and dry, filled with choirs of songbirds and cicadas.

"Take some pictures for me," he replies, blowing across the top of his coffee, eyes already back on his screen. "Don't want to lose my momentum here."

I apply a layer of sunscreen—I burn easily—and try to shake the disappointment as I tie the laces on my new hiking boots a bit too tightly. They were a purchase we really couldn't afford, but necessary for the terrain. Tennis shoes won't cut it out here. Seth's hikers, also brand-new, remain by the front door.

Then I leave on my own, letting the screen door slam loudly as I do, chastising myself for romanticizing our time here. I envisioned traipsing through the woods seeking shared adventures, reading our precious words aloud to each other at night, naked and unencumbered, maybe a juice glass of something strong shared between us. But it's only the first day. There's plenty of time.

It only takes ten steps or so for the boots to begin pinching my feet. I'm going to wind up with painful blisters on each heel, and I already regret not breaking the boots in first. I should have known better. This is hardly the first hike I've been on, though it has been a long while.

The forest beyond the cabin's perimeter is dense—only a tiny parcel of land was cleared for building, and the balsam firs and red pines stand tall in a protectionist-like circle around the log structure. Moving away from the cabin and deeper into the woods, I stay on what looks like a trail, but then the path meanders to the left, then the right, before disappearing entirely. Soon enough, I'm lost.

Glancing around, I see what looks like a clearing to my left and make my way toward it. Once there, I'm surprised to find water open up before me. On the far side of the lake's inlet is what appears to be a log cabin, significantly larger than the one we're staying in. I climb up on a rock, its top conveniently flat, positioned near the edge of the lake, and take the lens cap off the camera hanging around my neck. Holding it to my eye, I use the zoom lens to home in on the cabin.

Flanking the log structure are two similar cabins, though offset and so more hidden by the heavy brush. The whole place appears abandoned, the shrubbery growing up and over the porches, vines winding around the rails, the logs weathered and split, and the windows—what's left of them—fogged by layers of pollen and grime.

I take a few photos and am about to check them on the screen when a male voice behind me says, "Hey there."

I scream, and then, embarrassed by my reaction, put a hand to my chest and laugh to try and cover my shock. The man seems not at all alarmed by my outburst.

"Sorry for scaring you," he says.

"Oh, no problem." I give another short laugh, but I hear the nervous edge to it. I am acutely aware that I'm currently lost in these unfamiliar woods.

"I'm Aidan," he says, extending his hand. I hop off the rock and shake his outstretched hand, gripping firmly so he knows I have some strength behind me. He's still smiling and I notice he has nice teeth. As someone who does event photography, I spend a lot of time whitening teeth during editing. I wouldn't have to do a single touch-up to Aidan's.

"Hi, Aidan. I'm Rowan." Too late, I consider the wisdom of giving him my real name, my city-girl instincts humming. Aidan takes a small step back—casually, subtly—and I understand he's trying to let me know I'm safe with him.

"I like your shirt," I say, willing my fast-beating heart to slow.

Aidan glances down at his T-shirt—off white with faded moss green lettering that reads: "We don't make mistakes, just happy accidents." One of the more famous quotes from the late painter and television host Bob Ross. My dad, who loves gifting advice, is a fan.

"Thanks," he replies, giving me another warm smile.

"Also, sorry. For the scream. That was dramatic," I say. "I wasn't expecting to run into anyone else out here."

He points to the right of where we stand. "My place is that way, not too far. I usually take an afternoon foraging walk."

Aidan holds up a small, well-used canvas tote. It has dirt and stains over its surface, and a Stanford University logo that is peeling off. He opens the bag and I step closer, peering inside. There are a dozen or so mushrooms, with chestnut-colored caps and thick whitish stems, along with a few small evergreen branches.

"Bay bolete mushrooms and hemlock needles for tea. A pretty decent find today."

"Hemlock needles?" I take a second look at the light green needles resting on the bottom of the canvas bag. "Isn't hemlock poisonous?"

He nods. "I like to live on the edge."

I take a step back, but when I look up at him and see his amused expression, I realize he's messing with me.

"The toxic version of hemlock is a plant. These are from the eastern hemlock tree, and if you mix the needles with hot water, it's a pretty pleasant beverage," he explains.

"Interesting, I'll have to remember that." I'm fairly sure I won't be making hemlock tea anytime soon, in case I mix up the whole plant/tree thing. "So, you live here? Like, permanently?"

"Yep, almost ten years now," Aidan replies. "Jess and I came out here for a research project, and, well, we just never left."

"Jess?" I repeat, realization dawning. "I think we met her yesterday! She helped us with some chickens that were blocking the road."

Aidan lets out a laugh. "That's Jess for sure. We're ornithologists, and she's always had a soft spot for chickens. She has them better trained than most family dogs."

"Ornithologists? Bird experts, right?"

"The very same," Aidan replies.

"Well, being able to call your chickens with a whistle does seem a handy skill if you live in the woods and work with birds."

"I suppose that's true." He gestures at the camera in my hand. "Hobby or profession?"

"A little of both." I shrug. "We've rented a cabin here for a month. Looking for some inspiration."

"Well, this is as good a place as any for that," he says. "These woods have a lot of stories to tell."

An unexpected shiver moves through me as I remember the cabins on the other side of the lake. I point in their general direction. "What's the story with those cabins?"

"Ah, yeah, Camp Callaway, or what's left of it. It was one of the Great Camps of the Adirondack Park, but it hasn't been in use since the mid-seventies."

"'Great camp'?"

"They were these retreat compounds built by wealthy and influential families in the 1800s and 1900s so they could come and enjoy their summer weekends in nature. To escape from busy city life," Aidan says. "Most are still privately owned, and a couple have been taken over by conservationist groups. Camp Callaway is the only one left abandoned."

"Why was it abandoned?'

"The owner—Eddie Callaway—went missing in 1975, and it closed shortly after that," Aidan replies.

Another shiver moves through me. "Did they ever find him?"

"Her. And no. The camp was passed down to friends of hers, but it never reopened after that summer, as far as I know."

I look back at the cabins, more curious than ever. "Are you allowed to walk around the property? Explore a bit?"

"Technically it's private property, but I doubt anyone will give you trouble.

"I wouldn't go into the buildings, though," Aidan adds. "They're pretty sketchy, after all these years."

I nod, feeling an inexplicable pull to peer inside the cabins to see what's behind those grungy, cracked windows. I scratch absentmindedly at the bug bites on my arms.

"Anyway, Rowan, it was nice to meet you, but I'd better get back to the homestead. Frittata for dinner, and these mushrooms are the star ingredient." Aidan cinches the canvas bag closed, then puts it over his shoulder.

I say goodbye, and Aidan responds with a wave as he heads off into the dense woods.

It's only after he's out of sight that I realize I forgot to ask for directions.

CHAPTER 6.

GREAT CAMP CALLAWAY:
A BRIEF HISTORY

The land on which Camp Callaway resides was originally purchased by the self-made shipping tycoon Theodore Callaway in 1896. Reportedly, Callaway fell in love with the Adirondack wilderness during a hunting trip, after which he bought a 1,250-acre parcel of land with the intention to build his wife, Rosemary (Rose) Epstein Callaway, heiress of the Epstein Banking fortune, a luxurious summer home to be shared with their two young sons, Theodore Jr. (b. 1892; d. 1901 of tuberculosis) and George (b. 1894). Construction of the sprawling Camp Callaway took nearly two years, and was completed in 1898.

Following Theodore Callaway's death in 1932 and Rose's in 1934, Camp Callaway was bequeathed to their only living son, George Callaway, who continued the legacy of the family's Gilded Age Adirondacks life. Along with his wife, Delilah Callaway, and their daughter, Edith Jane Callaway

(b. 1925), George maintained the property for decades, hosting extravagant summertime parties (during Prohibition alcohol was brought in from Montreal, Canada, by train), before declining health forced the elder Callaways to remain at their estate in New York's Suffolk County.

The camp remained in the family fold, with George and Delilah's daughter, Edith Jane, inheriting the grand retreat upon her parents' deaths, both in 1968. The camp sat mostly unused until Edith Jane—who changed her name in 1970 to Eddie Callaway following her divorce from Dr. Stewart Hoffman (inventor of Dr. Hoffman's Medicinal Powder)—made the Callaway camp her primary residence in 1971.

Eddie Callaway ran self-funded wilderness retreats, exclusively for women, out of Camp Callaway from August 1971 until she disappeared on July 7, 1975. The camp was abandoned in the fall of 1975, and remains so at the time of this printing. While today the camp is a dilapidated relic, you can revisit its former glory in a June 1948 feature in *Architectural Digest*, which includes photos of the camp's stunning Adirondack-style craftsmanship and other unique touches, among them life-size wooden animal sculptures commissioned by George's parents for his birthday in 1929, and an open-air bowling alley.

While Camp Callaway has now largely returned to the wild, Eddie Callaway's mysterious disappearance continues to make it one of the Adirondack region's most intriguing settings.

*Excerpted from *The Great Camps: Jewels of the Adirondacks* (2011), by Jason Malther

EDDIE, 1975.

Until we can understand the assumptions in which
we are drenched we cannot know ourselves.

—Adrienne Rich, "When We Dead Awaken:
Writing as Re-Vision" (1972)

B EING A WOMAN IS THE GREATEST GIFT,"
Eddie Callaway liked to say.

Not in a superior way, Camp Callaway's leader was
always quick to point out, because wouldn't that make women
just as bad as the men who believed them to be merely a soft
place for the patriarchy to land? No, being a woman was better
than anything else because it was the perfect blend of warmth
and power, of grace and strength.

More recently Eddie had come to learn that not all women
characterized themselves so neatly. While there were benefits
in belonging, there were also drawbacks if the knit of the fabric

was too tight. A group's power could only be as potent as its individual parts. For that reason, in the summer of 1975, Eddie included a follow-up to her infamous statement:

"I believe being a woman is the greatest gift . . . and I welcome you here to discover what *you* believe."

To the Wild Women of Camp Callaway:

It was delightful having you with us, and we hope this handbook provides an anchor to your experience here. May it also inspire you, once you leave our sanctuary, to continue on the path you've so bravely started to walk. Head up, heart full, third eye open.

As I have shared, I was once a perfectly ordinary girl with extraordinary privilege, heiress to a vast fortune. My life was filled with both heady luxury and heavy responsibility. I was expected to carry on the Callaway name and fulfill my legacy as the matriarch of the family, while never stepping outside the boundaries of my role. I remain hesitant to speak of strife, as my life was never particularly challenging. However, because the expectations held for me were finite and contrived, I never learned I could ask for more. I already had so much!

You might have assumed my transformation from socialite housewife to Camp Callaway's Head Goddess was simple, because if there was a fight to be had, it was only within myself. Yet the unlearning of old beliefs, of previously held assumptions, will always be difficult, regardless of where you start from. Dwelling on the past is an enormous burden. We must learn from it and move forward, carrying with us only the most precious tidbits we'll need for what lies ahead.

Like you, I am on a path with a clear beginning but no end. There is no room to be tentative with our intentions. The length of this journey remains one of life's great mysteries, and time is a fickle thing. That's why, dear friends, I started these retreats at my family's camp. To grant you that time, as well as to offer refuge and compassion for your own miraculous unfurling.

If there is one thing I hope you take home and make a part of your daily life, aside from Samuel's recipe for Pineapple Upside-Down Cake (page 16) and my morning ritual to start every day off right (page 4), it is this truth: Your wildness is a gift that must remain uncaged.

I will close with one of my favorite musings, from Betty Friedan's "The Feminine Mystique," and leave you to answer for yourself as I bid you farewell for now:

"Who knows what women can be when they are finally free to become themselves?"

In love and awe,
Eddie Callaway xx

*From *Camp Callaway's Wild Women Handbook*, 1975

JUNE.

JUDITH BRAIDED A SECTION OF EDDIE'S HAIR, her fingers nimble and deft. She tugged gently, the pieces weaving together quickly in a long strand that lay over Eddie's bare shoulder. Judith shifted to face her, sitting naked and cross-legged. She grasped Eddie's narrow braid midway between two fingers. "I wonder what was happening in your life right here? When these strands of hair were only this long?"

Eddie, used to these sorts of queries from Judith, who was only twenty-four but somehow as chock-full of wisdom as she was of curiosity, gently shrugged her shoulders.

"Your history—*your stories*—live in this braid," Judith continued. "In every strand of hair on your head. It's a mindfuck, really, when you think about it." Eddie smiled, drawing a long pull on the joint she had just lit.

"If that's true, why do you ever cut your hair?" she asked. Judith kept her hair short—a close-cropped pixie cut that Eddie could never have pulled off.

Judith shrugged, taking her own pull off the joint. She held her breath, then exhaled slowly. "I prefer the stories to change, I guess."

"Fair enough," Eddie said, her eyes fluttering as the grass took its sleepy hold of her body. She lay back onto the pillows. While marijuana was her preferred indulgence—unless you counted chocolate milk—Eddie only smoked it on Mondays, which, happily, today was. She held few rules for herself anymore, having escaped a life bordered by expectations, but "Grass Mondays" were an exception.

So, why only Mondays?

"Why not?" Eddie would have replied, even though the truth was Mondays were a hard day for her because of a particularly tragic one six years earlier. The lull of weed helped soothe the still-sharp edges of that memory, dulling it into submission, at least temporarily.

Judith exhaled, lying back beside Eddie on the mattress, a pillow of smoke hovering between them. The young woman wore only a necklace—an enameled third eye hung on a strand of leather—which settled between her small, buoyant breasts. She rolled slightly to grab the notebook on the nightstand, setting it onto her bare stomach. A pencil was tucked into the crevice of the book's spine, holding a page. "Want to hear it again?"

Eddie nodded, and Judith began reading.

Judith was a talented writer, and Eddie loved these evenings when she read aloud to Eddie from her notebook. Judith was sharing her most recent poem with Eddie—boldly, without disclaimers or explanation.

Eddie watched as Judith arched her back, stretching. The notebook somehow stayed put, and Judith gave a contented sigh as she handed the joint back to Eddie, who watched appreciatively as Judith stretched again, lazily, like a cat coming out of a deep slumber. Her body was long and lithe, her skin velvety and golden from the early-summer sun, nary a blemish anywhere except for a small birthmark beside her navel.

"You are beautiful, Jude."

"I know," Judith replied easily before closing her notebook and flipping over onto her stomach. The younger woman seemed completely unencumbered by the insecurities that too often gripped her gender, which Eddie found nearly as intoxicating as the grass. Eddie had never imagined being intimate with a woman prior to Judith, but had since learned what her heart and body were capable of, which had been a delightful discovery.

Judith rested her head in her hand, and watched Eddie in the candlelight's glow. The room was heady with the smoke, some of it sweet from the grass and some spicy, thanks to the incense burning nearby. "You're beautiful, too, Eddie."

"Hmm," Eddie said, crushing the joint into the clay ashtray. As a younger woman, Eddie hadn't always seen the beauty of her own face or body. But over these last few years, and in particular thanks to Judith, she had learned of its feminine power and pleasure. Though she was also quick to acknowledge that a youthful body was wasted on the young. Eddie couldn't even imagine the ways she would enjoy her thirty-years- and thirty-pounds-ago body, if she could somehow try it on again.

She turned on her side to face Judith, feeling the soft parts of her fifty-year-old body droop with gravity. Her lines were not smooth, her skin a map of stretch marks, age-related moles, and skin tags, a white puckered semicircle scar across her lower belly, which was where the doctors had pulled her one and only child, Theo, from.

"So, tell me. Tell me what I need to hear, wise one," Eddie murmured.

"Eddie Callaway, you are going to change these women's lives," Judith replied on cue, reaching out to lay a hand on Eddie's cheek. Judith's pixie cut framed her petite face, its features delicate—she had killer bone structure—and she held Eddie's gaze. "Just like you changed mine."

She leaned toward Eddie, kissing her softly at first, then with more ferocity. Eddie had loved Judith's lips from the moment she first saw them, and they had lost none of their appeal over the past two years as Judith worked alongside Eddie at the camp. She'd arrived at Camp Callaway in the spring of 1973, only twenty-two years old, with a Wild Women retreat pamphlet in hand (given to her at a college party by a former guest—a common way for the camp's offerings and message to spread) and the desire to be a part of Eddie's "mission."

While Judith Swann's arrival at Camp Callaway had resulted in a seismic shift within Eddie, the young woman's origin story was quite conventional—raised upper middle class in the suburban Midwest by loving, earnest parents who supported her artistic side and urge for independence. Though she was Eddie's junior by many years, Judith had always been the one in charge when it came to the two of them—"my old soul," Eddie would lovingly call her, referring to Judith's confidence and self-assuredness. Eddie would never take power away from any woman who embodied it, viewing age as a mere detail.

"I am going to change these women's lives," Eddie repeated, then allowed Judith to gently push her onto her back. With the change in position Eddie's breasts slid sideways, her soft stomach sinking into itself and flattening in a way that pleased her. Some days Eddie felt vain about her body, remembering how her breasts used to be transformed into something more becoming by a lacy, structured brassiere. But now she most appreciated the freedom of letting things be as they were. She

could have been embarrassed by this betrayal of her body to hold its original shape, but Judith had helped her see things differently. Eddie closed her eyes as Judith's probing hands and warm lips trailed the outlines of her softened, mature body, allowing herself to be taken in by the electric sensations of a swift and invigorating orgasm.

LATER, AS JUDITH slept—Eddie having covered her with a light quilt—she sat out on the front porch of her cabin, the sky alive with stars and the sounds of singing cicadas and wildlife roaming through the nearby woods. Eddie loosely rebraided her hair—which was becoming ever more streaked with silver strands, dozens, it seemed, by the week—into two braids. Though she used to wear her hair in a stylish neck-skimming bob, using rollers to create voluminous curls at its ends (the style her ex-husband, Stewart, preferred), Eddie's hair was now long enough to reach the middle of her back. Still, she remained high-maintenance about the salt and pepper strands— her hair one of the few holdovers from her former life. Normally she slept in rollers, though occasionally she would use braids, like tonight, to achieve a tighter curl. But her hair was always "done," and she made no apologies for it. Nor for the many tubes of lipstick that littered her dresser—Revlon Moon Drops in Lovers' Coral was her signature color. She liked her hair waved and her lips painted, even as she wore pants with functional pockets, hiking boots or sandals, and hadn't shaved in years.

Soon the camp would welcome its first group of the season— women from all over the country. Some came because they needed help to see their value. Others, to uncover their potential. While coming to a Wild Women retreat was a privilege, you did not have to be privileged to participate. That was one of Eddie's tenets for the camp; it was a welcoming place where women could find kinship and belonging. A simple letter or phone call—explaining how you heard about the camp and why you wanted to visit—was all it took to be invited, free of charge. Eddie had a generous spirit, and a long wait list.

Even though this would be the fourth full summer the camp had been running retreats, she remained anxious and faintly unsure. Eddie's role was to mentor these women, to provide community and enlightenment, even if at times she herself felt lost and alone.

Her guests' bravery to explore deep within themselves never failed to inspire her, as they shed their skins over mere days to reveal the surprises underneath. Above all else, that was when Eddie felt most useful. Helping women begin anew—even when it was messy and hard and full of questions without answers— was exactly what Eddie felt Mother Earth had brought her here to do. One person might not be able to change the world, but Eddie Callaway could certainly try to fix a sliver of it.

She glanced down at Judith's notebook in her lap—the cover made of pressed mulched newspaper with wildflowers glued on its surface—and opened it to the latest poem. Eddie wasn't invading Judith's privacy; she had written this poem for Eddie, as though knowing what she had been planning for months.

This poem was precisely what she had been looking for, in no small part because it captured two of Eddie's favorite things: the forest's trees, which had been her sanctuary since she was a child, and her adage that "sometimes you need to look down—so you don't trip, or step on a snail sliding a silver trail across your path—but never forget to look up, too." Some might say a better proclamation for Eddie and her retreats would be to "look forward, not back" as a way to capture her passion for growth, to become the next great version of yourself. But Eddie believed looking *up*, at the blue sky, the brilliant sun, the expansive tree canopy, brought someone the greatest treasure of all: perspective.

Judith's evocative words were the final piece to the puzzle Eddie had been working on. An adventure and life-changing opportunity like none other that she could offer this next group of women. A thrill moved through her, the shiver that followed causing her to tuck herself more deeply into the blanket around her shoulders. There was just one last thing she had to do with Judith's poem, but not until morning. Eddie couldn't wait for sunrise.

IF YOU ARRIVED at Camp Callaway midsummer, the first thing you'd see was staggered rows of purple and pink hollyhock flowers standing like brightly colored guards at the entrance. They had been Eddie's mother's favorite, and she'd asked for so many to be planted the gardener had warned they might crowd themselves to death—but somehow each seed and then plant had found the space it needed, and the hollyhock bundles had bloomed in unison year after year. However, before the hollyhocks woke up, the colors at camp were more muted—earth tones, sun-bleached woods, and the greenery that preceded bright flowers. While summer was lush and soul-filling, Eddie loved every season at the camp, including the dead of winter, when life was harsher and quieter but no less beautiful.

Though the Callaway family had always referred to the

summering spot as "quaint" and "charming," those descriptions would often garner well-deserved eye rolls, depending on the company. It was a sprawling compound, with acres of pristine forest land to explore. There was a massive dining hall, large enough to accommodate up to fifty guests, and a barn that used to house horses, cows, goats, and chickens, along with an open-air bowling alley that had been a highlight of Eddie's childhood, and then of little Theo's. There was also a robust vegetable garden, two boathouses, three lean-tos, and a dozen smaller cabins scattered across the grounds.

In the camp's heyday, Eddie and her family had stayed in the largest cabin. There had been a dozen staff, including a groundskeeper who lived at camp year-round, and the family enjoyed luxurious lodgings. Crisp linens from Europe and animal furs as rugs, which Eddie remembered being soft underfoot. When she moved to the camp permanently in 1971, Eddie rolled up the furs, laying woven-cotton rugs on the wood-planked floors. But the expensive linens remained. Everyone slept better in lovely sheets, Eddie believed.

"Good morning, Mr. Goat, Miss Betty," Eddie said to the two goats grazing on the grassy knoll in front of the barn. Along with six egg-laying chickens, they were the only domesticated creatures that remained residents of Camp Callaway. "How's the grass today?"

The female goat let out an enthusiastic bleat, and Eddie laughed. "I hear that. I love grass, too, Miss Betty."

She continued on her way to the outdoor bowling alley, rehearsing her welcoming speech for the soon-to-arrive guests. So lost was she in her own thoughts that she ran right into Florence Dwyer, a Black former teacher from Baltimore whom Eddie had first met at the buffet table at a Women's Action Alliance event in early 1971, as they both reached for the last deviled egg. The two were there to learn more about grassroots organizing (Eddie with her vision for Camp Callaway; Florence wanting to transform education, particularly for Black girls and women) and immediately hit it off. After splitting the egg and learning more about each other, they found common ground—an earnest desire to empower others, along with their shared love of deviled eggs.

"Oh, Flo! Sorry about that." Eddie righted herself, hands on Florence's shoulders.

"You're fine. No damage done," Florence said, placing her hands atop Eddie's. "Ready for a game?"

Eddie saw pins lined up at the ends of the two wooden lanes, the black bowling balls in a row on the return track. Luckily, there had been a spell of dry weather, and the lanes were polished and ready for play. If it rained, you needed to wipe down the wood, and the pins required hand setting, and all the parts of the alley necessitated tedious and regular maintenance.

Every time Eddie walked into the bowling alley, she was filled with nostalgia, which used to make her weep but now provided comfort. It had been one of her son's favorite pastimes at camp. He had been a damn fine bowler, too, though once he grew out of childhood, trying to get him to come to the camp was like pulling teeth. Theo, like all teenagers, wanted to be with his friends. And just like that, the days of "Momma, one more game? Pretty please?" from her only child ended.

"Is Sam coming?" Eddie asked, and Florence pointed across the front lawn to where a tall man in shorts, a T-shirt, and an apron still tied around his waist was just stepping down the stairs at the dining hall. Samuel Harrison, the only man who stayed at the camp, was a couple years older than Eddie. She had known Samuel much of her life, ever since she was seven years old.

The Harrisons had worked for the family for years, both in the city and here at the camp. Samuel had learned everything he knew about cooking from his father, Samuel Sr., who had run Camp Callaway's kitchen. His mother, Gloria, had been a house manager and one of Eddie's favorite people—she was kind and patient, and always snuck Eddie peppermints out of her pockets.

Samuel and Eddie hadn't been allowed to spend time together back in those days—despite them being the only children at camp, their lives were kept purposefully separate, Eddie white and Sam Black. Though, as children are wont to do, they found hidden places in the woods to play when the adults were preoccupied doing adult things. Their covert meetups became sparser as the years passed, as teenage Samuel no longer joined his parents for the summers, staying behind in the city to work. After Eddie left home to get married, she'd heard Samuel had made his way to college and then later to Vietnam, as a war reporter, which had cost him two fingers on his left hand.

Eddie never imagined their paths would cross again, though she thought of Samuel, and their camp summers, often. Then, a few months after she moved back to Camp Callaway, she was sweeping debris out of one of the lean-tos and heard a distinctive birdcall—ever familiar, though not one she had heard for decades.

IT HAD BEEN the summer of 1934. It was a particularly sweltering July day, and the tree shade offered a cool reprieve. The two lay in a straight line, head-to-head, on the mulch of the forest floor, a good mile away from the camp, staring into the tree canopy above. Edith, at only nine years old, could distinguish a bird by its call even when she couldn't see it in the branches.

She'd learned the differences between the songs of the brown-headed nuthatch, the chickadee, the common sparrow, the eastern phoebe, and the yellow warbler, among others, and could mimic many of their calls with great precision.

That afternoon she was trying to teach Samuel her particular gift of birdsong. They practiced the shrill scream of the blue jay, the coo of the mourning dove, the downy woodpecker's single-note whinny, the eerie wail of the common loon, but the only one Samuel could replicate with any authority was the throaty "caw-caw-caw" of the crow.

"Let's make up our own," Samuel had suggested, flipping onto his stomach and resting his chin in his hands. "It can be our secret call—we'll use it whenever we want to find one another, like the loons do." Edith had readily agreed. Their call became a sharp whistle, punctuated by two short, low-pitched hoots, followed by a long trilling note. That summer was the last Samuel spent at the camp, but their top secret birdcall was one she'd never forget.

So when she heard it the afternoon she was sweeping out the lean-to, she let the broom drop from her hands. Eddie had held her breath until she heard it again. Then she'd run out of the lean-to and found Sam at the gate—older, yes, but still looking so much like the boy she used to know. He had a small rucksack over his shoulder, his camera around his neck, and a smile on his face. Samuel had loved Camp Callaway (and Eddie), and after the war, sought a quieter, deliberate life. So he returned to camp, offering to help Eddie however he could.

SAMUEL JOINED THE women at the bowling alley's entrance, rubbing his hands together in anticipation. "Prepared to lose?"

"Dream on, Sam," Eddie replied. "I'm *never* prepared to lose."

She grasped a bowling ball, sticking her fingers and thumb into the holes. Back when she was a child, the alley used hardwood balls because her grandfather insisted they were the best. But then her father replaced them with these black Brunswick rubber balls, which Eddie loved, monogrammed with the camp's name. Eddie vowed never to replace them, despite polyester balls being more common these days.

She moved into position at the end of the lane, then, slightly under her breath, said, "Give us knocked-down pins, please forgive us all our sins. We're praying on our shins, to ask for wins, wins, wins!" It was a silly rhyme she and Theo had made up when he was young, and one they religiously spoke out loud prior to releasing their first balls.

With a decisive swing back, her legs moving into a well-practiced lunge, Eddie released the ball right down the center of the alley. She raised her hands and gave a celebratory shout as every last pin fell.

"Damn, why do I even bother?" Florence shook her head and then took her position at the end of the second lane. Eddie was a masterful bowler, and rarely missed getting either a strike or a spare. Florence, on the other hand, seemed to be perpetually sending balls into the gutter, no matter how many games she played with Eddie.

"Because one day I may just miss. Or maybe one day I'll throw a game, just for fun."

Florence turned to Eddie with eyebrows raised. "You would never."

"You're right, I would never." Eddie winked, then gestured toward the upright pins. "But I don't know why you think you can't get a strike on your first ball."

"Because I never have before?"

Samuel chuckled. "She's right about that, Eddie."

"Flo, *I believe in you*. You have a great arm! Just focus on what you want before you let that ball go. Come on. Show me what you've got."

Florence took a deep breath. She pulled her arm back and swung through.

They all watched as the bowling ball sped down the lane before smashing into the pins. Florence jumped up and down, clapping her hands. "A strike! A strike!"

Samuel gave Florence a congratulatory thumbs-up, and Eddie said, "I knew you had it in you."

"You're the only one!" Florence laughed. "But thanks for the boost, Eddie."

"Don't thank me. Thank the strike gods," Eddie replied, holding her hands up to the sky. "I'll reset the pins, then it's your turn, Sam."

She started making her way down the lane, careful to walk its edges. Suddenly, she heard Theo's voice—high-pitched and with a slight lisp as he said, "Give us knocked-down pins, please forgive us all our sins. We're praying on our shins, to ask for wins, wins, wins!"

Turning to her left, she saw her son in his seven-year-old form. His shoelace was untied, and she resisted the urge to retie it. Instead, she smiled at him and let her hand drop low enough for him to reach it.

Feeling his hand in hers, she let her fingers close gently, then whispered, "I miss you."

"Why, silly-billy?" Theo replied, using one of her nicknames for him. "I'm always here."

At that Eddie smiled softly, now at the end of the lane. "Of course you are," she said before bending to reset the pins.

"TIME FOR A break?" Samuel stood in the doorway of Eddie's cabin, which was three over from his own, without opening the screen door as the black flies were ravenous this time of year.

"Almost." Eddie waved Samuel in.

John Denver's "Sunshine on My Shoulders"—Eddie's favorite of all his songs—played softly on the eight-track, and she hummed along as she sat at the small kitchen table making pin-back buttons. The words "Wild Woman" were displayed in a bubbly white cursive font, bright against the tangerine-colored background of the paper discs. The button maker had been a somewhat recent addition to the camp, and Eddie was still trying to get the hang of it. She was delighted to see how straight the words on the buttons were with this batch.

"How many to go?" Sam let the screen door, which was spring-loaded, shut behind him.

"Three. Or four, now that you're here," she replied, half standing as she pulled the long metal handle toward her, firmly pressing together the button pieces: the metal front, the art and clear acetate cover, and the pin back. Then she released the handle and pulled out the round metal contraption, which was about three inches high and held inside it one finished pin-back button. "Perfect," she murmured, setting it into a lime-green Tupperware container along with the others.

Samuel left his sandals on the mat, then came to stand across from her at the table. Eddie looked up at him and set her reading glasses on top of her head, the frames nestling into her curled hair, and pushed the container of buttons toward him. Samuel took one and pinned it to his T-shirt.

"Is it straight?" he asked, glancing down at the button. It was slightly askew, but Eddie nodded.

"You wear that well," she said, and Samuel smiled.

"Help me with the coins?" She pointed to another green Tupperware bowl—part of a set—and then looked over her shoulder. "The foil is on the counter."

Samuel retrieved the aluminum foil from the kitchen counter, then sat across from Eddie, his knees splayed to the side due to his height. "Cake smells good."

"I hope it is," Eddie said without raising her eyes from the button maker, where she was carefully fitting another metal disc into the holder. The aforementioned cake was cooling on the countertop, and Eddie's entire cabin smelled of doughy sweetness. "Butter pecan with vanilla frosting was the request."

It was Judith's twenty-fifth birthday the following day, and as was tradition at Camp Callaway, she was getting a homemade cake of her choosing. Eddie had only started baking cakes once she took over the camp—before that, any cooking or baking was relegated to her kitchen staff. Even though she had since made many cakes, she didn't see herself as much of a baker. Her cakes were always slightly uneven, sometimes a touch overdone. It was a skill, no question. Samuel, who was far more talented than Eddie in the kitchen, would have been happy to take on the birthday-cake making, but it had become an important tradition for her. Making things for people she loved was a privilege.

Samuel started wrapping the coins, mostly dimes and quarters with a handful of Eisenhower dollar coins in the mix, in small squares of foil he cut with the kitchen shears.

Eddie chuckled at his precision. "I would have just ripped bits of foil. I may put you on coin-foil duty from now on."

"Aren't you ever worried someone will bite down on one of these?" Samuel asked, continuing to cut foil squares and then wrapping them around the coins. He held up one of the foil-wrapped dollars. "This could break a tooth."

"Every birthday cake I ever ate as a child had coins baked in it," Eddie replied, pulling the button maker's handle toward her again, grunting slightly with the force required. "No one broke a tooth. But to your point, that's why they now go into the frosting instead of the batter."

The first time Eddie experienced the joy of a slice of money cake was her fifth birthday. The tradition had been passed down from her maternal grandmother, who used to bake coins—without a foil wrapping—into her homemade chocolate cake. When Eddie had seen the glittering silver nestled inside the nearly black crumb of her birthday cake, she'd squealed, using her chubby little fingers to excavate the coin, then sucking it clean of the cake. She'd kept that silver coin in a jewelry box on her dressing table for years, believing her mother when she told Eddie fairies must have filled the cake with coins while no one was watching.

Once Eddie finished the final button—and Samuel was nearly done wrapping the coins—she took a Quik tin down from the shelf. "Want a glass?"

"Sure," Samuel said, and Eddie filled two juice glasses with cold milk from the small fridge. She added two heaping teaspoons of the powder to her glass, and a scant teaspoon to Samuel's. He didn't have the sweet tooth Eddie did.

Handing Samuel his glass, Eddie sat down again and took a sip before asking, "So, what do you need to talk to me about?"

"What makes you think this is anything other than a friendly visit?"

"Experience," Eddie replied, stirring her spoon to release some of the clumps gathering.

Samuel set his glass down, pausing for a moment, and Eddie whistled softly. "This must be a doozy."

He laughed, and Eddie downed her glass of chocolate milk. Then Samuel reached across the table, wiping the corner of

Eddie's mouth with his thumb, which was soft and warm against her skin. She held his hand there for a moment, then kissed his palm. "Okay, out with it."

"Before I tell you this, let me say there is no pressure from me, okay? I'm simply the messenger here."

She nodded, and then Samuel continued. "I have an old friend, Joe Connors—a journalist I met in Vietnam—who's since landed at the *New York Times*, and he reached out."

"About what?" Eddie asked, snapping the lid on the Tupperware container of buttons. Another task down. Now she just had to put the finishing touches on this summer's handbooks—an epic task that took months, but did provide excellent busywork during the quiet winter.

She'd purchased the mimeograph duplicator secondhand from the church in town, and had taught herself how to use it. The size of a large bread box, it had a hand crank on the side that was turned one complete circle for each sheet of paper. The handbooks were multiple pages in length, getting thicker every year, it seemed, so it was slow but meditative work. She had come to love the intoxicating smell of the paper as it came off the duplicator, the ink sweetly aromatic as it printed out the words she'd typewritten on the stencils. Each guest went home with a hand-bound copy (Eddie used a hole puncher and waxed thread), so they could carry a piece of Camp Callaway with them forever.

"He wants to do a story about Camp Callaway," Samuel said. "About you, specifically."

She barked out a laugh, then got up and laid a gentle hand on the top of one of the cake layers. Good. It was cool enough to ice. "About me? How *novel*."

This wouldn't be the first time Camp Callaway was deemed newsworthy of late—the *New York Post* ran an article in early 1971 about Eddie and her Wild Women retreats. She had opted not to be involved after the reporter seemed more interested in her former life (and half-truths, like that she had been a pill-popping heiress, with an addiction that led to her marriage falling apart) than in the retreats themselves. She'd never read the published article, and had politely but firmly declined nearly all interview requests since.

"His cousin came to a retreat two years ago and was singing your praises. It changed her life. She apparently started a macramé handbag company after being here, which he said has done incredibly well." Eddie remembered this woman (long blond hair, effervescent personality, a tote of textiles and half-finished macramé projects always on her shoulder) and was happy to hear the update.

"Anyway, he was intrigued about this place, and you."

"Was he now?" Eddie murmured, pulling the bowl of frosting out of the fridge so it could warm to a spreadable consistency. "Let me guess the headline . . ." She lowered her voice, using a stage whisper. "'The Wild Woman of the Woods: Libber Fruitcake or Savior for Lost Girls?'"

"Come on now, Eddie . . ." Samuel said, smiling. She loved his smile because there was no question it was genuine. It went all the way to his eyes, crinkling the corners, his long dark lashes framing deep brown irises. "You know you're both."

"Proudly so," she replied, laughing, then held up a finger in correction. "Though there are no girls here. Could you hand me those coins?"

He brought her the bowl of foil-wrapped change. Eddie had already started icing one of the cake layers.

"He's legit, Eddie. And I trust him. It wouldn't be a hatchet job." Samuel handed her a foil packet, then another and another as she placed them carefully into the frosted layer, barely a quarter inch apart.

"But no pressure. Not from me, not from Joe. I just thought you might be interested. What you're doing here, it's special. It's important. And more exposure, especially in a well-respected paper like the *Times* . . ." Samuel had read the 1971 *New York Post* article, which was what had prompted him to return to Camp Callaway, so Eddie couldn't view that piece as all bad. "Well, you could tell your side of the story. Help more women find you, and the camp."

Eddie continued placing the coins Samuel handed her in tight, concentric circles. *Maybe it's time to do this,* she thought. As long as it could be on her own terms. "Let me think about it."

Samuel nodded and handed her another coin, which she pressed into the thick vanilla frosting.

ROWAN, 2021.

FOR THE PAST TWENTY-FOUR HOURS I'VE been thinking of little but the abandoned camp, and its missing owner, Eddie Callaway.

I'm waiting for Seth on the front porch—we're already ten minutes later than we planned to leave. I'm hungry and antsy, impatient to get into town and find Wi-Fi to do research, along with a proper coffee and a few groceries. Seth ate the last granola bar while editing last night, and I'm irritated he didn't at least save me half.

The nearest town is a "blink and you missed it" spot with one main road down its center, whose shops we quickly scanned as we drove through on our way to the cabin. Along with a diner that advertises free Wi-Fi in its front window, there's a small school, a church, a hardware store, an art gallery that seems to double as an antique shop, and a post office. It's enchanting in that small-town way, with passersby offering friendly greetings, bursting floral window boxes outside the shops, litter-free sidewalks, a leisurely feel.

"Imagine living somewhere you can walk from one end of town to the other in, like, three minutes?" I say as Seth parks the car near Hopper's Diner.

"Nightmare," he replies, and I laugh.

"That's harsh," I say, though I don't totally disagree. Something about the town, even with its charm, is unsettling—like nothing could be private in a place like this, everyone knowing everything.

THE DINER HAS a 1950s vibe, with red leatherette banquette seating and black-and-white-tiled flooring, plus a vintage milkshake maker on the countertop. We take a seat at an empty table by the window and I log in to my email to see if Clara has responded. *Nothing.* My stomach sours.

"I just need to let it go," I say, sighing in resignation. Seth's eyes are on his menu, printed on the paper placemats in front of us. He glances up, his brow wrinkling in confusion.

"Let what go?" Before I can answer, a woman approaches our table. She has sparkling streaks of gray running through her dark hair and a carafe of coffee in hand. Her plastic name tag reads "Glenda."

"Morning, folks. Can I start you with some jet fuel?"

"Please," I murmur, turning my cup over. She pours the coffee, and I take a sip even before she's finished pouring Seth's. It's good and strong.

I quickly scan the menu items. "Two eggs over easy, please. Brown toast and half a grapefruit." Seth orders pancakes with a side of bacon, extra crispy.

As we wait for the food, I scan my inbox. I reply to my parents ("safe and sound . . . beautiful spot . . . working hard . . . checking for ticks nightly") and ignore an inquiry about photographing a gender reveal in September.

Seth wolfs down his breakfast and uploads our latest videos to YouTube. When he is done, he asks if we should get the bill.

"I'm going to have another coffee and take advantage of the Wi-Fi. See what I can find out about Camp Callaway." I push my empty plate to the side, feeling full and satisfied. "It's sparked an idea, for a script."

Seth offers to pick up the groceries while I poke around online. We accidentally left the list at the cabin (it had been under the car key, which Seth grabbed), so I jot down necessities to get us through the next few days: coffee and creamer; cheese; eggs; butter; fresh tomatoes, basil, garlic; olive oil; pasta; peanut butter and jam; bread; chips and beer; frozen lasagna. We've agreed to eat mostly vegetarian for the month, to save money, but I suggest some chicken if he can find it on sale.

After Seth leaves, Glenda returns to see if I need anything else. "Another coffee would be great."

"How about a piece of pie to go with it? I have fresh-made raspberry."

"Why not?" I don't have room for another bite of anything, but I love raspberry pie.

A few minutes later she tops up my coffee, setting the pie beside it. The crust is golden, its lattice pattern crackled with sugar crystals, and I know I'll eat every last morsel. "Anything else, hon?" Glenda asks.

"Actually, could I ask you a few questions? About the area? I'm a writer, doing some research about the park." I take a bite of the pie. It's tangy and sweet, the raspberry flavor intense, as though the berries were picked just this morning. "*Heaven*," I declare. Glenda smiles at the compliment.

"Happy to help if I can," she replies. "Time for a break, anyway. Just let me start a new pot of coffee. Back in a jiffy."

A few moments later Glenda sits across from me, a mug of coffee in her hands.

"Have you lived here a long time?" I ask.

"Born and raised. Though I did leave for a time, for school. But came right back to get married, have my kids." I briefly wonder what she went to school for, but that isn't the question I really want answered.

"Did you happen to know Eddie Callaway? Or know of her?"

Glenda nods. "You don't grow up in this town without knowing about Eddie Callaway."

"What can you tell me about her?"

"I didn't know her personally, and this is going back a few years now." She offers an apologetic smile. "My memory isn't as elastic as it once was."

"No problem. Anything you can remember would be really helpful."

"Well, I was about twelve or thirteen when Eddie Callaway moved back here for good in '71. Her family's camp had sat unused for some time after her parents died, so the locals were happy to see her back. Most were, anyway. Always a few bad apples in a bunch, but they could never create much bluster." I wonder about the "bad apples" and their gripes.

"You see, this town relied on the Great Camps over the years," she explains. "Summers are busy, as you can imagine, but back then camp owners like the Callaways really kept us afloat during the off seasons."

I nod, taking another bite of the pie.

"Eddie Callaway was . . . eccentric. I'm not sure how else to put it. Granted, it was the early seventies and so women coming into their own were a dime a dozen, but she was different. So vibrant and *passionate*. A force to be reckoned with. Caused headaches for some, though." Glenda raises an eyebrow.

"The 'bad apples'?" I ask.

"Mmm-hmm. Some townspeople saw Eddie as too brazen about her beliefs, her way of life. Downright intolerant they were, to be honest." Glenda leans toward me, lowers her voice. "Small towns can breed small views, and though things are better these days, this place was no exception back then. There were also stories of infighting between a few Great Camp owners. But you never can be sure what to believe, especially with how gossip flies around.

"Anyway, I met Eddie once, the summer before I left for school. She came one afternoon in her old pickup truck, to get three dozen pies for her Wild Women retreat. I was working in the diner that summer, so I helped my aunt with the baking and packing up." She chuckles. "It was a damn lot of pies—largest order we ever got."

"I bet. That's a lot of pie." I press my fork into a smattering of crust crumbs. "What was a Wild Women retreat?"

"Camp Callaway ran these weeklong sessions during the summer months. Only for women, and completely free. Eddie apparently paid for everything, and the crew that helped her out with the sessions were all volunteers. It was a real seventies commune. Rumor is they even grew marijuana on the property." Glenda raises an eyebrow, offers a knowing smile.

"Anyway, at these retreats the guests took part in meditation, yoga, and arts and crafts workshops, that sort of thing, along with some more, ahem, *controversial* sessions on . . ." She lowers her voice again, even though there's only one other person in the whole place, and he's on his phone. "*Female genitalia.* There was one session, oh, what did she call it . . . something clever. I can still picture the flyer. Eddie used to tack them up around town." Glenda snaps her fingers. "'Be Your Own Vulva Voyeur.' I think that's what she called it. Or something similar."

She lets out a hearty laugh.

"You can imagine that as a young lady I thought she was so *cool*. But like I said, not everyone approved. Eddie Callaway's retreats were polarizing, no question."

"I bet," I murmur. I write down "Wild Women retreats" on my notepad.

"Not long after that day at the diner Eddie Callaway disappeared. There were countless search parties. Big police presence and scent-tracking dogs, plenty of reporters camped out in town. Everyone here helped out, too, however we could. The diner was jam-packed most days."

I try to imagine this sleepy town, this diner, becoming the bustling epicenter of a missing person investigation.

"The searches went on for months. Everyone in town was questioned, including those bad apples I mentioned, as well as the other camp owners. But nothing came of it, and they never found a trace of poor Eddie. After that the camp closed for good."

"So, no one knows what really happened?"

"Nope. There were plenty of rumors, of course." She begins enumerating them with her fingers. "She fell into a bog on one of her hikes. Drowned in the lake. Met some guy and took off with him. Then there was chatter for a while she'd left to join a cult in California. And then that she started her *own* cult. Either way, no one ever saw or heard from her again."

Neither of us speaks for a moment, until the quiet is interrupted by the sound of the front doorbell chiming. A woman and a young child walk in, then sit in a booth a couple down from where I am.

"Thanks for taking the time to chat," I say, knowing Glenda has to go serve the new arrivals. "I hope I didn't keep you too long."

She waves a hand. "No worries, hon. I own the place, so I can pretty much do what I like."

"I'm Rowan, by the way." I laugh. "I probably should have started with that."

Glenda smiles, points to her name tag. "Glenda, as you can see."

"Very nice to meet you."

"Likewise," she replies. "Hope we'll see you again before you head out of town?"

"I expect you will," I say. "Especially now that I know about this pie."

Seth texts that he's done shopping. I thank Glenda again and ask for the bill. While I wait to pay, I download as many articles as I can find about Eddie Callaway.

I TRY TO read one of the articles out loud to Seth (who has now caught my curiosity bug about Camp Callaway) in the car, but the twisty roads make my too-full stomach uneasy. Setting my phone down, I crack my window, waiting for the wave of carsickness to pass as I watch the landscape change, from meadows and fields to the dense woods that mean we're close to the cabin.

I'm about to ask if Seth wants PB&J or egg salad for lunch before we hike to the abandoned camp, when an old metal sign partially obscured by the foliage catches my eye.

"Stop," I say, my head whipping around so I can keep an eye on the sign's location.

"What?" Seth takes his foot off the gas, glancing quickly my way. The car slows.

"Stop the car, Seth!"

He does, fairly abruptly, and my seat belt digs into my chest and abdomen, my breath momentarily restricted. I unclick my seat belt. The relief is immediate.

"What's wrong?" Seth looks in his rearview mirror, then at me, confusion and concern on his face.

I'm already out of the car, Seth calling after me, and I jog back to the sign.

CAMP CALLAWAY

Some of the lettering on the metal sign is chipped and faded, but all in all, it seems to have weathered well. Since Camp Callaway has been abandoned since 1975, this sign has been here for at least fifty years. I run my fingers over the embossed letters, and feel a similar chill as when I looked over the lake at the cabins.

Seth catches up to me, the soles of his feet slapping against his flip-flops, making a rhythmic sound in the relative quiet.

"Are you okay?" he asks, then reads the sign I have my fingers resting against. "Huh, look at that."

"Maybe we don't have to hike in after all," I say.

Fencing stretches on both sides of the gate, long grasses swooping in between and over the metal and wood slats. The driveway—gravel, narrow—is long overgrown. However, the path of it remains visible through the underbrush, so I know we can walk it on foot.

"Let me grab my phone, then we'll take a closer look."

"What about the groceries?" It's warm, and I imagine the eggs baking hard in the sun, the romaine wilting to become paper-thin and slimy.

"We'll be quick. Now that we know where it is, we can easily come back."

As he jogs back to the car to grab his phone, I stare down the overgrown driveway, wondering what we're about to find at the other end of it.

NOT FAR DOWN what used to be Camp Callaway's driveway is a metal gate, a rusting chain and padlock keeping it closed. A "No Trespassing" sign with bright orange letters is zip-tied to the gate, above which the name "CALLAWAY" is spelled out in a majestic arch, the letters created from bark-stripped sticks held together by something we can't discern from our position—maybe short nails?

Hopping the gate—only for one brief moment questioning whether we should—we continue down the path until we reach a clearing. Nature has taken over, the soft, tall grasses and wild-flowers covering what was likely a sizable lawn at one point. The grasses tickle the bare skin on my ankles as we walk, and though I'm sweltering, I'm glad for my leggings.

Soon we come upon a large building, clearly the center-piece of the camp. It is wide and impressive, with stacks of logs creating its structure and a massive wraparound porch. It appears mostly intact, at least from the outside, though the glass in the windows is broken. Littering the porch are empty beer cans, liquor bottles, and other paraphernalia that prove we aren't the only ones who ignore "No Trespassing" signs. There's also a large cast-iron bell near the door, attached to a metal post protruding from the logs. Seth rings it, swinging the chain that drops from the bell's center, and amazingly it still works. Its metallic yet melodic clang echoes through the emp-tiness, and I glance around, feeling anxious about disturbing the peace.

"This is sick," he says, and asks me to take a video of him ringing it again.

Then we peek through what remains of the front windows, noting that there's not much inside except for a few errant beams that have fallen and are partially propped up against the walls. It's dark inside, so I cup my hands around my eyes to see better. But the building remains mostly empty, hollowed out at some point between 1975 and now. I catch a glimpse of something tall near the farthest corner of the room, and for a moment I lose my breath, goose bumps rising on my forearms. It looks like a shadowy figure, standing alone in the dark. But upon second glance, I see it's actually a statue. A bear carved out of a tree, standing on its back legs with front paws extended as if to play a game of patty-cake. I laugh at myself—at my jumpiness—and take a photo with my phone, but it's too poorly lit and grainy to make out.

The front door is also nearly off its hinges, so we *could* easily go in and poke around more. See what else was left behind. But we decide it doesn't look safe enough (and I invoke Aidan's warning about the buildings' unknown integrity). Instead, we split up to investigate a few of the surrounding cabins and outbuildings, including a barn, with its center entirely collapsed like a failed soufflé, and a surprise find: an open-air bowling alley that has a tree growing in its center, straight through a hole in the gabled roof. The forest has mostly reclaimed the cabins, and many of the buildings are at least partially obscured by winding vines and branches crowded with leaves.

There's a sudden breeze, which feels inexplicably cool. The hairs on my arms rise with the slight shift in temperature, and with it I feel a hint of apprehension. I blame it on a mild case of trespassing anxiety, though it likely has more to do with the setting. It's eerie to stand among the ruins, to see the ghosts of what used to be.

"YOU HAVE TO check this out." Seth's voice finds me in the cabin next to the one he's exploring. He isn't shouting, but because the glass is long gone and the cabins are side by side, it's not hard to hear each other.

"What?" I step gingerly, being cautious about my footing as I walk across the creaking wooden floors.

Seth holds up an old tin, rectangular in shape, the words "Nestlé's Quik" still easily legible on the yellow label.

"My grams used to drink this all the time," Seth says. "When I went to her apartment after school, sometimes I would sneak spoonfuls when she wasn't looking."

I make a face. "Remember how the powder would just sit on top of the milk?"

He laughs. "It never, ever mixed in. No matter how hard or fast you stirred. Like sand in a glass of water. But look at this."

As he turns the vintage tin toward me, I see the word "Inside" written in black paint down its side. There's another word, too, at the top, but I can't read it. The paint has been smudged, and there are a few black fingerprints on the sides of the tin.

"Wonder what that means?"

"Not sure," Seth replies. "But something's in here." He shakes the tin then, and I hear the faint sound of something rustling inside.

"Where did you find it?" The cabin is bare except for an old, moldy-looking blanket in one corner and a few crushed beer cans—same brand as the ones on the porch.

"In there." Seth points his phone's flashlight into what seems to be a small pantry, the space filled with a few shelves, layered with dust and remnants of spiderwebs.

"The whole place is ransacked. Why leave this tin?"

"Well, it wasn't easy to find," Seth says. "It was tucked into this nook on the shelf, way at the back. See?" His hand disappears, presumably into this nook. "I was feeling around the shelf, otherwise I probably wouldn't have noticed. Found this, too, right behind the tin."

He points to some sort of notebook on the kitchen's wooden countertop. It's thin, hand-bound with heavy thread tied into small double-knotted bows. The front cover is printed with "Camp Callaway's Wild Women Handbook, 1975" in purple ink. There's a distinctive crease running horizontally about a third of the way down the cover. The notebook is taller than the pantry shelf, which explains the fold.

I'm worried it will be flimsy and fragile after all these years, but the pages hold together just fine as I pick it up. I carefully open it to the first page, to a typewritten letter. "To the Wild Women of Camp Callaway," it begins. I quickly scan the letter, my breath catching as I get to its end and see the signature.

"Whoa," I murmur. "I can't believe it."

I flip through a few more pages; they're filled with typewritten quotes, recipes, notes, and hand-drawn sketches.

"What can't you believe?" Seth shines his flashlight into the pantry, double-checking he hasn't left anything behind.

"It's . . . some sort of manifesto, I think. Apparently Camp Callaway used to host these Wild Women retreats in the seventies—this has to be connected, because look." I point to the name at the bottom of the letter, to Eddie Callaway's signature.

"Shit. That's wild. No pun intended." Seth takes the book from me, a little too roughly. I bite back the urge to tell him to be more careful. A lot of effort clearly went into making it. Plus, it's forty-six years old, so a treasured find worth safe-guarding.

Seth turns his attention back to the tin, and I take the note-book from him, relieved it's back in my hands. He starts to pry off the lid—a round metal circle embedded in the tin's top—but then stops.

"Wait, let me film this." Seth sets his phone to video, hands it to me.

Camera on, he playfully shakes the tin again and does a brief intro. Talks about finding it inside "this old, abandoned cabin in the woods," and says it clearly has something impor-tant in it . . . *but what?*

"Should we open it? See what's inside?" he asks, setting fin-gernails underneath the lid's lip, holding eye contact with the camera.

The lid won't budge. "Damn, it's rusted," he mutters. He tells me to stop the video, saying we'll pick it up again once we get back to our cabin and can get something sharp un-der it.

"I don't know if we should take it," I say. This is private prop-erty, and that tin certainly belongs to someone (not us).

"Who's going to miss it?" Seth replies, tucking it under his arm and heading for the cabin's front door.

"What about this?" I'm still holding on to the Wild Women handbook.

Finders keepers! I hear someone say. It's quiet, though, and somewhat muffled.

"What did you say?" I ask Seth, who turns back toward me.

"I didn't say anything," he replies, shrugging. "That book has clearly been here for decades. I can't imagine anyone is coming back for it now."

Again, that sense of foreboding. Followed by a tingling

numbness in my fingertips, which could be explained by how tightly I'm holding on to the notebook. I release my grip slightly; the tingling lessens.

I suddenly have no doubt this book is coming out of the cabin with me.

Tin and book in hand, we step out onto the porch—I tell Seth we've left the groceries long enough, and should head back to the car.

"Now that we know how to get here, we can always come back. Put this stuff back where we found it," Seth says. "It can't hurt to take a closer look and you can—"

But whatever Seth is about to say is lost in the loud crack of wood splintering, and then he disappears from beside me.

"Seth!"

He's fallen through one of the porch slats, which has given way due to rot, based on the moist blackness of the splintered wood. Only the top half of Seth's body is visible, the rest of him swallowed up by the hole. He grunts with pain, and I crouch, trying to figure out how hurt he is.

"Careful, Rowan," he says, through gritted teeth. "I don't want you falling through, too."

Still in a crouched position, I shift my weight from foot to foot, and the boards seem secure underneath me. "Are you okay?"

He sets the tin (somehow still in hand) down, then pulls himself up, grunting with the effort. Swinging his legs around, he shimmies away from the gaping hole in the wooden slats.

A deep cut yawns open on the side of his calf, up near his knee. Blood streams down his leg.

"Ah, shit," he says, glancing at the cut. "That's not great."

For a moment I'm woozy. Suddenly I'm back at the accident fourteen years earlier where my arm was split open, bleeding profusely onto my brand-new hoodie I'd saved my babysitting money to buy. Remembering how the paramedics held my arm with gloved hands, putting pressure on the deep laceration as they spoke urgently using terms I didn't completely understand.

I take a deep breath to clear my head and then support Seth as he hops down the porch steps. We sit on the bottom step to take a better look at the injury.

"You might need stitches. Probably a tetanus shot too." Blood oozes from the cut, creating rivulets through the hairs on his leg. The contrast between his fair skin and the blood's deeply hued red makes my dizziness return, and I pinch my arm—hard.

"I had a tetanus shot a couple of years ago. After I stepped on that rusted beer can on the beach. Hey . . . you all right?" Seth asks, holding my gaze. He knows how I got the scar on my arm, and that I'm not a fan of blood.

I nod, pinching the webbed spot between my thumb and first finger to distract myself. It does the trick.

"I don't have anything to clean this up." I look around, which is useless because there's nothing resembling a first aid kit anywhere. I take my sweatshirt from my waist, rolling it like a burrito.

"That's your favorite sweatshirt," Seth says.

"You're worth it," I reply, wrapping the rolled sweatshirt around his leg and tying the arms as tightly as I can to create some pressure on the wound. "Now, think you can walk on it?"

Seth winces when he puts weight on his leg. "Don't have much choice. Unless you're going to piggyback me to the car?"

"Hop on," I say, turning around so my back is to him.

He limps past me. "That is not happening."

I laugh, then slip under one of his arms. "Here, lean on me. I'm stronger than I look."

I QUICKLY SET the handbook on the car's hood and the tin on top of it, then search for the first aid kit in the glove box. But it's a cut-rate one, holding only a few plastic bandages, a roll of gauze, and a small ice pack. Not good enough, as blood is seeping into the heather-gray fabric of my sweatshirt, tied around Seth's injured leg.

I suggest driving back to town to find out where the nearest hospital is. He clearly needs stitches. Also maybe antibiotics, because who knows what germs are living inside that rotted wood.

Seth tries to convince me he doesn't need a doctor, and definitely not stitches. "A few Band-Aids and a cold beer ought to fix it."

I tell him he's being ridiculous. He tells me I'm being melodramatic.

It's then we see a couple walking toward us—it's Jess and Aidan. I briefly consider how strange it is that we keep running into them, knowing what Jess said that first day about the isolation out here. They wave, and I wave back.

"Rowan and Seth, right?" Jess says once they're in front of us.

"Yes! Nice to see you again," I reply. "Seth, this is Aidan. Who I was telling you about."

"The mushroom guy." Seth reaches out a hand, and Aidan shakes it, laughing.

"I like that," he says, turning to Jess. "I should get a T-shirt made."

They both look down at Seth's leg at the same time. "What happened here?" Aidan asks.

"Seth cut his leg on—" I begin.

". . . a, uh, tree branch. I tripped and it got me," Seth says.

Jess casually looks over her shoulder to the Callaway sign

and driveway entrance. "Lots of those around here," she says, nodding. My cheeks grow hot, and I nod weakly in response.

"Looks like it's bleeding pretty good." Aidan bends to get a closer look, and Seth tugs the sweatshirt down an inch or so.

"Wow, where did you find that? That's a relic." Jess now points at the Quik tin resting on the car's hood. The painted word "Inside" and the smudge aren't visible from Jess's viewpoint.

"Oh . . . um." I glance to Seth, and he opens his mouth to respond, but then shrugs.

"In one of the cabins." I give the couple a sheepish look. "We probably shouldn't have been in there."

"You certainly aren't the first," Jess says.

"Also, I didn't really try and dissuade you," Aidan adds.

"You *did* say not to go in any of the buildings," I reply. "Can you tell us where the nearest hospital is?"

"Rowan, it's fine." Seth reaches down to remove the sweatshirt. I know he's worried about the cost of a hospital visit. "The bleeding has stopped, all good."

For a moment this seems true, and then the river of blood resumes.

"So, the hospital?" I look back to Jess and Aidan.

"It's a bit of a drive." Jess kneels, checking out Seth's leg. "I could stitch it up for you."

"What? You mean, like here?" Seth's voice is strained, and he turns pale.

"I don't know . . ." I start. "I mean, we wouldn't want to bother you."

Aidan waves a hand to show it's no bother. "Jess does beautiful stitches. She has field first aid training. She could take out your appendix, right here, if she needed to."

"Seriously?" I'm all the more curious about this woman who whistles for chickens and is a bird scientist and can apparently stitch up a wound, or remove an organ, in the middle of the woods.

"Seriously. Though I'd probably suggest the hospital for the appendix," Jess replies, chuckling.

Aidan bends his arm, showing a reddish scar on his elbow, about two inches long. "See this? Perfection. Tricky spot, too. Had a run-in with a nail."

"Unfortunately I don't have any numbing agents, though," Jess adds.

I ignore the look of panic on Seth's face. "Where to?"

ABOUT FIVE MINUTES later we pull into a driveway, also gravel but with edges much tidier than those of Camp Callaway's.

"You can park there, beside the greenhouse," Aidan says. I'm driving, Seth in the passenger seat, Aidan and Jess in the back. I pull into the spot where Aidan directs me and put the car in park. Along with the glass-paneled greenhouse, there are two other buildings—one large yurt and a smaller one—and they look no-fuss, but well maintained.

The couple get out of the car, Aidan carrying the grocery bags with the perishables inside. "We have a fridge," he says. I linger a moment longer and turn to Seth, lowering my voice. "Are you sure you're okay with this? We can still go to the hospital."

But Seth gives me a grin, holding up his phone. Mood completely shifted. "This is going to be great content."

"Of course it is," I mumble as Seth climbs out of the car.

"THIS IS REALLY nice. I've never been inside a yurt," I say. The wood dome and lattice paneling contrast the white canvas that serves as the structure's walls, which makes the large tent-like structure feel light and bright. There are plenty of creature comforts, including an espresso machine in the kitchen and a tiny television in the living room space. It's open concept, the kitchen to one side, the living room to another. There's also a loft upstairs, which houses the bedroom. The decor of the entire place is homey and cozy, with billowy curtains framing the many windows and large embroidered cushions on what appears to be a bamboo floor.

"I was expecting something more 'off the grid,' you know?" Seth adds. He's on the living room's couch, his leg elevated on a pillow. I'm pressing a dish towel firmly on the cut.

"Oh, we are off the grid," Aidan says as Jess returns with a white metal box in her hands. "We're fully hydroelectric—thanks to the river that runs through the property—and we have a composting toilet, plus solar panels to power our lab and the greenhouse."

"I'm impressed," I say. "I can barely keep a plant alive under perfect conditions."

Jess laughs. "It takes some practice and patience, that's for sure. But now we grow a lot of our own food. And we always have fresh eggs—you remember the chickens. Plus, Aidan is a master fungi forager." She smiles at Aidan, who mouths the word "T-shirt." We all laugh.

"Okay, let's take a look." Jess pulls out two chairs—one for her, one for Seth, who gives me a slightly panicked look. His earlier bravado is fading.

He reluctantly rises, limps over the few steps to the chair, and glances back at me. "Can you grab the camera?"

"Sure." I look between Jess and Aidan. "Would either of you mind if I film this?"

Aidan shrugs. "Fine by me."

"And by me, too. Though can I ask why?" Jess lays out supplies—including a small glass bottle with a clear liquid inside, and a hypodermic needle.

Seth pales, seeing the needle, so I answer. "It's for a You-Tube channel."

Jess's eyebrows raise. "Ah, so you're 'YouTubers'?"

Before I can clarify anything (what exactly do I hope to clarify?), Seth speaks up. "We are. Our channel has over 900,000 subscribers."

Aidan says, "Wow," and a wave of embarrassment passes through me.

"I'm also a screenwriter, and Seth is writing a novel," I add. "YouTube is a side hustle. To pay some of the bills, just for now." I don't look at Seth as I say this.

"That all sounds pretty creative," Aidan says. "Jess and I are science nerds, so writing anything that isn't a research note is way out of our league."

"True story," Jess replies. "Now *I'm* impressed." She smiles at me, and I'm grateful to her. Because it's more than a polite smile—it's one of understanding, though I don't know how Jess is able to do that so easily. To notice the things that aren't being said, and acknowledge them quietly.

"Ready?" Jess has gloves on and finishes cleaning around the cut with an alcohol wipe. She picks up the glass bottle and needle, then looks at Seth's face—his eyes are shut as he breathes deeply, in and out of his nose.

"Hey, Seth," Jess says, her voice smooth and calming. He opens one eye. She holds up the needle, filled with the clear liquid. "I was joking about the no numbing part. We're well stocked here. Lidocaine. A few needle pricks and you're golden."

Seth nods in relief, then closes his eyes again. I see his fingers clench into fists.

I hit record on the video just as Jess slides the needle into his skin.

SETH'S STITCHES ARE perfect. A pristine row of small black whiskers holding the edges of the cut neatly together. He only needed four in the end, and Jess was deft at the task. Seth relaxed by the second-to-last stitch, talking animatedly into the camera I held, which I transitioned between his face and his leg. Then we did a few thumbnails as Aidan and Jess looked on, and I felt self-conscious again, seeing the production of it all through their eyes.

We also have learned more about this off-the-grid couple who came to the Adirondack Park seven years earlier as part of a research team of ornithologists searching for a rumored gynandromorph cardinal (a rare finding where the bird is half male, half female, Aidan explains), which had been observed by a hiking birder. Jess and Aidan fell in love, and then, once the study ended, they decided to stay. They continue supplying research for the university, which is how they pay the bills now, and agree wholeheartedly they'll never go back to urban living, despite both having grown up in busy metropolitan cities—Chicago for Jess, and San Francisco for Aidan.

While Aidan takes Seth for a tour of the greenhouse and lab, I enjoy the chance to chat with Jess alone. She shares that she was the one to push for living off the grid, but says that now it's Aidan who is most enamored of their lifestyle.

"It suits me, absolutely," she says. "But he's passionate—he even built our waterwheel out of an old washing machine, and practically has a PhD in edible plants."

I chuckle, remembering the hemlock.

"I don't *want* to go back to city living," Jess says. "But I don't think Aidan ever *could* go back."

"I'm jealous," I say. "Though not about the composting toilet." Jess admits that one has a learning curve.

"You both seem happy out here," I add. It's a bold observation, I realize, as I don't really know either of them. I wonder if loneliness ever seeps into their seemingly idyllic life in the woods. "Or settled, maybe? Though I'm not sure that's the right word either. But something along those lines."

" 'Settled' is exactly the right word." Jess pours us iced tea from a glass jug—peppermint, a hint of sweetness. "To be settled into a life that fits you well—around all your bumps and imperfections and sharp edges—well, there is nothing better."

My eyes fill with tears, and I try to hide my emotion with a subject change. If Jess sees me welling up, she doesn't let on.

"Before I forget, I wanted to ask about a bird that keeps visiting our cabin. Pretty sure it's a crow. But it might be a raven? I'm not entirely sure what the difference is, to be honest."

I describe the jet-black bird, with its urgent, throaty "caw-caw."

"That's a crow. Ravens are larger and have a different call. More 'kronk-kronk' than 'caw-caw.' And it's really deep, the crow's song." Jess then does an excellent impersonation of the bird that has been visiting our cabin, and I tell her so.

"Comes with the ornithology territory," she says. "You should hear Aidan's tufted titmouse. He's really good."

"Maybe I'll ask him later. Be warned, Seth will probably want to record him for the channel," I reply, with an eye roll. "One strange thing about the crow. It has, like, a pure-white feather. On its wing."

"Ah, interesting. That's called leucism—a leucistic bird is

missing melanin, the pigment that makes the plumage jet black, so it has feathers absent of color."

"What causes it?"

"Could be genetic. It can be passed from one generation to the next. Might also be from an injury. Hard to say, but it's not that uncommon, actually, even though it's pretty cool," Jess says.

I agree, before adding, "This might sound weird . . . but it sort of feels like this crow is waiting for me? To give it something when it visits?"

She nods. "My guess is someone at your cabin has left food out in the past."

"So, it's like a pet crow?" I laugh. "Is that even a thing?"

"It could be. Honestly, they're one of my favorite birds."

"Why?" I ask, genuinely curious.

"The Corvus birds, crows and ravens, are often overlooked because their plumage—usually, not counting your leucistic friend—is all black, with none of the vibrancy of, say, the pileated woodpecker or the yellow warbler, or the purple finch, which looks like it has been dunked in a glass of raspberry juice." I nod as though I have a clue about what any of these look like. I'm entranced by Jess's enthusiasm, the way her face lights up when she talks birds.

"But crows are amazingly intelligent. Some species can actually craft tools to forage, by bending wire to create a hook. They also teach their young the way humans do, by modeling behavior, and this learning is passed down through generations. And they've been shown to remember human faces, so I suspect your crow friend is looking for a familiar person. Someone who has left food before."

"Maybe the cabin owner?"

Jess says it's likely, as the crow is comfortable enough to land on the porch railing when a person is present.

"What do you think they were leaving out?"

"Peanuts would be my guess. Crows love peanuts." Jess takes a sip of her iced tea. "Now, I should tell you not to feed the wild birds, and that does stand as an overall rule, particularly out here."

I murmur, "Of course."

"But clearly this crow has a relationship with your cabin. So look around in the cupboards. I bet you'll find a bag of peanuts somewhere."

THE NEXT MORNING I set a few in-the-shell peanuts—which I find in a crinkled paper bag tucked up in a cabinet above the stove—in a row on the railing. Seth asks what I'm doing, and I tell him they're for the crow.

"What crow?" His face is inches away from his laptop screen as he works through the final video frames. I can see the close-up of Jess tying one of the stitches.

"The one that keeps coming by. Jess said someone was probably feeding it. Did you know crows can live up to thirty years in the wild? Like, this crow *could* be as old as I am."

For someone usually so enamored of random facts, Seth seems fairly uninterested in my newfound crow knowledge. "Hmm. I haven't seen a crow" is all he says, eyes never leaving his laptop screen. I breathe through a prickle of irritation, feeling dismissed by his lack of interest.

The peanuts are there, untouched, an hour later when I head out for a walk. Alone again, as Seth remains buried in editing. I hike back to the spot by the lake, across from Camp Callaway, and sit cross-legged on the large rock with a flat top. I pull out my notebook and pen, and my phone. Time to do some reading.

Like Aidan said, the Great Camp was shut down in late 1975 after its owner—Eddie Callaway, heiress of the famed and wealthy Callaway family (who, according to the article, had close to Rockefeller-level wealth)—mysteriously disappeared that summer while out for an early-morning hike. The camp was bequeathed to two friends after Ms. Callaway was declared dead, the common-law time of seven years after her disappearance—though neither is mentioned by name—and the camp never changed hands again; Eddie Callaway's disappearance remains unsolved.

I tab over to the next article. It offers mostly the same information, though there's a mention of a 1971 *New York Post* article—apparently the only interview Eddie Callaway ever gave about the camp's retreats. I jot that down in my notebook, already planning another trip to town to scan the paper's archives.

This article also mentions the infighting Glenda talked about, specifically between Eddie Callaway and another Great Camp owner named Victor Valence. There had been "bad blood" between them (it offers nothing specific, aside from referencing an incident the morning she disappeared), and Victor Valence was a primary suspect early on. However, he had a "solid alibi," the journalist writes (plus, a body was never found), so he was never charged with any crime.

The rock is warm through my shorts, having soaked up the morning's sunshine, but I shiver nonetheless as I think about Eddie Callaway meeting some sort of nefarious end, perhaps in these very woods. I stare across the lake to the cabins we walked through yesterday, and the back of my neck prickles. But there's no obvious reason for this sensation of impending danger, no sounds to pique alarm. I'm being silly. There's no one else out here.

Thinking about what's left of Camp Callaway, I wonder how a place once presumably so vibrant could turn into this empty shell. With rotting wood floors and jagged glass windows and trees growing through holes in the roof—neglected, handed back to the flora and fauna for safekeeping. Only a tin of chocolate powder left behind on a pantry shelf to prove it wasn't always this way . . .

The tin. *The handbook.*

With a start I remember the Quik canister and Wild Women handbook, placed into the trunk before we drove to Jess and Aidan's, and then forgotten by both of us after the stress of Seth's injury. I immediately text Seth to get them out of the car, but the message doesn't go through. *Of course not. No signal.* I sigh in frustration, then pack up with hurried hands.

I hike back to the cabin with urgency, my lungs and legs burning with the effort. Thinking about the handbook, what we might find inside the Quik tin. Wondering what, if any, significance the items carry about Eddie Callaway and her disappearance. I'm already imagining the opening lines of my script. Ideas crowd my mind, and I bask in them—it has been so long since I've felt this creatively inspired.

I'm lost in thought and at first don't notice what's different as I approach our cabin. But then, one step onto the porch, I see the bare railing and abruptly stop. The peanuts are all gone, and in their place is one small rock—mica, its surface glossy black, speckled with stardust that glitters in the sunshine; it's beautiful.

I suppose that rock could always have been there, unnoticed before today. But somehow I understand it's a gift, for the peanuts, from the white-feathered crow.

EDDIE, 1975.

If you want to transform, you can't be tentative.

—Eddie Callaway

*From *Camp Callaway's Wild Women Handbook*, 1975

EDDIE WAS SETTING UP THE WEEKEND'S "freedom fire" trash can in the enormous stone firepit, which was situated in the middle of the compound. She had gotten the idea from the 1968 Miss America protest on the Atlantic City boardwalk, where a trash can became a vessel to hold items women felt were indicative of forced femininity—false eyelashes, makeup, hair spray, girdles, corsets, and bras. But while the protesters hadn't lit the items in that bin on fire, Eddie made sure whatever ended up in the camp's bin was burned. It wasn't merely ceremonial; she had learned firsthand how healing these fires could be as the women watched physical representations of their oppression go up in literal smoke.

She had just finished placing the rocks around the metal can to prevent any spread of fire from possible sparks—they needed rain, everything sun-crisped—and was touching up the word "Freedom" with a small can of white paint when she heard Florence call her name.

"Fred's here," Florence said.

Glancing toward the front gate, she saw the short, round man coming toward them, his strides purposeful. Victor Valence went by Vic V, but Florence and some of the others called him Fred, as in Fred Flintstone, the animated television character from the sixties, because he was loudmouthed and sexist. Once, during a discussion about the road's annual brushing bee, Victor suggested the camp wives (including Eddie) make sandwiches while the men did the trimming, because "no one wants to see a woman handle a brush-cutter!" Eddie had shown up without sandwiches and with a brush-cutter in hand, and she and Victor had been disagreeable with each other ever since.

Victor Valence had bought the neighboring property, Balsam Lake Lodge, in 1965, a few years before Eddie came back to live at Camp Callaway. He and his wife, Sandra, had four children, plenty of wealth from his construction empire, and explicit disdain for Eddie's chosen way of life.

As he approached now, his face was beet red, and he clutched a rolled-up paper in his hand. When he got close enough, he unrolled the page and held it tautly by its edges in front of Eddie's face. She glanced at it, then planted her feet a touch wider than hip distance apart and kept her body tall, like the trees surrounding the camp.

Edith Jane Callaway had always been a performer. First as a child for her parents' many friends, when she made up songs and dances for the parties held at the family's compounds, her mother accompanying her on the piano. Then as a young woman, with the etiquette, outfits, and demure presence of a proper heiress to one of the great American fortunes. As a wife who understood her role both within society and her own home (look pretty, be a genteel and gracious hostess, smile softly but often, focus on domestic tasks). And now, in her latest evolution, as a woman free of the burdens of expectation. Except that wasn't quite true, as there remained many expectations on Eddie Callaway, and she still at times felt burdened by them. Like with Victor Valence, who only saw one side of Eddie and presumed nonetheless to know the whole of her.

So she continued performing, like a chameleon changes colors, conforming her persona to the needs of whatever—whoever—was in front of her. A mentor for the camp visitors, even as Eddie herself struggled to find her footing; a fearless leader of Camp Callaway and its caretakers; a powerful woman unafraid of Victor Valence and others like him who were put off by her "wild" ways.

While she worked diligently to hide it from those who might use it against her, Eddie's fear of being dismissed, of making mistakes, of being alone, *was* ever-present, even if she had mostly harnessed it by now. As she stood in front of a clearly irate Victor Valence, she remembered Amelia Earhart's famous words: "Use your fear. It can take you to the place where you store your courage."

Eddie gave Victor an easy, relaxed smile.

"Nice morning, isn't it?" Eddie kept her voice honey smooth, her shoulders down.

"Callaway, you have to stop this horseshit," Victor said. He pointed at the paper, jabbing the air. "This is not appropriate."

"What's not appropriate?" She remained calm, only shifting position to swat away the flies that were trying to get underneath the rolled bandanna around her neck. Noticing the look of disgust that settled on Victor's face at the sight of her unshaven armpit hair, she kept her arms up a beat longer.

"Why do you have to advertise *these* sessions?"

"Which sessions are those?" Eddie asked casually. Florence, who had now joined them, linked arms with Eddie.

"I know you're not dense, Callaway," Victor said, looking briefly between the two women—at their entwined arms. He scowled, likely remembering the first time he'd met them.

"This is upsetting Sandra. So stop putting your filthy flyers all over town, okay?" He often used his wife, Sandra, as the example of who was most upset by Eddie and her "radical libber" displays, but she had met Mrs. Valence and found her warm and friendly.

The flyers Victor referred to were advertisements for Camp Callaway's retreats. Not only did they list upcoming dates, they also outlined what one could expect in participating. Along with workshops on yoga and silk-screening and making garden satchels were others that some could view as more provocative. Like the "Women of Color" session, meant to explore the particular challenges of Black women in the liberation's movement, which Florence had created and ran. Or the "Target Your Pain" workshops, in which Eddie put hunting rifles (unloaded, of course, as there were no longer bullets allowed on Camp Callaway property) in the women's hands, as a metaphor for harnessing power and "shooting" away fear.

The flyer Victor was huffy about today promoted a personal favorite of Eddie's, the popular "get to know your cervix" session, which was called "Voyage to the Vulva and Beyond."

"This is pornography," Victor said, with disgust. "Children might find one of these, the way you've strewn them all over town."

That was hardly the case, as Eddie had dropped two flyers each at the library and the diner in their small town, where only about a few hundred people lived year-round. Eddie had been warmly welcomed back in 1971 (even if her retreats pushed the boundaries for some) because of her family's legacy and the camp's ongoing support of the town's shops and businesses. Though at times she felt the locals' eyes on her when she went into town, and occasionally heard unpleasant mutterings directed her way, she did her best to ignore the less-than-friendly fuss. Instead, she focused on those who greeted her with kindness (like Carole, at Hopper's Diner) and otherwise held her head high, for Eddie knew she had nothing to feel shameful about.

"And across from God's house, of all places!" Victor continued. He was angry, but also flustered and uncomfortable, Eddie could see—the red flush on his neck, the inability to hold eye contact with her. She made a mental note to take another flyer to the library, which was across from the church, as that was where Victor had clearly removed this one from.

"This isn't 'pornography,'" Eddie said. "It's a chance for these women to better understand their bodies, which is something we should all strive for, don't you think?"

His face screwed up like he had sucked on something sour. Clearly he did *not* think so.

"Nothing nefarious happens, I assure you. Simply a mirror and a speculum for each workshop participant so she can visualize her own cervix. It's truly beautiful, the cervix. Have you seen one?"

Victor stared at her, his mouth falling open, and Eddie nodded. "I didn't think so. Anyway, it looks like a glistening pink balloon, with a dent"—she used her pointer finger to mimic making a hole in the air—"right in its center."

"Personally, I think it looks like half a rose-colored apple, without the stem," Florence said.

"Oh, that's a fantastic visual, Flo!" Eddie replied, watching Victor's face grow redder still.

"Enough of this nonsense," Victor retorted. "All this libber bullcrap . . . You are everything that's wrong with this 'new' world, Callaway. You and the rest of your *radicals*. I'm going to ask you one last time. Cut it out, or you'll regret it."

Eddie turned toward Florence. "Did that sound like a threat to you?"

"It's not a threat, it's a warning," Victor retorted.

Eddie cocked her head. "Those really are the same thing."

She released Florence's arm and stepped closer to Victor. He held his ground, puffing his chest out. Eddie was a tall woman, had inches on Victor Valence. She rolled her shoulders back and jutted her chin forward to show he did not—would not—intimidate her.

"Why can't you mind your potatoes, Victor? Let people live as they choose? No one's asking you to participate." Then she gave him a pointed look. "Though you would probably learn a thing or two."

Victor seemed uncertain what to say to that, so instead furiously balled up the flyer and dropped it at his feet. He turned to leave as Eddie said, "Didn't you forget something?"

She nudged the balled-up flyer toward him with the toe of her well-worn hiking boot—scuffed ruddy brown leather with bright red laces. "Surely you don't want to get a reputation as a litterbug?"

Vic scowled, but bent down to retrieve the page nonetheless before striding back the way he came, furiously shoving the paper into his shorts pocket as he did.

"Do let me know if you'd like one of our educational pamphlets!" Eddie shouted after him, unable to stop herself.

Florence chuckled and shook her head. "Eddie, you're bad."

"HEY, FRIENDS. COME join me," Eddie said to Judith and Dot, patting large patchwork pillows on either side of the one she rested against in the camp's "wisdom tent." The humble lean-to had been transformed—soft muslin sheets swathing the walls, fairy lights strewn across the ceiling—to give the space a feeling of tranquil coziness. It was one of Eddie's favorite places to relax in the entire camp, and while she reserved Mondays for marijuana, she often drank her bedtime chocolate milk in there while watching for shooting stars in the night sky. In a few days it would be full of retreat guests and clouds of fragrant smoke, so she was enjoying some quiet contemplation while she could.

Dorothy "Nurse Dot" Tartt was a mother of two, a sixty-year-old former nurse from the Chicago area who had worked with the Jane Collective in its early days, and had heard of Eddie's camp from a fellow activist. After retiring from traditional medicine, and Jane when it disbanded in 1973, thanks to the *Roe v. Wade* ruling, Dot left Chicago and her now-grown children to join Camp Callaway as its summertime "healer." She used the bounties of the forest and garden to create her tinctures, salves, and teas, and was also a big fan of grass, believing in its many healing properties ("Better than an apple a day!").

Judith held up a joint as Dot settled onto a pillow beside Eddie. "Do you mind?"

"Of course not," Eddie said. She moved to the end pillow to allow Judith and Dot to be side by side. Judith put the joint in her mouth, and Dot sparked it with a lighter from her pocket.

Eddie was bursting to tell her friends about what she had planned. A first-ever offering for the camp guests—a first for the camp, period—and it was a doozy.

The idea had come to her the past winter as she'd shivered violently under heavy quilts, feverish and delirious with a bout of influenza that had passed through town, and then the camp.

It had actually been Eddie's mother, Delilah—or rather the

ghost of her—who had planted the thought in her mind. At the slightest sign of childhood illness, Delilah Callaway used to insist that slices of raw onion be placed around Eddie's sickbed and through the rest of the house, believing the old wives' tale of the vegetable being both protective and preventive. It was a holdover from Delilah's childhood—her own family's nurse believed in the onion's healing powers, slipping the vegetable into a sock and placing it at the end of the bed whenever illness struck. Eddie still found the pungent scent of raw onions oddly comforting.

That afternoon Samuel, who was recovered now from his own fever, had brought Eddie a mug of soup made from their winter stores of potatoes and onions. The scent of it had reeled her back in time, and suddenly Samuel was gone and Delilah was the one spoon-feeding Eddie the soup. She had grabbed for her mother's warm hand, tears shining in her eyes as her heart ached with longing.

"How are you here?" Eddie had croaked out.

"You are my greatest treasure," Delilah replied. "Where else would I be?"

Then her mother had pointed to her old jewelry box, gathering dust on Eddie's bookshelf. "You should really polish that, my darling," she said. "So it's ready to be found."

After Eddie's fever broke, Samuel revealed he'd almost driven her to the hospital when she began speaking gibberish, and she apologized for worrying him so. But she couldn't stop thinking about her otherworldly visit with Delilah, which in the end inspired the most delicious secret Eddie had ever kept.

"Here you go, Eddie. Sharing is caring," Dot said, exhaling a stream of smoke into the open air of the wisdom tent as she held the joint out to Eddie.

"It's not Monday," Judith said, pinching the joint between

two fingers. "Nothing stronger than chocolate milk for our fierce leader here."

"I admire your discipline, Eddie," Dot said, her voice strained due to her holding her breath. She released the smoke in a long hiss and then lay back against the pillows.

"I believe my chocolate milk consumption suggests I have *no* discipline," Eddie replied.

The other two women burst out laughing, their giggles lasting until Dot got the hiccups. Eddie was envious of how her friends felt in that moment—a soft-minded, body-to-liquefied-gold sensation that came from smoking great grass. But she had learned years ago it was best to keep boundaries around her grief, and to not let herself get taken in by mind-numbing drugs. She held a lot of sadness inside her, and self-medicating didn't serve her well.

Soon Dot got up in search of a slice of lemon or spoonful of sugar for her hiccups, weaving slightly as she walked away from the lean-to. Even though she had disappeared into the night darkness almost immediately, the fairy lights only reaching so far, Dot's sharp hiccups echoed.

Judith reached out to hold Eddie's hand, their fingers linking together. "I heard you had a run-in with Vic V today."

Eddie turned her head toward Judith. "Did Flo tell you he threatened me?"

"Flo told me you got the last word in." Judith let the tips of her fingers tickle Eddie's palm in slow, methodical circles. Eddie had the desire both to pull her hand away and to press it more tightly to Judith's. "You know that's what he wants, right? To get under your skin?"

"I know he probably doesn't know the difference between the cervix and the clitoris, nor could he find either even with a detailed map," Eddie replied, scowling.

Judith laughed. "Possibly quite true. But he's not who we're fighting, Eddie."

"Of course he is. Him and all the other small-minded women-haters." A sudden flash of heat engulfed her—something that had been happening more often of late. She knew this was "the change" knocking at her door, and while she found the hot flashes uncomfortable, she didn't fear what they meant. Delilah Callaway hadn't breathed a word about her own change of life to her daughter, something Eddie found most unfortunate. She made a point of not hiding the changes her body was undergoing so the younger generations could be empowered when their own time came.

Between dips in the lake to cool off and an iced tea Dot concocted (made of black cohosh root, which grew wild on camp property), Eddie generally managed the flashes just fine. Tonight, however, the heat wouldn't abate, and she groaned in frustration as she held her hair off the sweaty nape of her neck.

Judith fanned Eddie's neck and chest with her notebook, creating cool puffs of air, and the redness and heat finally started to fade.

"That feels good," Eddie murmured. "Thank you, sweet Jude."

"You're welcome," Judith replied. She set the notebook to the side, then placed her palm against Eddie's chest, right over her heart.

"You need to protect this beautiful fighting spirit of yours. Vic V is a *distraction*. What we're doing here—what the movement on the whole is trying to accomplish—it's far bigger than him. You are no one's stereotype, Eddie Callaway. So don't give Fred Flintstone the satisfaction of turning you into one."

"You're right." Eddie sighed, placing her own hand atop Judith's. "How do you always know what I need to hear?"

"Because we are one soul divided," Judith replied, nestling into the crook of Eddie's arm once she lay back down. "'Love is born into every human being; it calls back the halves of our original nature together, it tries to make one out of two and heal the wound of human nature.'"

Judith had introduced Eddie to philosophical literature, and Plato's *Symposium* had become a favorite.

"We were once a human with four legs, four arms, two hearts, and Zeus, fearing our power, split us clean down the middle. We've been looking for each other ever since, and are now reunited, here in this lean-to," Eddie murmured.

"Precisely," Judith whispered, tilting her head to kiss Eddie.

They were quiet for a moment, and then Eddie's voice—threaded with tension—broke the silence. "It's worth it, right? I mean, all of this."

"It is." Judith's reply was swift, certain.

Nonetheless, Eddie's brow creased. "It's so much work. I know these weeks exhaust the hell out of all of you, too. But none of you ever complains. I'm really grateful you're here, Jude."

"There is nowhere else I would rather be," Judith replied, her voice sleepy and smooth thanks to the grass. "I will always be here with you."

She then sat up and pulled a small canvas bag toward her. "I brought you something."

"Another poem?" Eddie asked.

"Not this time." Judith reached into the bag and brought out a stack of letters. "I thought you might need to hear it from someone other than me."

Eddie had read these letters before, but she was touched by Judith's recognition that this was precisely what she needed to-night to tamp down her insecurities. Judith fluffed one of the pillows and folded it in half to rest under her head. "I'll lie with you while you read."

"Thanks, Jude." Despite all her talk of independence, Eddie hated being alone after dark.

As Judith snuggled beside her, Eddie made her way through the letters—two dozen or so, written by grateful women who had attended a past Camp Callaway retreat. They used words like "life-changing" and "empowering" and "inspiring" and told tales of lives made better for having had the experience.

After she finished the last letter, Eddie returned it to its envelope before settling in beside Judith, taking the younger woman into her arms. They fell asleep under the twinkling lights to the melancholy sounds of the loon's cry and those of a night forest having come alive.

JULY.

THE FIRST RETREAT GUESTS WOULD ARRIVE later tonight, and there was much left to do. Standing among the herbs in the camp's garden, Eddie took off her sandals and stood barefoot in the dirt. The sun had risen, but wasn't yet at full strength. Eddie performed five morning sun salutations, sweeping her arms up and overhead, arching her back slightly, feeling the long, delicious stretch through her muscles. Normally she'd hike first thing, but today's to-do list was long and she needed every minute she could harness.

After sliding her sandals back on, she checked growth patterns and grub and fly infestations (things were looking good), stooping to rub a fuzzy, pale green leaf between her fingers. She brought the scent to her nose. *Sage.* It was spicy, abundantly potent to her senses, and it reminded her of Christmas holidays as a girl, when sage-and-butter-rubbed roasted turkeys would adorn the Callaways' dining table.

The sage still sharp in her nose, Eddie walked around the pile of goat manure, which was vital for curing the garden, and over to where the vegetables were planted. Eddie ran her fingers through the hexagonal holes in the chicken wire, which protected the growing plants. With a gentle touch she coaxed the juvenile tomato leaves toward the sky to gather the sunlight they needed, murmuring encouragement to them as she did.

The dirt on her hands mixed with the dew from the stems and leaves. Thin, muddy streaks crisscrossed her palms, gathering in their creases. She pressed her hands against her denim patchwork jeans—her preferred gardening pants—and smiled at the two faint earthen handprints left behind on her thighs, remembering . . .

IT WAS JULY 1971. Camp Callaway had been left to Mother Nature's whims years earlier, after her parents' poor health kept them from making the trip, after the seasonal staff had been let go, after Theo, Stewart, and Edith couldn't seem to find the time to visit. The dichotomy between Eddie's vision for the camp and what she returned to was vast—perhaps an insurmountable task, she worried silently. However, it was never going to be easy. Edith Jane Hoffman was used to easy; Eddie Callaway thrived on a challenge.

Though she'd grown up at the camp, Eddie was truly a fish out of water that whole first year. She was in transition, straddling the line that demarcated her "before" from her "after." At least she wasn't alone, thanks to Florence and Samuel. They toiled alongside her and propped up her confidence, believing in Eddie more than she believed in herself. What she did to deserve those friendships, she didn't know, but she was grateful for them. They had become her chosen family, and the antidote to her loneliness.

That July day was a soggy one, as it had been raining for three days straight. Those drenching summertime showers that kept everything green and lush in the Adirondack Park, but made Eddie feel blue. Eddie and Florence were in what used to be Camp Callaway's abundant vegetable garden, mucking about. Neither of the women had any idea what she was doing, Florence having grown up in the city surrounded by concrete, and Eddie in an environment where she merely enjoyed the results of hard labor performed by others. The only thing the women knew at this point was that resurrecting a garden was damn hard work. Plowing, shoveling, raking, pulling, tilling—all before a single seed could be planted. Eddie and Florence had been living at the camp for almost four months, since the first signs of winter's thaw. Samuel had arrived at the gate in the middle of May. Camp Callaway's very first retreat guests—a small group of eight women—wouldn't even step foot on the property for another month. Then Judith and Dot would show up the spring of 1973, after which Eddie's core camp family was complete.

Back in the mess of a garden, Florence's rubber boots had gotten stuck in the mud. "Ah, a little help here?"

"Hang on," Eddie replied, taking the few short steps over to Florence. She went to grab her friend's arm, but stumbled, her own boots sinking in. For one chaotic moment Florence tried to keep Eddie upright, and Eddie tried to avoid taking Florence down with her. Soon both women lay prone in a muddy trough beside the burr bush, the Velcro-like balls clinging to their hair, near where the zucchini would later grow large enough that you needed both hands to hold one.

"At least I got one foot out!" Florence stuck her one leg in the air, her sock haphazardly hanging from her toes. The rubber boot remained in the muddy hole.

After they helped each other stand, Florence pulled her T-shirt, which used to be pale blue but was now soaked in dark brown mud, over her head. Eddie followed suit. Then she dipped her hands into the mud and pressed her palms against her chest—the muddy handprints covering her breasts.

"What do you think? New camp uniform?" she asked, spinning around once for flair. Florence did the same, so the women had matching handprints. They observed their handiwork for a moment before busting out laughing, which caused Eddie to have to tightly cross her legs, as she was at risk of peeing through her shorts. Her bladder was never the same after Theo's difficult delivery.

"Uh, hello there?" A man's voice echoed out from behind them.

Eddie and Florence stopped laughing, and gave each other a questioning look—people didn't generally pop in for a visit out here. Florence was the first to face the unexpected visitor, and with her mud-encrusted breasts on full display replied with a friendly "Hey there, yourself, how can we help you?"

Victor Valence and his wife, Sandra, had come to Camp Callaway that morning to welcome Eddie to the Great Camp community. Not realizing, or not caring, that she had been there long before he had, third-generation camp owner and all. Sandra, who stood beside her husband in a lime-green sleeveless tennis dress, held what appeared to be a loaf of some sort in her manicured hands as she said, "Sorry to drop by like this, but your gate was open and Victor thought it would be fine."

Victor Valence didn't know where to look, a redness creeping up his neck and into his ears, but Eddie swore she saw the corners of Sandra's mouth turn up in amusement.

Sandra lingered politely after her husband huffed out a goodbye and swiftly headed back to their car. She handed Eddie the baked loaf (carrot, and quite delicious) and said, "We have a great gardener, if you're looking for help. I'd be happy to pass his name along to you."

"I appreciate that," Eddie replied. "But I think Flo and I have it covered."

Sandra Valence had given the women—and their mud handprints—a final glance, and with a warm smile had replied, "I can see that you do. Have a wonderful day, ladies!"

EDDIE OFTEN REMEMBERED this moment when she came to the garden, now flourishing, and inevitably the laughter would bubble back through her belly and she would have to cross her legs and wait it out.

With a few minutes yet before breakfast, Eddie walked the perimeter of the plot, pausing for a handful of bib lettuce, which she tucked into her mouth and chewed, the buttery green flavor mellow and sweet.

She was both eager and anxious for this session to begin—more so than in the past. Much like a kid on Christmas morning, or before the first day of school, she felt a humming anticipation grow inside her with each passing moment. While the camp was ready for this session's guests, Eddie herself still had a few secret boxes left to tick before she could settle.

Picking up the bag of peanuts she'd brought with her, Eddie set rows of the shell-on nuts along the fencing that bordered the gardens. "Busy hands quiet a busy mind," she used to say to Theo, always honoring his little-boy energy with activities like fishing or hiking or paddling in the camp's canoe. Turned out the same was true for Eddie, and she felt a release of tension as she lined up the nuts.

While Eddie enjoyed all the birds that called the nearby woods home, she had a soft spot for the camp's family of crows—some of whom she believed to be the descendant of the black-feathered birds of her childhood, due to an odd feather marking.

Holding a peanut shell in her open hand, she let out a gruff "caw-caw-caw-caw" and waited. A moment later she heard it—the responding call clearer and deeper than her own as it echoed through the warming air.

"Hello, Jack Frost!" she replied with delight as the mostly black bird, with a smattering of white feathers on its head, which looked almost like the icy patterns left on wintertime windows, swooped in. The crow landed on the nearby fence, right beside her hand holding the peanut.

"I was hoping to see you this morning," Eddie said. "We have guests arriving soon, so fill up and let the family know, all right?" While Jack Frost and the other crows seemed comfortable around the Camp's core crew, they often disappeared when the retreats started.

"Just save some for the chippies. Peanuts are their favorite treat, too." The crow appeared to listen, giving a series of sing-song clicks before nabbing the peanut from Eddie's hand and flying away. She shielded her eyes from the sun, watching it soar, screeching out its call to alert the others about the nuts.

A tense unease suddenly filled her belly. Eddie could write it off as hunger pangs, but ignoring her qualms only bolstered them. So she closed her eyes, pressed her hands against her stomach, and turned inward, resurrecting her old self for a moment.

"Edith Jane, you can rest easy," she whispered. "I know sometimes it feels like what we're doing isn't enough. That it doesn't always make sense. That someone else might be—would be—better to lead the charge." Eddie smiled softly, eyes still closed. "But you are here. I am here. And together we can do this. No, we are doing this."

The dining hall's bell rang out—Samuel announcing the morning meal would soon be ready, and it was time for the rest of the crew, including Eddie, to set the tables—and her eyes popped open. Waves of calm moved through her, the uneasiness dissipating and giving way to a proper stomach growl. With a sense of pleasant eagerness, Eddie quickly scattered the last of the peanuts for the chipmunks, then headed toward the dining hall to join her friends.

The Seduction of Sun Salutations

I know of no better way to welcome the day than greeting the sun! Ground your feet to the earth (barefoot, ideally) and sweep your arms out to the sides and up as far as you can toward the sky. Repeat five times, remembering to use your breath. The sun will nourish you, and the ground will anchor you.

Afterward, hug a tree, caress a flower, leaf, or stem, or press your fingers into the soil to tickle an earthworm. Then, if possible, take a swim in the nude. There is no greater morning ritual to bring out your inner goddess.

—Eddie C. xx

*From *Camp Callaway's Wild Women Handbook*, 1975

ROWAN, 2021.

I RETRIEVE THE QUIK TIN AND HANDBOOK from the car's trunk. While Seth searches for some tool to get under the rusted lid, I look more closely at the book. There are eighteen printed pages, with five blank ones at the end. Curiously, there's some sort of marking on its back cover. It looks a bit like a wide, smudged fingerprint, in black ink or maybe paint. I touch it and feel texture—the left side slightly more raised. Paint, I guess. Likely whoever (Eddie Callaway herself?) smudged the tin also left this mark on the handbook.

When I read the opening letter again, Eddie's earnestness, her depth of passion, leaps off the page. Flipping through, I see a recipe for a green sauce to go over pasta, with "nettles" being a main ingredient. There's a hand-drawn sketch of a plant at the bottom of the recipe, with the words "stinging nettle" written beside it.

"Did you know stinging nettle is edible?" I ask Seth, but he's digging through one of the kitchen drawers and doesn't seem to hear me.

I flip back to a page titled "The Seduction of Sun Saluta-tions." I begin reading the typewritten text—I know of no bet-ter way to welcome the day than greeting—but am interrupted by Seth, who has found a small paring knife he thinks will work. I set the book down.

"YOU HAVE TO get it under . . . No, Rowan. Under the edge, yeah. Just don't slip—it's sharp. Here, let me try. Hand it over." Seth tries to pass me the phone. We're recording our attempt to remove the lid, which is not going well. We've been at it for almost twenty minutes.

I shift, taking the tin with me so it's out of his reach. "I don't need help."

I'm annoyed by his impatience and determined to get the lid off myself, one way or another.

"You could have fooled me," he mutters, exasperated with me as the knife slips again, nicking me this time. A minuscule line of blood, an eighth of an inch long, reveals itself on my finger. "Careful! Jesus, Rowan, *careful* . . ."

Checking the small slice in my skin, which is barely bleeding—no more than a paper cut—I tell him to relax. *I have this under control.* And then . . . success. The rusted metal gives way with a tiny crack, freeing the round lid from the tin with a scrape and then a pop.

"See? Told ya." I'm triumphant, for both Seth and the camera. He'll edit out our bickering later, no doubt. I place the paring knife down and carefully pry off the lid using only my fingertips.

"Easy—that lip might be sharp," Seth says.

"I got it." The lid lifts, and the first thing I notice is the smell—faintly dusty. Stale. Like nothing has disturbed its at-mosphere for a long time. Not dissimilar to how our cabin smelled when we first arrived, before we got the windows open to air it out. But then, as quickly as it came, the scent fades. I peer inside, then play it up for the camera because that's how it's done—exaggerated reactions, plenty of flair. I'm trying to have fun with it because I'm tired of arguing.

"There's something in here . . . ," I say, dropping my voice to a loud whisper.

"What? What do you see?"

Using my phone's flashlight, I point it into the depths of the Quik tin. Then I look up at Seth and grin. "Wanna see?"

"Yes!"

Putting my phone down, I turn the tin upside down and shake it a couple of times. The square of paper inside shifts, but as it's slightly larger than the tin's opening, it doesn't fall out with the movement. However, a dried nub of an evergreen branch slips out, a few of its no-longer-pliable needles sprinkling onto the table. Moving the browned evergreen needles aside, I shake the tin again, and Seth makes a strangled sound, telling me to just get it out already. "The suspense is killing us, Rowan!"

Laughing, enjoying this light moment between us, I play it up for a few extra seconds ("The camera loves you, Rowan!" Seth will say later, and despite my reticence, my ego will enjoy the compliment . . .) before tugging out the paper, which is folded upon itself numerous times. I unfold it, carefully. Four times, until it's a full page—the size of a personal notebook.

"What does it say?" Seth asks, nearly breathless with anticipation. The video continues rolling.

"It's . . . It's a poem." Typewritten, the ink the same purple shade as the handbook's text.

I sit down, page in hand. Seth continues filming me as I scan the page, then flip it over to read what's on the other side.

"What is this?" I murmur.

"What?" Seth asks.

"Turn the camera off, Seth." Before he responds, I look up at him and say, "I'm serious. Turn it off. You need to read this."

A short time later we drive into town, excitedly discussing what we found and what we're going to do about it.

Tucking ourselves into a corner booth at Hopper's, I introduce Seth and Glenda before ordering club sandwiches with fries. Soon we're both focused on the task of learning everything we can about what we discovered in the Quik tin.

I'm careful to wipe all vestiges of French fry grease from my fingers before I smooth the paper out. On one side is the poem, authored by "Jude," the year 1975. The poem references the forest, its trees in particular, and is somehow both ominous and hopeful. On first read, I wasn't sure of its significance. Until I turned the paper over and read the note.

<u>Congratulations!</u>

Dearest adventurer(s): You have found the first clue and now the fun begins! There is a treasure hidden on Camp Callaway property, and it is now yours to find.

The accompanying poem, written by the impossibly talented Judith, is beautiful, haunting, and full of truths. It is also meant to inspire you in your search, and be a compass for what lies ahead. If you follow that inspiration to the place where it lives, an adventure like none other awaits you! All that is required is a willingness to open your mind and your heart, and to explore the world around you without trepidation or expectation.

Good luck, and always remember to stop and LOOK UP, because if you don't, you're missing half of what our

Great Mother Earth has created for us . . . and possibly a clue. Happy treasure hunting, Wild Women of Camp Callaway!

In love and awe,

Eddie Callaway xx

I've been studying Eddie's note since we discovered it, wondering if the "treasure" she refers to is literal and legit. As I'm now rereading the poem, I see something I haven't before, because I was focusing on the words and message and not the shape of it as a whole.

"Can you see what I'm seeing?" I ask Seth.

"Hmm?" His eyes are trained on his computer screen, as he searches for anything related to "Adirondacks + buried treasure."

I lay the page on the table between us, the deep creases impervious to my attempts to smooth them, then shift Seth's computer out of the way. Pointing at the poem, I run my finger along its edge, following the pattern. "I think this is a tree."

Seth leans forward, elbows on the table. The vinyl seat squeaks as he shifts closer.

"See how it starts with one word and gets slightly longer with each line, then shortens again? Like an evergreen tree, and these lines here are supposed to be branches, I guess? And then this last part is the trunk."

"A concrete poem," Seth says. "That's next level."

I nod, bite my lip as I consider the shape of the poem again. Then, more intrigued than ever, I turn back to my phone. It's not a very strategic search, and my expectations are low, but I type in "Judith + concrete poem + Camp Callaway." My screen fills with results and I scan them, stopping at one about

halfway down: a Wikipedia page about Judith Swann, a celebrated American poet.

"Um, hang on a second . . ." I read the Wikipedia page, my
eyes stopping on something familiar: "Camp Callaway."

*Judith "Jude" Swann, the award-winning poet, is also the
owner of Camp Callaway, the now-abandoned Great
Camp in the Adirondacks that once belonged to the
wealthy Callaway family.*

"I think 'Jude' might be *the* Judith Swann."

"The poet?" Seth asks, turning the poem around to look at
it properly. "Damn. If that's the case, we may have an unpub-
lished original here. That's gotta be worth something, like
maybe a lot." He lets out a low whistle.

I'm bothered by his jump to the monetary value of the
poem versus the incredible sense of discovery that comes from
realizing you have something in your hands that may have
never been seen before.

"I wonder how *the* Judith Swann ended up owning Camp
Callaway?" Seth asks.

I shrug, fingers already typing into the search engine. "Let's
see if we can't find out."

WE SPEND AN hour, heads down, researching our find. I
concentrate on articles about Eddie Callaway and Judith Swann,
while Seth gathers information about the supposed hidden
treasure, in particular anything connecting it to Camp Callaway. We're jazzed up on caffeine and sugar (today's pie was

bumbleberry, a medley of blueberries, blackberries, and raspberries, which Glenda says was inspired by a vacation to Eastern Canada), and hyperfocused. At one point I glance up at
Seth, who has a look of deep concentration on his face. He
senses me watching him and gives me a big, disarming smile
before reaching out to squeeze my hand. He goes back to his
screen, but his hand remains a moment longer, his fingers gently caressing my own. I think, *We're a team again*, and a pleasant flush fills me.

I find an address for Judith Swann, though Seth suggests we
don't email her yet. "Let's wait until we figure a few things
out," he says. But to me it seems the quickest way to get information, right from the source, so while Seth's in the washroom,
I type out a quick note ("Dear Ms. Swann . . . We recently
found something at Camp Callaway we believe is yours . . .")
and attach a photo of the poem before hitting send.

AN HOUR LATER Seth and I are back at the cabin, scouring
the articles we've downloaded. After a few minutes, my heart
rate increases as I scan a local news item. *Jackpot.*

"Seth," I say, urgency in my tone. When he doesn't respond, I walk over to where he lies on the rag rug, staring up at
the ceiling—his "I'm thinking" position. His laptop rests beside him.

"Listen to this." I sit cross-legged on the floor and start
reading from my phone.

"'Heads up, amateur treasure hunters—the mysterious Eddie Callaway (née Edith Jane Callaway) is back in the news,
and if you've ever dreamed of finding buried treasure, you'll
want to keep reading.'"

Seth sits up.

"'A park ranger doing a security check of the long-abandoned Camp Callaway unearthed an old chocolate milk powder tin on the property, tucked among a collection of other similar tins near what used to be the camp's shooting range. Inside this newly discovered tin (the words "Look Inside" were painted on its exterior) was a note, which included an evergreen-tree-shaped concrete poem (the poet employs graphic patterns of letters, words, or symbols to convey meaning) as well as suggestions for using the poem's clues to discover a hidden treasure. The note was signed by none other than Eddie Callaway.'"

I pause to take a breath. "'Edith Jane Callaway, who later went by Eddie, was a Long Island socialite and sole heir to the Callaway Shipping fortune. Eddie Callaway, who was notoriously eccentric, according to locals in town, held nature retreats for women at her family's Great Camp after her divorce from Dr. Stewart Hoffman. These retreats ran in the summers from August 1971 until she went missing in July 1975, after heading out for a morning hike. She was never seen or heard from again, despite an extensive search that lasted nearly two months, covering miles of wooded areas surrounding the camp. There has been much speculation about her disappearance, including the suggestion of foul play or a kidnapping attempt, though no ransom demand was ever made, nor was any evidence found to support those theories.'"

Seth's eyes widen; I keep reading.

"'Camp Callaway has been abandoned since shortly after Eddie Callaway's disappearance. The camp changed hands once she was declared deceased (in 1982) and was left to two of the heiress's friends. Unlike other Great Camps in the area, Camp Callaway was never refurbished or sold and, due in large part to the mystery shrouding Eddie Callaway's disappearance, remains one of the Adirondack Park's most captivating settings.

"'While this recently discovered note suggests long-ago rumors of a buried treasure on Camp Callaway property may be true, local law enforcement is reminding the public that trespassing will not be tolerated. Consider yourselves warned, treasure hunters.'"

"When is that from?" Seth asks.

"Ummm . . ." I scroll back to the top. "September 22, 2008."

"That has to be the same note, right?"

"It has to be." I pick up the paper with the poem and the message. "I mean, it was in an old chocolate milk powder tin with 'Inside' painted on it, and it's signed 'Eddie Callaway.' She must have hidden more than one tin?"

"That article is thirteen years old," Seth said. "Do you think the treasure was ever found?"

"Hang on . . ." I scan through the other articles, trying to see if there are any related keywords. "Oh, here's something. From 2015.

"'While many people claim to have figured out the clues within the poem, none have been successful in finding the supposed buried Callaway treasure. There are those who believe Eddie Callaway never buried a treasure at all, but rather fabricated the entire thing in an effort to promote her retreats.'"

I look at Seth. "Unless we missed something, it seems like the treasure's still out there. I mean, if there ever was a buried treasure."

"Let's do it."

"Do what?" I'm still scrolling through the articles, my eyes on my screen looking for anything more recent than 2015.

Seth jumps to his feet. "Let's try and find the treasure."

I laugh. "Seth, we don't even know if there *is* a treasure to find."

"So what?" He crouches beside me, elbows on his splayed

knees. His grin is infectious, and I start to feel what he's feeling—a burst of tantalizing possibility.

"We found the tin. We have this poem. We have the time . . . We're here, like, *right here*," he says, pointing at the forest through the nearby window. "What are the chances it all lines up? It's a sign, Rowan."

"Okay, so let's say we do this." I set my phone to the side, on the rug. "What does that even look like? I've read this poem a dozen times and I have no idea what these supposed clues are. And the park is, like, massive." About *fifteen thousand* square miles massive.

"It has to be within hiking distance of the camp, right?" Seth says. "The note says it's on Camp Callaway property. So that would shrink our search parameters a lot."

"And what about the whole trespassing thing?" I give him a dubious look.

He grabs for my hands. "We'll figure it out. I read some of the camp's property was sold to the state, in the eighties. So maybe it's not even on private property anymore? And we can film all of it, of course."

My grin falters somewhat at the last part, but the energy crackling between us is intoxicating. I've never been able to say no to this version of Seth: engaged, excited, animated.

I nod. "I'm in. Let's go treasure hunting."

Seth throws himself on top of me and I laugh, but it's squeaky because the weight of him restricts my breath. He rolls us so he's underneath me, then kisses the tip of my nose. "I love you," he says.

"I love you, too." I do—so much. Though it's the last time I'll feel that emotion without a flurry of others complicating everything.

EDDIE, 1975.

T HE RETREATS BEGAN IN THE EVENING, AF-
ter the camp bus (a converted school bus) picked the
guests up at the train station. The long gravel drive
that led to camp was lit up with lanterns, as was tradition at
Camp Callaway to welcome its guests. Eddie had set and lit the
kerosene lanterns herself, always careful with their placement
to avoid a fire (an ongoing concern for all local owners, particularly during drier months). It was one of her favorite tasks, and
the final one before the guests arrived. The effect of it was
magical, setting the stage for what would come when they ex-
ited the bus.

Eddie was thrilled to see the new faces—thirty-four of
them, to be exact. It was the largest group so far. The dark sky
was illuminated by the moon's soft glow and that of the many
lightning bugs that circled in lazy patterns. The women were
ushered into the main barn, the only light now coming from
the crew's flashlights. Though the barn housed the animals
in the off-season, the chickens were moved to a nearby coop
and the goats to a lean-to during the summer.

The space had been modified for workshops, twenty hewn

stumps providing seating, along with a few wooden benches. There was an area for yoga practice, and an art installation of sorts on one wall, where former guests had painted dozens of notes beneath a handmade sign reading "Wishing Wall."

"I need you to know three things," Eddie said to the group gathered before her. "One, Mother Earth has provided us access to her home and all she asks is that we respect it. This means no cigarettes or unsupervised burning of any kind."

A woman close to the front, her long hair hanging so straight it looked iron-flattened, itched two fingers on her right hand together. She frowned as she tucked her hand into the pocket of her cutoffs.

"The one exception to the no-burn rule is the wisdom tent, and grass is available for those who are interested," Eddie said, smiling at the woman, who had stopped rubbing her fingers together and looked relieved. "We grow it on property, though we won't mention where."

This had been one of Dot's projects, and she grew the marijuana surreptitiously in the sunflower garden behind the barn. The plants were tucked between the tall large-flowered stems, and so relatively inconspicuous.

"We appreciate your discretion," Eddie added. Most heads nodded in understanding.

"Now, two. This is a women-only retreat. Yes, we do have a man living at camp—Samuel, 'Sam,' who provides us with nourishing food, and who I promise you makes the best pineapple upside-down cake you've ever had—but outside of him, we choose to be with our sisters here at Camp Callaway." More nods around the group.

"And on the note of mealtimes, breakfast, lunch, and dinner are served buffet-style here at camp, and we expect you to scrape your plates and stack them in the bins after you've finished. Though I doubt there will be much left behind, as Sam's meals are delicious." At that, there was a mild murmur of laughter from the women.

"And three, we are here to guide you—as equals. We will never control you or force you into anything. Our purpose is one of light and love and peace. Your knowledge is your power, so don't dismiss your inner voice." Eddie paused for a moment, for effect.

"I know our time together is short, but I promise you it will be meaningful."

Eddie made eye contact as best she could with each of the women. It took well over a minute to connect with everyone, but Eddie didn't rush. In their faces she saw myriad emotions— she had learned to recognize subtle differences between excitement and trepidation, sadness and anxiety, optimism and yearning. She saw all of this in the women before her, and suddenly felt choked up. Overwhelmed that the women were putting their trust in Eddie, in the others who ran the camp with her. She was impressed as hell with their willingness and courage, and told them so.

"Most importantly, we are going to have a lot of fun. So, who's with me? Who wants to have the most incredible week of her life?"

Eddie raised her hands above her head and pumped her fists as the women cheered and whistled and shouted affirmations, and no matter how much work and dedication it took for Eddie to do this—week after week, year over year—she experienced the same exhilaration she did every time.

THE NEXT MORNING Victor Valence was back, though this time he was not alone. He and another one of the private owners, Alfred Bell—whose property, Whispering Pines, re-sided on the other side of Victor's—stood at the front gate.

While Eddie and Victor had a caustic relationship, she had remained neighborly with Alfred whenever their paths crossed. Alfred Bell was old money, too, his camp a multigenerational one as well. Though unlike Eddie's, Alfred's lineage remained robust, with four living children and fifteen grandchildren.

Alfred and his sons had on occasion joined George Calla-way's hunting groups, back when there was more socializing between the camp families, with summer picnics and July Fourth parties. Eddie had also played with the two youngest Bell children, daughters, during those summers, but it had been years since she'd spoken to any of them. Naturally she'd heard rumblings of dissatisfaction with how she chose to use her camp, but the Bells (at least until today) had kept their opinions to themselves.

Eddie sighed as she walked toward the men. She had better things to do than deal with whatever nonsense issue had brought them to her gate today. The first camp sessions were starting soon; Eddie hoped this impromptu visit was brief.

"Morning, Victor. Alfred." Alfred Bell, with his thick, wavy stark-white hair, towered over Victor and Eddie. She stuck her hand over the gate, having decided on *polite and friendly*, with a tinge of assertiveness as required.

"Eddie," Alfred said, stepping forward to shake her hand. The older man was nothing if not socially appropriate. Vic-tor, however, remained where he was, arms crossed over his chest.

"Enjoying the sunshine?" Eddie asked the men, to which Victor replied, "This isn't a friendly visit."

Don't give him the satisfaction.

"Ah, well then. So, what business brings you by?" Though

she was now a woman who felt comfortable staking her place in the world, old habits die hard, and Eddie found herself crossing her own arms protectively across her chest. As soon as she realized what she was doing, however, she uncrossed her arms and let them rest easily against her sides.

"You need to keep your girls here, Callaway," Victor said.

"First things first, they are *women.*" Eddie worked hard to keep her cool.

Victor pressed his lips together, and Alfred placed a firm hand on his shoulder before addressing Eddie.

"As you know, our properties are private. Vic V's simply here to ask your *women* visitors to respect the boundaries of camp lines," Alfred said.

"Did something happen?" Eddie asked. The guests had just arrived the night before. As far as she knew, she was the only one who'd ventured out for a hike this morning.

"Well, he came across a couple of your guests in, uh, a delicate position in his north boathouse." Alfred raised an eyebrow, which was as white as his hair and furry like a caterpillar. Victor looked like he was going to blow a gasket.

"I see." Eddie felt a flush of annoyance toward whoever had decided Victor's boathouse was an appropriate place for this intimacy. She had been quite clear that the guests needed to stay on property. After all, there was plenty of room to accommodate *all* needs. Not to mention that would have been quite the middle-of-the-night trek! Victor's camp property was across from Eddie's, though slightly south, with a solid few miles separating them.

But she also wanted to burst out laughing, imagining Victor discovering these two women. Oh, he must have had a fit.

"I expect you to deal with this. It can't happen again," Victor said.

"Well, not in your boathouse at least." Eddie shouldn't needle Victor, but it was like scratching a mosquito bite—it made things worse in the long run, but was deliciously satisfying short term.

Besides, she was done with all this meddling in her affairs. Perhaps she had been naive, had misjudged the depth of irritation the other camp owners felt toward her and her retreats. Eddie had assumed any discontent would eventually blow over—after all, no one was being harmed, even with this current trespassing incident.

Never mind, Eddie told herself now. She would tuck that issue away for another day. *You have more important things to focus on.*

Keeping the easy smile on her face, she stepped back from the gate. "Gentlemen, I need to return to my *women* guests. Alfred, Victor, I hope you have a lovely rest of your day."

EDDIE HAD GROWN up in the woods around the camp, so there wasn't a single foot of the forest on her property she didn't know intimately. It had been a place she sought adventure, wisdom, peace, refuge, and healing—especially in more recent years. It was therefore a great pleasure and honor to be able to introduce the women who visited Camp Callaway to these cherished woods, and help them connect with nature in a way they might not have before.

She had only one request for the retreat guests she led on these hikes—aside from asking for their trust that she would not lead them astray—and that was to remain silent during the trek. "Learning to listen while deep in the belly of the forest teaches you to listen to the depths of your own heart and soul," Eddie explained as they set out.

Today's hikers abided by the ask, and for an hour all you could hear—except from the sounds of labored breathing—was the wind's gentle whistle through the treetops, myriad bird-songs and -calls, and the crunch of hiking boots cracking forest debris underfoot. The only time Eddie spoke was when they walked near the lake, where a large patch of stinging nettle grew.

"Nature offers such bounty," Eddie said, pulling gloves and a canvas tote from her small backpack. She slid on the gloves, and firmly grasped one of the stems of the tall green leafy plant. "This is stinging nettle. You may have seen some in our vegetable garden as well—it's a great babysitter for the tomato plants.

"You never want to touch it with your bare hands, because see?" She snapped one of the plant stalks, then showed the group. The women leaned in, murmuring that yes, they did see the baby-hair-like stingers.

"But once you steam or boil the leaves, they are not only safe but delicious. You won't believe how good nettle pasta is—there's a recipe in your handbooks." Eddie snapped a dozen more stalks, being sure to leave plenty behind, then crammed the plants into the canvas tote before putting it, and the gloves, into her backpack again. "Okay, let's carry on then."

Soon they came to a familiar landmark of Eddie's—a large rock that was pyramid-shaped, ice-blue lichen dotting its surface—and she paused for a beat, her eyes following the barely noticeable trail that split off the main path, to the right. Eddie didn't follow that trail now (she traveled it only once a week, on Mondays, during her usual morning hike), instead leading the women to the left, on a more well-trodden path.

The hallowed spot the trail on the right led to had been Eddie and Theo's discovery almost twenty years earlier. A secret clearing deep in the woods, with a tree whose leaves "danced" in the breeze, and where the two would laugh and dream in the happiest of times. It was tucked between pockets of dense forest, literally off the beaten path, and so without knowing the critical landmarks—the triangular blue-lichened rock; the two trees whose trunks had grown together, like a chocolate-and-vanilla soft serve twist; a small meadow bursting with vibrant green fern steps from the clearing—you might never find it twice.

After hiking for another half a mile, Eddie held up a hand and the women all stopped walking in unison. In front of them were two logs lying perpendicular to each other, propped up on both ends by flat-topped rocks to create benches.

"That was a sweaty one, well done! Expect everyone has worked up an appetite?" Eddie used the bandanna around her neck to mop her face, asking the group to find seats on the bench—the informal meet-up location she liked to use to get to know the women better. The guests sat on the benches as Eddie pulled the hearty granola bars Samuel had made from her backpack, chock-full of nuts, seeds, and carob chips, and sweetened with maple syrup.

This group of hikers Eddie led into the woods consisted of five women. There was Nancy, a young mother of two from New Jersey, who had apparently told her husband she needed to visit her ailing aunt when really what she needed was an escape from family life. Beside Nancy sat Ingrid; willowy and slightly older than Eddie, she had been quiet since arriving at Camp Callaway—more an observer than a talker, Eddie figured. Then there were two friends, Shirley and Patricia, barely twenty, who had traveled from Boise in a camper van and were the women Victor had found in his boathouse (rather than chastise the young women, Eddie had simply reminded the entire group to stay on Callaway property). Rounding out the hikers was Rebecca, a middle-aged woman who seemed painfully shy and had kept to herself thus far. When Rebecca had pulled up her long sleeves during the hike, Eddie noticed, but didn't comment on, a couple of suspicious-looking bruises on her arms. Rebecca now explained that her younger sister had suggested the retreat.

"She insisted I needed the break," Rebecca said with a halfhearted shrug, and Eddie wondered what precisely she needed a break from.

"If I were a genie and could grant you one wish, what would it be?" Eddie then asked the women, after they'd started in on the granola bars and shared why they'd come to Camp Callaway.

Nancy spoke first. "I wish I could stop time. But not for myself. I'd like to stop everyone and everything around me—I have seven-year-old twins," she explained, smiling. But she looked tired, with dark circles under her eyes.

"So if the world stopped, even for a day . . . heck, for an hour! I might be able to catch up." Nancy chewed on her fingernails, and one of the hangnails started to bleed. She tucked the bleeding hand under her thigh.

"Not the first time I've heard a wish for a time machine, Nancy," Eddie said, smiling warmly at the frazzled mother. "Who else?"

Shirley and Patricia wished for enough money to travel through the rest of the United States in their van, and then maybe spread their wings around the world after that. They held hands and grinned at each other as they spoke, and Eddie encouraged them to add this to the Wishing Wall in the barn. The art wall was a recent installation at Camp Callaway, started the summer before, and the barn boards served as a canvas for retreat guests to record their greatest wishes. It provided a physical manifestation of dreams for the visitors, who used colorful oil-based paints to draw and write on the Wishing Wall. Eddie loved how it transformed the interior of the barn, and how the kaleidoscope of words and pictures changed the feel of the space. She couldn't wait to see what it looked like another few summers from now, after more visitors had left their marks.

Ingrid, up next, hesitated before revealing her wish. "I want to be a mother," she said. Nancy quickly looked up from the ground, guilt stretching across her face.

"I'm too old now, obviously." Ingrid glanced down at her hands, clasped in her lap. She was so slender her veins popped across the tops of her hands, like blue ropes under her pale skin. "And I know being a single mother won't be easy. But I'm on an adoption list, so . . . we'll see."

Eddie thought of Theo, and how she might feel if she had never had him. If the yearning for a child would have continued long after her body was capable of creating one. She did know that once he left her, she never wished to be a mother to any other child. She only wished for him to return, somehow.

"Where there's a will, there's a way," Eddie said. "I will fervently wish for that to come true for you, Ingrid." She made a mental note to speak with Dot—who herself had been a single mother, after becoming a widow—about adding a workshop to the camp roster specifically for women facing that unique parenting challenge.

Then she turned to the last woman in the group. "What about you, Rebecca?"

She looked over at Eddie, her face blank. "I stopped wishing for things a long time ago."

"Maybe it's time we change that, huh?" Eddie asked softly,

holding Rebecca's gaze. She then pulled Judith's notebook—handmade, with pressed wildflowers on its cover—out of her backpack.

"I'd like to read you all something. In another day or so, you'll understand the significance," Eddie said. Flutters of anticipation filled her. "I have a surprise, but it's not quite time to share it. So for now, please just close your eyes and listen with your whole being."

Nettles, if not grasped firmly, will sting. It's how they protect themselves, an outer shell meant to keep them safe—not unlike the shell we sometimes wrap around ourselves, hoping it provides protection from trauma. However, with a bit of heat nettles are transformed, and so, too, can you be. Grasp your life firmly so it won't sting you like a nettle, but rather be soft as silk.

—Eddie C. xx

Green Sauce Noodle Salad

Blanch nettle leaves in boiling water (this removes the stinging hairs), then pop about a half a cup of blanched nettle into your blender, along with garlic, walnuts, and a few shakes of grated hard cheese, like parmesan.

Blend until smooth and enjoy over chilled pasta shells or noodles.

*From *Camp Callaway's Wild Women Handbook*, 1975

ROWAN, 2021.

J ESS CALLS THE NEXT MORNING, INVITING
us to take a hike with her to see more of the area. I readily agree. My quick acceptance of her offer makes me
realize how friendship-starved I have been lately. And not just
since arriving at the cabin, but really since leaving LA. Things
have felt so transient of late, and I miss the cadence (not to
mention fun) of nights out, of Runyon Canyon hiking dates or
a simple beach day with my LA friends, most of whom I've
failed to keep in touch with. Between the pandemic and the
move back to Ann Arbor, I've been so focused on my own shit
that I've been a lousy friend. And after a while, people stop
reaching out.

Jess tells me she'll pack a picnic and to make sure we wear
the "serious" bug repellent. Before grabbing my camera, I slip
on my thick hiking socks to avoid blisters. Seth barely looks up
from his laptop when I mention Jess's offer. We've been studying the poem, looking for clues, and my eyes and brain feel
scrambled—I need a break, I tell him.

"You go," he says, barely looking up from the poem. "Have fun."

"COME ON IN," Jess says as she opens the yurt's front door. "Just getting my pack ready."

"Just me," I say, stepping into the yurt. "Seth is head down on something at the moment. I'll tell you about it while we hike."

Aidan turns from his easel to say hi, brush in one hand and wearing an oversized T-shirt covered in paint splatters. I catch a glimpse of what he's working on: a mountainous landscape, partially complete, two long dark brown brushstrokes ready to become trees.

"That looks great," I say.

"Thanks, Rowan," Aidan replies, swirling his brush into the brown watercolor paint. "You a Bob Ross fan?"

"My dad is," I reply.

"Aidan is obsessed," Jess whispers, sliding her backpack over her shoulder, and I laugh softly.

"We once got a Bob Ross Chia Pet for my dad," I tell him. "As a birthday present."

"Oh yeah?" Aidan's eyes light up. "I'd love one of those. For my collection." He flips around the mug he's using to clean his brushes and I read the caption.

"Let's Get Crazy."

I raise an eyebrow at Jess, and she mouths, "See?" Then she hugs Aidan from behind, her arms encircling his waist. He leans back into her in a sort of reverse embrace, and with stabs of envy I think of Seth's distracted goodbye.

Aidan kisses Jess's forehead. "Say hi to the birds for me. And remember, in the words of our good friend Bob . . . 'There's nothing wrong with having a tree as a friend.'"

"Well, if Bob says so . . ." Jess opens the yurt's door. "Ready to go make some tree friends, Rowan?"

"Can't wait." I follow her out into the sunshine.

"SO WHAT'S YOUR guilty pleasure?"

Jess laughs. "I don't believe in guilty pleasures. There are only things you enjoy or don't, and guilt should never be attached to anything that brings you pleasure."

"I never thought about it that way, but you're so right."

"But if you're asking what's my Bob Ross equivalent?" Jess is slightly out of breath, while I'm finding it difficult to talk at all—we're on a particularly arduous part of the trail, and I'm out of shape. We pause at the top of a hill, which is steep with craggy rocks and unreliable footing.

"Cheeseburgers. And needlepoint," she answers.

"Cheeseburgers?!" I laugh, feeling less winded now that we've stopped for a minute. "For some reason I assumed you were vegetarian?"

"I am, mostly," Jess replies. "But a couple times a year I get a cheeseburger at Glenda's diner in town. They're handmade and have a thick slice of sharp cheddar on top. With pickled onions."

"I've met Glenda, but not her cheeseburger. I'll have to try it. And needlepoint, huh?" I shake my head. "You talk about being science nerds, but between his painting and your needlepoint, I don't know. Pretty creative and artistic, if you ask me."

"Well, you haven't seen my needlepoint."

We laugh easily again, and I realize how relaxed I am. Happy, even? It has been a while since I've felt that so purely, without shadows of other emotions. As we press on, I occasionally pause to take pictures. Bright green caterpillars inching across branches. Two trees that have merged trunks, as though embracing. Tiny white flowers blooming out of impossibly narrow rock crevices. A gentle trickle of water carving a path through the mulch underfoot. Jess points out birds as we go: a bay-breasted warbler, its throat bright orange; a yellow-bellied sapsucker, the only woodpecker in the park, Jess says, that is completely migratory; an American bittern, with its distinctive "pump-er-lunk" song.

As we hike deeper into the woods, I fill her in on what we found. The Quik tin and its curious contents. The Wild Women handbook, which provided insight into Eddie Calla-way's musings and perspectives, at least in 1975. We talk about the buried treasure, discuss its veracity.

"That rumor has been swirling for years," Jess replies.

She says that when she first met me and Seth, that's precisely why she thought we were visiting the park: as amateur treasure hunters.

"I wasn't confident about your success, though," she adds. "Anyone lost on the main road probably won't have much luck in the woods."

I laugh, acknowledging that neither of us is particularly directionally gifted.

"I've explored miles of these woods, and I've never seen anything resembling a treasure. But I'm always distracted by the birds," Jess says. "I'd probably have to trip over it."

Soon we take a proper break, and when I remove my backpack, my T-shirt sticks to my sweat-slicked skin. I tug it away a few times, letting air circulate under the material.

Jess hands me a hard-boiled egg from a stainless steel container. It's cold and rubbery against my fingers.

"Thanks." I add a shake of salt to the egg. "Can I ask you a personal question?"

"You bet." Jess salts her own egg.

"How old are you?"

Jess looks amused. "How old do you think I am?"

"Honestly, I have no idea!" I reply after swallowing a bite of egg. "Seth and I can't figure it out. And it doesn't matter, but..."

"I'm fifty-three."

"You are not." I turn to face her, half-eaten egg still in hand. Jess chuckles at my shock. "What? How? I will never believe it. Fifty-three?" My own mother is sixty-three, and Jess looks closer to my age than my mom's. "Wow. Hashtag aging goals."

"Okay, my turn," Jess says.

"I'm thirty, and I look my age." I give her a wry look.

"You're aging just fine, Rowan," Jess replies. "But that's not my question. I'd love to know how you ended up becoming a writer."

"Hmm. I think I love the challenge of it? Of creating something tangible out of a simple idea. Plus, it's *fun*. Even when it's not." I laugh, a touch bitterly. "I can't believe I said that. It hasn't been much fun lately."

At that I go quiet, thinking of my pitch sitting somewhere in Clara's inbox, long buried now. Of the screenplay that took me two years to write. About how I deprioritized my writing when the bills piled up—something I promised myself I would never do.

I feel exposed despite Jess's knowing none of this, and my cheeks burn hot.

"How come?" Jess asks.

I shrug. "I thought I had it all figured out. I had a timeline. A *plan*. But what's that they say about best-laid plans?"

Jess smiled. "They go awry."

"They do. It did."

Suddenly, there's a light tickle on my wrist. It's a daddy longleg spider making its way up my arm with its spindly legs and pinhead-sized body—moving in a straight line, as though following my scar. I see Jess glance at my arm, at my scar. The spider shifts direction, finding a safe path across my elbow, down my thigh, and to the ground below.

"I almost died when I was sixteen," I say, tracing the length of the scar with my fingertips. "After that I promised myself I wouldn't be one of those people who *hesitated*, you know?"

Jess nods, listening.

"But lately it feels like all I do is *hesitate*."

And then, in a moment of clarity, I see precisely what's happened. What's behind my despondence of late. Why I pushed to return to Ann Arbor when we ran out of money. Why I got drunk and made that unfortunate live confessional. Why I was so keen to get us to the small cabin in the big woods.

I've been wasting my own precious time, shifting my focus to meeting Seth's needs. Pretending it doesn't matter which one of us finds success, as long as one of us does.

(We succeed together or fail apart.)

What if, somewhere along the way, I stopped believing in myself?

"I WAS OUT walking with my mom after dinner. It was early fall, my favorite time of year," I tell Jess. "I was all about my fleece hoodies back then."

My mom, via some parenting book she read when we were young, had decided nightly walks with us girls—never as a group, always one-on-one—were the answer to keeping the parent-child relationship threads intact. Because my two older sisters had left home by this point, the walks with my mom were almost nightly now, as I was the only chick still in the nest.

"We had this orange-spice tea, in travel mugs, and walked our usual route—about a forty-minute walk." I pause, finding it hard to catch my breath. Jess comments how much she loves orange-spice tea, especially iced.

"Me, too." I clear my throat. "One minute we're sipping our tea and laughing about a funny moment I shared from school— someone in my class had swapped a live frog for the cadaver ones we were dissecting in biology, and our teacher nearly dropped to the floor when the frog jumped from the table!"

Jess laughs easily. I join her, before stopping abruptly.

". . . Then the next I'm lying on the ground ten feet from my mom. All I could hear were the sounds of a radio blaring and someone crying."

I also remember the thick smell of burning rubber in my nose, making me feel sick to my stomach.

We found out later the driver, who was only nineteen, had dropped her cell phone. When she reached down to grab it, she swerved, and when she looked up again, she was about to jump the curb. Panicked, the young woman hit the gas instead of her brakes, and plowed right into me and my mom.

It was a miracle we lived, everyone said. My mom's leg, which was pinned between the car's bumper and a nearby tree trunk, couldn't be saved. Neither could the tree. But because my mom had pushed me as far from the car's path as possible, I ended up only with injuries I could heal from. A concussion, a sprained ankle, and a deep gash on my arm (right through my fleece hoodie) from the metal on the car's passenger-side door, which had been torn mostly off with the impact. The only physical reminder I have is my long white scar.

"Thanks for listening to that very depressing story." I smile, but it's fleeting. "I never really talk about it. Which is sort of weird, isn't it? Maybe because no one asks anymore."

"Thanks for telling me," Jess replies. "You know, I have learned stories, particularly hard-to-tell ones, are a lot like birds. You have to let them come to you, in their own time."

"IT WOULD BE so easy to get lost out here." As we hike back the way we came, I look around at the thick-trunked trees, the saplings reaching toward the canopy, the rocks covered in blue lichen surrounding us. They all look identical to the trees, rocks, and plants we passed fifty paces back.

"One of my favorite things to do is to get lost in the woods," Jess replies. "I try to do that at least once a week."

I think about perspective. About how while losing my way in the forest feels terrifying to me, especially if I'm alone, for Jess it's a positive experience. Even more, it's something she *seeks*.

"Do you ever miss things? Like, the creature comforts of city life? Being able to get to a Target in under five minutes? Or spontaneously going to a restaurant for dinner? Having drinks with friends on the weekend?"

"Oh, for sure," Jess replies. "The luxury of picking up groceries daily, or walking into a coffee shop and getting a hot cappuccino someone else made for you . . . with a fancy design in the foam." She lets out a small, wistful groan.

"I have learned I make truly terrible coffee," I say. "I could blame the ancient coffee maker at the cabin, but I don't think that's it. I'm spoiled, I guess."

"Nah, blame the old-ass coffee maker." Jess grins, then pulls out her water bottle.

"I don't really miss the crowds, or the hustle of that life," she says, looking up at the tree canopy overhead. My eyes follow hers. A slight breeze makes the leaves tremble, allowing rays of sun to reach down to the smaller saplings below. Jess's bare shoulders are swathed in patterns of dancing light. "Did you know trees talk to each other?"

"Really?" I say.

Jess nods, still looking up. "They communicate what they need, and then send each other nourishment."

She crouches, digging her fingers deep into the moss and soil underneath. With gentle fingers she unearths a spindly white root. It has tendrils of baby roots covering its surface, like new hair growth. "They use networks of fungi, buried deep underground, to spread the nutrients around. Like the way electricity moves through wires."

Jess carefully tucks the root back into the earth, and stands. "I know I'm a bird lady, but trees are cool as hell. It's all connected."

Suddenly, everything around us seems more vibrant. More alive.

"I used to feel like something was missing, in my old life. There was this *void*, even though I was surrounded by people. By things I really didn't need but felt compelled to collect," Jess says. "But now, surrounded instead by all these beautiful, magical trees and the birds that call them home, that sense of emptiness is gone. Even though we're so isolated out here, I'm never lonely. Funny, isn't it?"

"It is," I reply softly. Sometimes all I see is what's missing.

Jess takes a drink from her water bottle, and I notice a crescent moon of black earth under her fingernails. I stare at the slivers of dirt for a moment, thinking about what she said.

How messed up it is that the trees—without brains, without hearts, without words—are better at communicating their needs than I am.

THE SHRILL "CAW-CAW-CAW" interrupts my lunch-making efforts, and I glance up through the cabin's open front window. I'm making toasted tomato sandwiches, thanks to a fresh one I picked from Aidan and Jess's garden after our hike yesterday. I'm feeling good. Humming as I spread mayonnaise on thick slices of sourdough bread. I had a productive morning writing, and am still on a high.

Seth has only moments before returned from town. He said he wanted to ask Glenda a few questions about the buried-treasure rumors, and I happily handed him the car keys, told him to take his time. I relished the solitude to brainstorm my new script idea based on Eddie Callaway's camp and disap-pearance. My hike with Jess wriggled something loose inside me. Suddenly, everything feels limitless.

As Seth was leaving, he asked to borrow my phone, as his was nearly out of battery.

"Fine with me," I said. I prefer old-school writing sessions: pen to paper. My only request was that he download any new emails, which he said he would.

Now, hearing the crow's throaty call, I set my mayonnaise-laden knife on the cutting board and grab the peanuts from the cupboard. "Shoot. I forgot to put these out."

Seth is at the kitchen table, waiting for his sandwich. He makes an annoyed sound, though I can tell it's put on. "Really? You're leaving your starving-to-death fiancé for a bird?"

"Didn't you just eat a giant plate of Glenda's pancakes?" I say. "Besides, that's not just any bird. It's our crow friend. Did you know they can build tools? And remember people's faces? And pass lessons on to their young?" I slide my feet into slip-on sneakers by the front door, the peanut bag tucked under my arm.

"Mmm-hmm. I did know all that," Seth replies, for I have already told him what Jess shared with me about Corvus birds.

"I'll be back. Feel free to slice that tomato." I open the screen door, and the crow, with its white wing feather, gives another "caw-caw." Its black beady eyes follow me—or, more specifically, the bag of peanuts—as I set nuts out on the far side of the railing.

"Sorry I'm late today," I say. The crow cocks its glossy head, as though listening.

"There you go. Enjoy the snack." I take a couple of steps back, readying to sit in the chair on the porch. I like watching the crow enjoy the peanuts, and it doesn't seem to mind my company. But it flies away, cawing loudly as it goes. I sigh, a little disappointed, then set out another row of nuts on the railing it just vacated, hoping once I go inside it will return.

Just as I'm opening the screen door, the crow swoops back toward the cabin, landing effortlessly on the railing covered in peanuts. It has something shiny in its beak, but I can't make out what it is.

"What have you got there?" I squint, focusing on the object. "Another rock?" Something glints gold, and ever more curious, I take a tentative step toward the crow.

"Don't be scared. I'm a friend."

The crow sets the object on the railing, then takes a peanut in its beak and flies to a nearby tree branch. I pick up what the bird has left behind, turning it over in my fingers. It's a small enameled pin, with a yellow happy face on its front. The outside edge is rimmed in gold metal, which also outlines the oblong black eyes and smiling mouth.

"Is this for me?" I look over at the crow in the tree. No "caw-caw" answer, but it also doesn't fly away.

I glance back at the pin. Its metal back and pin have rusted, but the front smiley face is in excellent condition. "Huh," I say softly, and then, more loudly to the crow, "Thank you!"

My eyes are still on the curious pin when I return inside, so I don't immediately notice what Seth is doing.

"The weirdest thing just happened. I think that crow brought me . . ." My voice trails off as I see Seth, seated at the table, quickly shuffle papers over my phone. "What are you doing?"

Seth swallows hard. His face pinches up like he's in pain. "Rowan, I need to tell you something."

"Did something happen to my phone?"

He looks ill and places his hand atop the papers, holding them in place. Like you would if there was a big gust of wind.

"What's the matter?" A cold dread fills my stomach because I know his face and its expressions, and what I'm seeing there in spades is guilt. I move closer to the table, so I'm right in front of him.

"I'm sorry, Rowan. So, so sorry."

I clutch the smiley face pin—its edges sharp against my palm. This must be worse than a cracked phone screen. "Sorry for what?"

Seth sighs, then moves the stack of papers off my phone and hands it to me.

I take my phone and look at the screen. It's not cracked. Everything looks fine until it doesn't.

My inbox is open, and an email stares back at me—a message I've never read. At first I think it's a new email Seth downloaded in town. But I notice it isn't bolded, like an unread message would be. And then I notice the date—July 6. This email is almost a month old.

"What is this?" I whisper, staring at the message. Trying to scan it while also staying focused on Seth's response. I look over at him, dumbfounded, my throat constricting.

"I moved it back into your inbox when I was in town." He scrapes his fingers through his dark hair. Once, twice. Linking his fingers behind his neck, he pulls his elbows together, his face shifting downward so I can't see his expression.

"*Back* from where?" My heart races as understanding slowly dawns.

He sighs, doesn't look at me. "I'm sorry."

I turn my gaze from Seth to my phone. I read the email in full. Then I read it again.

"This is from before we even left!" My breath catches, realizing the implications now. This email arrived less than a week after my drunk-on-tequila night when I live streamed. *"Why haven't I seen this email, Seth?"*

"Because I stuck it in a folder."

I have well over a dozen folders for my emails—I like the organization it provides, so my inbox stays manageable. I rarely go into the folders, however, unless I'm searching for something specific.

"What?" I sputter. "When? *How?*"

"Does it matter?" He shrugs, looking dejected, then clears his throat. "I honestly meant to tell you. Before we left Ann Arbor. But then I just . . . I fucked up. You have no idea how sorry I am."

I stare at him, speechless, trying to catch up.

"So you did this . . . *on purpose?*"

"Rowan, I have no . . ." Seth presses his lips together. "I'm sorry, I—"

"Stop saying you're sorry!" I pace the small room, trying not to burst into tears.

Seth strides toward me, hands suddenly on my upper arms to stop me from pacing. I shake him off, but he's determined to have me near him, and approaches again.

"It was so stupid. I almost can't even explain anymore why I did it in the first place! But . . . I was mad about that live broadcast, okay? Really mad. And, I don't know, worried maybe you wouldn't want to come here to the cabin if you read this email? I needed you . . . *I need this*, Rowan. For my book. But we also need this time together. You know it as well as I do. Things haven't been easy since we left LA. For a while, actually."

My mouth falls open. "This is about punishing me?"

"No!" Seth says quickly. Hotly. Then he shakes his head. "It's not like that. It just seemed we were at a crossroad. And I was worried we might end up going in different directions if I didn't *do something.*"

I shrink back, crying now. Tears of frustration, betrayal, and crushing disappointment. We're supposed to be a team! Our ambitions tied together in a way that makes us stronger than we could ever be apart.

"Do you even know what you've done?" I say.

"No, no. Rowan, *listen to me.* It's not too late." Seth reaches out to wipe away my tears. I let him, mostly because I'm in shock.

"I'll drive us back into town right now so you can reply. Or even call her, okay?" He gestures to the corded telephone in the kitchen. "You can still set the meeting. We can leave to-morrow morning if we have to. Or even tonight. You can be in LA the day after. It's going to be okay. Please, please say it's okay, Rowan."

"Let go of me," I mutter, pushing him away. He holds his hands up, regret and sadness etched on his face.

Some part of me understands that Seth's childhood baggage includes a deep fear of being abandoned. Of being left behind, all alone. It's why I think, aside from the money, he's obsessed with building our subscribers—proof people want him around, care about what he has to say. Seth practically raised himself. It was not a happy time in his life, and he was adamant he would never again let someone determine his trajectory. He always said he wouldn't make the same mistakes with us, with his own family. *Our family.*

Before now I saw this as stoic and brave—Seth pushing past his sad upbringing and promising history would not repeat itself. Despite the lack of role models, he would be the best partner. But now, as I watch him tear up about a situation he has no business crying over, I realize he wasn't thinking about me or considering *my* future at all. Only his own.

I grasp for the screen door's handle, awkwardly as I'm still holding my phone in one hand and the pin from the crow in the other. Then, without a glance back, ignoring his pleas to *stay, listen, talk,* I slam the door behind me as hard as I can before running away from the cabin.

EDDIE, 1975.

EDDIE THREADED THE SQUIGGLING WORM onto the hook, using great care to ensure no part of the metal would glint under the water. Once satisfied, and after a silent but earnest "thank you" to the worm for its role in what would come next, she cast the rod. The water was smooth as glass this early in the morning, the sun beginning to peek over the tree line across the lake, bathing everything in a soft golden glow. The camp and its guests were still quiet, slumbering, and Eddie had awoken with a desire to fish rather than to take her usual morning hike. Really, it didn't matter which she chose. Both gave her time with her son.

She fished in bare feet (a necessity for sun salutations, which required the soles and toes to grip the dock's wooden slats), something she would never have let Theo do. Errant hooks could easily sink their barbs into skin and flesh.

The rod was light because of its bamboo construction, the cork handle smooth from use. The only sounds were the whip of release from the rod's tip and the plop of the worm as it hit the surface of the water before sinking quickly, the finely braided cotton line barely visible.

As she waited for a tug on the line, Eddie allowed reminiscence to envelop her. She liked to remember Theo at the camp. How he learned how to bait a hook from his grandfather at only four years old, both of them so proud when he did so without pricking his own finger in the process. The way Theo would tread water until he got cramps in his legs so as to offer his head as a resting spot for the blue-bodied dragonflies that flew about. Then there were the epic raspberry-picking sessions the two of them embarked upon, returning to the camp's kitchen with buckets of sweet, juicy fruit to go into pies, cobblers, and jams. Or the time the smallmouth bass fought so hard it pulled Theo off balance and right into the lake (though he never let go of his rod, he'd excitedly told everyone).

"I think we got one!" Eddie exclaimed now as the line went taut, the fish fighting for release. She felt exhilarated as she began reeling it in—the muscles in her forearms straining with the effort. This was a good-sized fish, she could tell.

Then she heard Theo's voice, cracking and shifting from high to low, the way boys' voices do during the preteen years, shouting, "Keep it steady, Mom!" She caught a glint of the metal-and-nylon net in her peripheral vision, noted Theo's tanned arm holding the net above the water. He was ready to catch the fish when Eddie reeled it close enough. She focused on the rod, clutching the cork handle tighter as she reeled with some effort. Eddie suddenly felt a *pop!* reverberate through the handle before the line went slack again.

"Shoot," Theo said, to which Eddie replied, "We'll get it next time, my sweet boy." She turned to give him a smile, but now there was no tanned arm, no net. No Theo. The bubble of joy she had experienced a moment earlier burst. She reeled the line in slowly, sensing the next memory that wanted in.

The day Eddie lost everything—the tragedy that changed her forever.

She cast the rod and let it come, having learned long ago it hurt more to fight it.

IT WAS A celebratory evening—April 14, 1969. Theo's eighteenth birthday. Edith had been planning it for weeks—the menu (Theo's favorite foods, including fried chicken and scalloped potatoes, plus the Callaways' traditional money cake, all of which Edith would only pick at, as she was watching her figure), the guest list (his closest friends, including Mary Ann, his girlfriend of a year, and a dozen or so guests from the Hoffmans' social circle), the decorations (tasteful yet youthful), and Theo's gift (an apple-red Pontiac GTO convertible).

Delilah and George Callaway had both died the previous year. Their deaths, only months apart, had unmoored Edith, filling her with a melancholic heartache that wasn't abating. As such, she'd been trying to get Stewart and Theo to go to Camp Callaway with her, but they had plenty of excuses and apparently no time, or inclination, for a family vacation. Theo would be starting at West Point in the fall, like his father and grandfather both had, and Edith could feel time slipping through her fingers. At least the planning for Theo's birthday party had breathed some energy and joy into her.

Edith had met her husband, Dr. Stewart Hoffman, at Camp Callaway when she was nineteen years old. Stewart, ten years her senior, had been invited as a guest of her parents for the summer weekend. He was dashing and accomplished—he had invented a medicinal powder for indigestion and headaches that had made him incredibly wealthy—as well as an avid outdoorsman and hunter. They married after she finished college, at her parents' estate in Greenwich, Connecticut, and honeymooned in Italy. Their marriage was not only a solid match, but also a pleasing one. Stewart doted on Edith in all the right ways. She never complained or gossiped about Stewart when she lunched with her friends, most of whom had sharp tongues for their own husbands. What would she complain about, after all? They were happy. In love. Theo was born a few years later, and her love expanded again. It was a heady, joyful time in Edith's life.

However, all good things must come to an end.

As "Mrs. Stewart Hoffman," Edith had four main roles: keeping the home immaculate by managing the household staff; hosting the many events and parties at the Hoffmans' estate; mothering their son; and maintaining her twenty-seven-inch waist (which she measured daily with a sewing tape), so as to wear her fashionable clothes well. She did most of it with relative ease, stepping into the role she'd been primed for.

However, as the years passed, she and her husband spent less and less time together—a dangerous thing for any marriage. Stewart worked; Edith mothered. Then, when Theo was old enough to not require his mother's constant attention, Edith finally looked up, only to find Stewart's attention had shifted elsewhere. It was at that point that she realized how much of her life was transactional, everyone playing the part they had been given. Even her closest friends were both exactly like her and exactly like one another: all high-society wives, their roles as rigid and scrutinized as Edith's, living in their husbands' peripheral visions. Edith's external life might have been grand, but her internal one felt less so.

Really, it was only a matter of time before the cracks between Edith and Stewart became irreparable.

The day before Theo's birthday party Edith had been in the kitchen, reviewing the menu with Anna, their live-in housekeeper, who also managed the kitchen staff. She had been surprised when Stewart came home because it was only two o'clock in the afternoon and she had not been expecting him until much later in the evening.

As Stewart walked into the kitchen, Anna quickly stood up from the table to take his jacket.

"Thank you, Anna," he said, his voice deep and warm. One of the things Edith appreciated about her husband was how kind and thoughtful he was with the staff. Her father had been the same way, and she hadn't realized what a wonderful—and rare— characteristic it was. "Would you mind giving us a minute?"

"I'll come and find you as soon as we're done here," Edith had said to Anna as the housekeeper retreated into the cavernous mansion. The Hoffmans lived in an English-style manor home in Suffolk County that boasted ten bedrooms, seven bathrooms, a formal dining room and two kitchens, a study for Stewart to work in, and a library and sitting room where Edith spent much of her time. Their home was gorgeous, palatial, and absurdly large for their family of three and full-time staff of five. It said something about you when you had more staff than you had residents of the house, but at that time Edith wasn't aware of precisely *what* that said about her.

She walked over to where Stewart stood, leaning back against the marble countertop. He looked tired. Drawn. "Are you all right?" When he didn't answer, she placed the back of her hand against his forehead.

"I'm fine, Dee. Fine." He gently removed her hand and held it. "We need to talk."

Somewhere between when they had last been happy and this moment, Stewart had fallen in love with someone else. *Could there be a more clichéd way to end a marriage?* she wondered. Edith had started to shake as Stewart admitted the affair. She didn't cry, though. Women like Edith were taught to be stoic during difficult times. You cried alone if you had to, far from prying eyes—including those of the help.

Edith, upon later reflection, wouldn't be entirely surprised. She and Stewart had been little more than companions for years now. Their once enjoyable sex life had diminished after Theo was born. His birth had been arduous for Edith—she labored for twenty-three excruciating hours—and ended in an emergency cesarean section (she was advised not to try for a second child) and weeks of healing. Then she was too tired, or had a headache. When they did have sex, maybe once a month, Edith would mentally disengage, planning menus and outfits for upcoming parties and events while Stewart lay heavily on top of her. While she'd stopped enjoying sex years earlier (though Stewart didn't seem to notice), she still recognized her responsibilities as a wife.

After Stewart confessed his affair, she asked him for only one thing: to not tell Theo what was going on until after the party. He'd readily agreed. If she had one consolation about how everything had happened, it was that Theo never knew his parents' marriage had fallen apart. Edith held her head high at the party, the split down her middle—right through her heart—visible to no one and hidden behind her stunning sapphire-colored brocade dress. The only sign of struggle within Edith that evening were crescent-moon fingernail marks on her palms, as she clutched her hands too tightly, trying to hold herself together.

The party went exactly as planned—*flawless*—and after dinner Theo took Mary Ann for a spin in his new convertible. And then, just after Stewart had poured nightcaps for the lingering guests, they received a call that would shatter her heart into a thousand pieces.

"The tree came out of nowhere," Mary Ann had later sobbed from her hospital bed—her badly broken leg requiring surgery. Theo had not been so lucky. They'd had to cut him from his brand-new car, on his eighteenth birthday, and he lived long enough to ask the ambulance attendant to tell his parents he was sorry he'd wrecked his present.

FOR SIX MONTHS following Theo's accident, Edith and Stewart remained living in the same home, despite Stewart's declaration of loving another woman. Even with their shared grief, they spent little time together. His betrayal of her still raw; her sadness too intense, like an inferno you can't get close to. Many days Edith wouldn't get out of bed. Others she spent in Theo's room, the door locked, holding his clothes to her face and breathing in his scent, trying to resurrect him. Their home began to feel like a mausoleum—they held no further parties, rooms were kept darkened, friends stopped coming by.

After Theo died, Edith understood how a child's existence flows through your blood, becoming intricately woven into the sinew of your body before finally settling into your bones. The love of a child comes from a higher place and can't be expelled from your marrow, and so she saw no other option. It was all-consuming, her grief, sucking the oxygen out of every room she walked into. Finally, Edith asked Stewart to leave. He was reluctant at first, but then acquiesced when she insisted. Of course, what he hadn't understood was that Edith needed him gone so she could fulfill her plan.

So Stewart left. And on her forty-fifth birthday—January 18, 1970—nine months after Theo died, Edith took two full pill bottles from her medicine cabinet. Pills she had easily procured over the years, as a doctor's wife, to deal with various ailments (tennis elbow, C-section pain, baby blues . . .). She washed them down with a tidy glass of red wine, told Anna she was ill and going to bed, and then locked her bedroom door.

Stewart had called to wish Edith a happy birthday (they remained friendly, as what was the point in being bitter now?) and, upon hearing she wasn't well, asked Anna to put her on the phone. When the bedroom door was discovered locked, he told Anna to use the master key to open it. She found Edith in a deep slumber, unable to be roused—the pill bottles on the nightstand, empty. At Stewart's insistence, not willing to wait for the ambulance to arrive, Anna forced her finger down Edith's throat to save her life.

It took most of the next morning for the housekeeper to remove the vomit stain from the bedside Persian rug. Then, at Stewart's request, Anna cleaned out the medicine cabinets. Later, when Edith left her Suffolk County estate for good to move to Camp Callaway, she gave Anna enough money to see her through the rest of her life comfortably. It was the least she could do.

A COUPLE OF months after Edith's overdose, an old friend of hers from college, Genevieve "Gin" White, told her it was time to rejoin the land of the living. Gin wanted to take her somewhere special the next day, somewhere "important"—she wouldn't take no for an answer. Edith was to be ready to go by six a.m. the following day, Gin said. The only other stipulation was that she had to wear a skirt.

"Why a skirt?" Edith had asked.

"Because that's the dress code," Gin had replied, offering nothing further.

The next day at precisely six a.m. Gin gave a couple of short honks, and Edith stepped out into the still-dark morning, the chill of the air making her breath come out in little puffs, and then climbed into Gin's warm car. Gin was high society like Edith—the heiress to a sugar fortune—but she was the most independent woman Edith knew. She had never married nor had a child, but had plenty of beaus to accompany her to the events a woman of her class was required to attend. Essentially, Gin did what she wanted, when she wanted to. Edith had always envied that about her friend—she couldn't imagine being so rebellious.

The two ended up in New York City, just under a two-hour drive from Suffolk County. If Edith had envisioned a day filled with shopping and dining and city fun, she soon realized Gin had something else in mind.

"What's going on?" Edith had asked as they walked up to a crowd of women outside Saint Peter's Church on Lexington Avenue, all dressed similarly in skirts and heels and winter coats. She had smiled shyly at a few of the women as they got closer, and though Edith couldn't explain it (as she had no idea why they were there), her palms grew sweaty and she felt a trickle of excitement course through her. It had been so long since she'd felt anything but paralyzing grief.

Gin, holding her hand, had tugged her into the crowd until they were swallowed up. There was an air of anticipation and the hum of chatter, until one woman asked for everyone to break into smaller groups—only three people at most. Gin and Dee linked arms, and then Gin turned to a woman next to her and said, "Would you like to join us?"

The woman, who seemed to be around Edith's age and breathtakingly beautiful, nodded and then linked arms with her.

"I'm Nellie. Nellie Murdoch," she said, smiling at Gin and Edith.

"I'm Gin White, and this is Edith Hoffman. Where are you coming from this morning, Nellie?"

"Greenville. You?"

"Suffolk County," Edith had said, and Nellie replied, "Oh, it's lovely there."

She was asking Nellie if she knew what was happening, and Gin was telling her to stop badgering poor Nellie ("You'll find out soon enough!") when the organizer came up to their group of three. It was just before nine in the morning.

"It's time," the woman said, directing Gin, Nellie, and Edith toward a building across the street from the church. "Once you get up there, don't let anyone make you leave. Don't worry—you won't be alone long. We'll all be inside soon enough."

THE HUNDRED OR so women—including Edith, Gin, and Nellie—crammed themselves into the 54th and Lexington Avenue office of the *Ladies' Home Journal* editor and publisher, John Mack Carter. It was Edith's first sit-in (she was only vaguely aware of the protests that had filled the news in recent years, her socialite life a privileged, protected bubble), and the energy of it—*the sense of purpose*—had been exhilarating. Over the course of eleven hours the group made demands of the magazine, which they felt exploited women, despite the publication's motto, "Never Underestimate the Power of a Woman." Demands such as free daycare for employees, the hiring of women of color based on the percentage of minorities in the US population, the creation of an entirely female advertising and editorial staff, and the request for Carter to step down and have a woman take on role of editor.

The sit-in participants advocated to upend the magazine's editorial content: Instead of columns dedicated to questions like "Can This Marriage Be Saved," the women wanted articles such as "How to Get a Divorce" and "How to Have an

Orgasm" and "How Psychiatrists Hurt Women, and Why." The women called for a focus on single parents, the Vietnam War, the impact of detergents on rivers and streams. They also smoked John Mack Carter's cigars, which left Edith buzzing and mildly nauseated.

While most demands were not met, progress *was* made. John Mack Carter refused to step down, but agreed to explore on-site childcare and gave the women an eight-page spread in the magazine, to be produced that August, under the title "New Feminism." It was the first time in her life that Edith felt a part of something that truly mattered outside of caring for her family, and the energy, camaraderie, and purpose of the protesters she shared the room with that day would change her forever.

She left that protest exhausted and spent, but with a most unexpected fire in her belly. She had a newfound appreciation for the plight of her fellow women and a resolve to *do* something about it. Edith didn't want to extinguish the fire; she wanted to fan it. Let it burn bright, like a wildfire consuming everything in its path.

But can one moment truly alter the course of your life?

"Yes. If you want it to," Edith would have answered, now knowing the truth of it.

"This feels extreme, Edith," Stewart said when she told him of her plan to resurrect Camp Callaway, to move there and run women-only retreats (though the details were still fuzzy at that point). He'd been encouraging Edith to find a hobby of late, maybe as a volunteer with the library board, as she did love to read. This plan of hers was beyond his comprehension, though. It had all sounded foolish, pointless, and, most worrisome, unhinged, to Stewart. "You're going to run a summer camp, for grown women?"

"Why would you *want* to do this?" he'd asked, upon realizing he truly didn't have a say in the matter.

To her, the answer was simple. "Because I can," Edith had replied.

And with that Edith Hoffman disappeared, and Eddie Callaway took her place.

"You have no idea how much your life can change in a year," Eddie liked to say to the Camp Callaway retreat guests. "Trust me, better late than never."

The Future You

They say you can't predict the future. But my fellow Wild Women, I believe you can! Once upon a time I was a very different woman. A woman with dreams, but without the confidence to chase them. When I wrote my initial Future You letter, after participating in my first protest, the truth is that I felt silly. I was far too old to believe in this sort of magic! However, I had much to learn about the power of our words, our thoughts, and our intentions. You would never be reading this if I hadn't written that letter, my friends. These retreats were born out of my willingness to imagine a future far different from my present and past, and to simply write it down. I would like to offer you the same opportunity, and fervently hope you take it.

Write yourself a "Dear Me" letter to be opened a year from today. Leave it with us here at camp and we'll mail it to you, or tuck it away somewhere that you won't forget about it (don't open it early, as the magic of the letter requires patience). When you do open that letter, into which you will have penned your hopes, dreams, aspirations, and ambitions, be prepared for the power of it. You predicted the future!

—Eddie C. xx

*From *Camp Callaway's Wild Women Handbook,* 1975

ROWAN, 2021.

I STOP RUNNING NOT LONG AFTER I LEAVE THE cabin, when trying to navigate the forest's uneven terrain proves too challenging. My feet are wet and slimy, the mulch that blankets the ground having found its way inside my flimsy slip-on sneakers. My lungs burn. I have a literal pain in my heart.

After about five minutes of waiting for Seth to follow me— the cabin still in my sight line—I realize he isn't coming. So I tuck the pin from the crow into the pocket of my shorts and start walking, hoping to put some distance between us. I need time and space to think.

About an hour or so later, having no idea where I am or how far I've hiked, I come to a small clearing with a steep embankment on one side. There's a fallen tree trunk, probably ten feet long, resting a few feet from the embankment's edge. The trunk is now mostly moss, though I can still make out its shape under the lush emerald-green rug. Feeling drained and physically spent, I sink down onto its soft and mossy surface.

Then I open the email Seth hid and read it again.

Hi Rowan,

So glad you took me up on this! I'm intrigued. Your pitch is fantastic, and Robbie agrees. Any chance you can get back to LA, like in the next week or so? We think this deserves an in-person meeting, and we'd love first dibs. Wine and oysters (for old times' sake) on us!

-C xo

Clara Cottingham
Development Executive
Film ARTS

Roberta "Robbie" Ray, the talented and successful Hollywood producer whom Clara works with, thinks my script pitch is "fantastic." But it has been almost a month since that email from Clara arrived. For all these weeks it was tucked out of sight in a folder titled "personal" (which held random, non-work-related emails, like one giving me my parents' new door alarm code). A folder I don't check regularly, because why would I?

This email is the "yes" I've been waiting for. And Seth—despite knowing how much I want this, and after telling me it was only a matter of time because I am *so very talented*—chose to hide it from me. Because he was . . . angry about the live stream? Jealous, maybe? Worried I would move forward, perhaps without him?

It's too confusing and hurtful to sort out—his motivation, his lack of respect, his *selfishness*, the fact that he almost got away with it—and so I turn my phone off. The email, and Seth's betrayal, going dark.

Setting the phone aside does little to calm me, and a wave

of fury begins to build. Soon I'm overwhelmed with anger, and I know the only option to get it out of me is to make physical contact with something.

So I crouch, shoving at one end of the moss-covered, decaying tree trunk, grunting as I do. My sneakers slip on the mulch, and I fall hard onto my knees. Ignoring the bruising pain, I'm up a moment later, releasing a guttural scream as I push the log as hard as I can. This time there *is* movement. A slight rolling from front to back, the connection between trunk and earth separating.

Feeling slightly better, I catch my breath and examine my scraped knees, when a hollow tap-tap-tap catches my attention. The sound is coming from a nearby maple tree. High up the trunk, I catch a splash of black and white, a dot of red moving in time to the tapping sound. Putting a hand above my eyes to block the sun, I watch as the woodpecker continues its relentless search. Then my eyes see a glint of something unusual in the maple's neighboring tree.

It's split in half, the remaining trunk jagged spires of splintered wood where the two parts separated. The rest of the tree, which looks to be about twice as long as the still-standing trunk, lies nearby on the forest floor.

On second glance I notice something else about the split tree. There's a dark hole in the trunk's bark, about seven feet up from the ground, though it doesn't seem to be connected to whatever trauma the tree has endured. The edge of this hole is smooth and rounded, as though it has always been a part of the tree itself.

"What is that?" I ask aloud, trying to get a better view, because now I see there's something inside the hole. I take a step back and stand on the moss-covered log, attempting to make myself taller. Something *is* nesting in the hollow, but it isn't from the natural world.

A small swatch of aqua-green patina stands out against the blackness of the hollow. I would never have noticed it if I hadn't looked up at the woodpecker.

I lean back a bit, squinting at the hollow. "What the—"

But I don't get the rest out because the mossy log gives way under my feet, rolling forward as I fall back. I hit the ground, hard, and lose my breath with the impact. For one second I think I'm okay—breathless but safe—until suddenly the ground disappears and I'm tumbling awkwardly, and quickly, down the steep embankment.

I pick up speed as I go, and sharp pains shoot through my shoulder, my hip, the bared skin on my left thigh. Luckily, the slant evens back out, and I finally come to a stop. I'm on my back, staring up into the canopy of trees above me, gasping like a fish out of water when my lungs refuse to fill with air.

Everything hurts.

I need to know if any of my searing pains are serious, so I shift onto my side. My breath returns, and I wait until the black spots in my vision clear. I prop myself up to a sitting position and move my arms. My one shoulder feels hot and tingly. I glance at my leg, see deep scratches from mid-thigh to shin, lined with dots of blood mixing with the dirt—the cuts seem superficial.

But that's about where the good news ends, because I realize where I am. And have no idea how I'm going to get out.

My phone is up top, not that it's much use to me out here. For a moment I sit still, marinating in the panic, and then my survival instincts kick in. The most important thing I have to do is get back up the embankment—before it gets dark.

I'll never know what draws my eyes to a crevice at the bottom of the embankment, where a narrow rocky outcrop has created a deep nook in the earth's wall, the exposed tree roots dangling down like a hairy curtain. Maybe it's seeing that jagged rock shelf and realizing how fortunate I was to have avoided sliding into it. Or maybe it's when I notice a precise shade of pink, barely visible behind the roots—a burst of unnatural color, like the aqua-green patina in the tree's hollow—that has no place out here in the woods, where everything else has been colored by Mother Nature.

Something about what you're seeing does not fit, my mind tells me. *Pay attention.*

I turn, crawling carefully along the ground to get a closer look. Closer still, almost there . . . I push the dangling root curtain aside, and when I see what's behind it, I let out a blood-curdling scream.

AFTER MUCH EFFORT, driven by sheer desperation, I claw my way back to the top, using roots as climbing ropes and small trees and rocks as hand- and footholds. I retrieve my phone with shaking, dirt-streaked hands, a couple of my fingernails ripped and bleeding.

"Please, please, please," I whisper, my throat sore and hoarse from crying and dehydration. But the "no service" message remains.

I have to get back to the cabin.

Tucking my phone into the shorts pocket with the smiley pin, I start running back the way I came. My lungs burn; the pain in my shoulder throbs with every step. Soon it's clear I don't know where I am, and my panic swells. Leaning against a tree, my legs quivering with fear and effort, I take one deep breath in through my nose, hold it for five seconds, then release it slowly. As my breathing slows, my heart rate also slows, and after a couple more breaths I'm able to think more clearly.

What did Jess tell me about getting lost in the woods? Aside from how frequently it happens to tourists visiting the park . . . *rivers and streams.* She said, "If you can find water, follow it downstream. It will lead you out, eventually."

I listen for running water. The forest is busy, the birdcalls ever-present, but no sounds of a stream. I walk twenty, then fifty feet, stopping every ten feet or so to listen. Finally, a faint trickling sound.

Crouching carefully near the edge of the stream—the last thing I need is sopping-wet shoes—I let the crystal-clear, cool water run over my fingers. Then I stand and follow the water downstream, cautious about my footing and always keeping an eye out for a path. More lucid now, I fill my mind with land-marks: a large tree split down its center, maybe from a light-ning strike, the two sides splayed out from its middle; three white paint slashes on three consecutive deciduous trees, hope-fully marking a trail; and then an oddly shaped triangular rock covered in deep green moss and lichens.

I START SCREAMING for Seth when I see the cabin. I'm unhinged by this point. As soon as I turn into our driveway, my legs grow so weak I can't take another step. Hearing my cries, Seth throws open the front door.

Without hesitation he jumps from the porch—clearing the stairs entirely, in his bare feet—and runs to meet me.

"Rowan! What the hell? Where have you been?" He holds me tightly, and I collapse against him, sobbing into his chest. Our fight—and the reason for it—the last thing on my mind now. I'm covered in dirt, bloody trails crisscross my shins and forearms from scratches, and there are bits of the forest stuck in my hair. "What happened?"

My teeth chatter, the adrenaline draining out of me now that I am safe. "We have to call the police. Seth, *we need to call the police.*"

Shock is setting in—fingers of cold wriggle their way through my body, and then my legs give out. Seth, thankfully, still has his grip on me and so when I drop, I don't hit the ground.

"Jesus, Rowan!" He grunts as he tries to prop me up. I will my legs to steady and hold my own weight, but it's pointless. I'm a limp rag doll. Seth finally just picks me up in his arms and carries me inside the cabin. He sets me on the couch, then wraps an itchy wool blanket around me and fills a glass with water. I guzzle it greedily after he hands it to me, his arm behind my shoulders to help me sit up. The water dribbles down my chin and neck, and into my T-shirt's V-neck opening. Once I have a few more sips, I set the glass on the table and rest against the back of the couch. Seth sits beside me, one hand on my knee, which is bouncing from leftover bursts of my fight-or-flight response.

"Talk to me. What happened?" He watches me closely, his brow knitting in concern.

"I was . . . There was this clearing and a log . . . with moss and I tried to . . . I was standing on it, and . . ." I gulp air, my whole body quaking. Seth runs a hand quickly up and down my arm through the blanket, as though trying to warm me up. I'm not cold, though I am shivering. And still thirsty, but also nauseated from drinking the first glass of water so fast.

"Take a deep breath. Try to calm down. There you go. Breathe in, breathe out." Seth keeps rubbing my arm and then my thigh through my shorts, pulling the odd twig or leaf out of my hair in between.

"Are you hurt?" he asks, glancing me over properly now. I shake my head, even though my shoulder is throbbing. But it's not serious, I'm pretty sure. Nothing can be as serious as what I found under that rocky ledge, at the bottom of the embankment.

"I don't think so. I jammed my shoulder, and some of these scratches are sort of deep, but I think I'm okay." I move my arm back and forth gingerly, and my shoulder complains, but it's not horrible.

He puts his hand on my shoulder, feeling around the joint. "It seems swollen." He goes to the kitchen and riffles around the small freezer.

Grabbing a bag of frozen peas, Seth sets the icy package on top of my shoulder, holding it firmly. I wince when the bag hits my skin, but the cold feels good.

"Start from the beginning, Rowan."

And so I do.

"I don't know exactly what happened, but the log slipped and I lost my balance. I fell down this really steep hill." My breath catches, remembering the fall and how terrified I was that I would never stop sliding. "Honestly, I don't know how I got out of there. It was *so steep.*"

Seth, still holding the icy packet to my shoulder, looks pained at my story. His mouth is a straight line, his jaw clenching rhythmically. I see a flash of remorse in his eyes before he looks away.

"But . . . it gets worse. There was something down there with me. Under the rock ledge." I whisper this, squeezing my eyes closed against the memory.

"What?" Seth asks gently.

I open my eyes, which fill with tears. "Something awful."

"Tell me. Please."

"There were bones." A sob escapes me. "And I think they're human."

SLEEP ELUDES ME, my mind circling back over my discovery. How the bones lay there, still recognizable in the shape of the body they once belonged to. A body that was once a living, breathing person.

There are 206 bones in the adult human body. I remember learning this in third-grade science class. My mom lost twenty-eight bones—the total in her lower leg and foot—after the accident. I wonder now where those bones went, after they took my mom's leg. If she misses them specifically instead of just missing her limb as a whole.

When dawn breaks, I get out of bed. Relieved the night is over. The plan is to take Seth to the spot where I found the bones as soon as there's enough light. That is, if I can find it again. While Seth was concerned, and alarmed by how rattled I was when I first returned to the cabin, he isn't convinced I saw what I thought I did. So we'll go back to "double-check," he says.

"Maybe you hit your head?" He ran his fingers through my hair, across my scalp, to feel for any lumps or bumps that might explain my story.

"I did not hit my head," I replied, starting to cry all over again. But enough time had passed, the shock turning to mind-numbing exhaustion, that I began to doubt myself as well. Seth was right: It *could* have been something other than human bones, really. Animal bones, perhaps, or even a collection of weather-bleached sticks. The mind seeks familiarity and pattern, especially when what's presented defies logic.

AFTER I DRESS, I do the dishes from the evening before—working through the ache in my shoulder—and set out peanuts for the crow (I need to keep moving, to keep *doing*). I decline breakfast, my stomach still off, but accept the banana Seth insists upon, and then we get in the car. We drive as far down the road as we can, hiking the rest of the way on foot.

There are a few wrong turns as I try to remember the landmarks and the path, but then we come upon the mossy triangular rock, and I know we're getting closer. I head right. There isn't a clear trail, like there is to the left of the rock, though the grasses and plants are flattened enough you could call it a "path."

"Are you sure this is the way?" Seth asks.

"Yes," I reply, though in truth I'm sure of nothing right now.

After another half hour of hiking, we reach the clearing. The mossy log lies closer to the center of it now, having rolled from its original spot when I fell. The sun shines in earnest, and I'm sweating—there's a tickle of moisture behind my knees and between my toes. However, as I take in the clearing, the embankment, I shiver violently.

I don't feel good, being back here. Even though everything looks perfectly fine now. Serene and natural: the sunbeams sparkling through the leaves, birds chatting in trees overhead, only a slight whisper of wind between branches.

"So, walk me through what happened," Seth says, glancing around the clearing, one foot up and resting on the moss log.

"I was . . . standing on that log, trying to get a better look at—" I quickly glance up at the large tree, the maple, nearby. The one the woodpecker had been using for his lunch break. My eyes move to the right, at the jagged tree trunk where yesterday a glint of something aqua caught my eye in its darkened hollow . . .

"A better look at what?" Seth asks.

"That." I point at the hollow in the still-standing half of the tree. Seth walks closer to the wide trunk.

"What is that?" he asks.

"I have no idea," I reply.

All of a sudden, Seth takes a few quick steps backward and then runs at the tree, jumping up when he reaches the trunk. He tries to latch his fingers into the hollow, but misses and clumsily slides back down the bark.

"Seth—you're going to get hurt." But he's undeterred, gearing up to take a running leap at the tree again.

The next time he jumps even higher and manages to hook his fingers over the splintered edge of the trunk, where the tree split. The gum soles of his hiking boots give him traction on the rough bark as his fingers hold tightly to the shards of wood.

"Am I close?" he asks. His voice strains, his cheek pressed against the bark.

"Another few inches to the right," I shout.

Somehow, he manages to hold on with one hand, using his right to feel around for the hollow. Now I'm helping support him, placing my body flat against the trunk, allowing his feet to rest on my shoulders. My injured one protests, but I don't dare move.

Seth wriggles the fingers of his right hand, and then hooks them over the lip of the hollow.

"Stand back, Rowan." He grunts and shifts with his effort, and I don't know how much longer I can hold him against the tree trunk.

"I don't want to let you go." I grit my teeth through the shoulder pain. "You're going to fall."

"Stand back, *now*!"

I do, and a second later something comes tumbling out of the hollow and crashes to the ground at the base of the tree.

Seth drops from the tree awkwardly, but rebounds quickly, unharmed. We stare at the object—a metal box—for a moment before Seth crouches, picking it up. He turns it over in his hands—it's larger than your standard jewelry box, and is bronze—or used to be, because after being exposed to the elements for a time, the surface color has transformed into an aqua-green patina. The lid remains closed with a small lock, which is rusted and doesn't carry the same patina as the box.

"What do you think this is?" he asks.

And then, suddenly and for reasons I will never be able to explain, I know precisely what it is. "It's the treasure."

He glances up at me, his confusion shifting to excitement.

"You think so?" he asks. He jiggles the lock. "Damn. I wonder if there's a key some—"

"No, don't!" I put my hands over his, stilling them.

"Why not?" He's puzzled. Then he nods, as if understanding my hesitation. "You're right." He pulls his phone from his pocket.

"Seth, stop." He's fiddling with his phone, opening the camera. "*Stop.*"

When he finally looks at me, I point shakily at the embankment. "There's someone . . . down there. And if this is *the* treasure, then I think that might be—" I swallow hard, my throat constricting. Bile rising. "Then that might be Eddie Callaway."

Yesterday's horror fills me too fast, like drinking from a garden hose on full blast. I kneel and retch, but nothing comes up. Seth crouches beside me.

"Easy, Rowan. Take a breath, you're okay."

"I'm going to throw up."

"You're not. Try to relax." He rubs at my back a few times, but I can feel his distraction.

Once it's clear the banana—the only thing in my stomach—is going to stay put, Seth says, "Why don't I go take a look?" He taps the top of the box. "Just don't try to open this until I'm back." I assure him I won't.

Seth walks to the edge, peering over. "Is there an easier way down?"

"It's slightly less steep over to the right. That's how I got back up."

And then, holding tightly to a nearby sapling, Seth sits on the edge of the embankment. He shimmies forward, then flips over so he's on his stomach before pushing himself off and disappearing from view.

"Be careful!" I say. Then, a scrabble of rocks, a loud grunt, some cursing. The sapling springs back when Seth lets it go. I hold my breath until I'm light-headed.

"I made it!" Seth finally calls out, his voice echoing. "Where were you exactly?"

I crawl over to the edge, the dizziness intensifying. Lying down, I starfish my legs and press my arms flat into the ground. It's the most stable position I can think of. I inch forward until I can see just over the edge. Seth's at the bottom. The rocky outcrop to his left.

"Just to the side of that rock ledge," I shout.

Seth glances over. He's about fifteen feet away. He struggles through the brush, pushing branches out of the way and slipping occasionally on the uneven ground.

"You are damn lucky you didn't hit this rock," he calls up to me, but I can't reply. I inch back, then roll over and stare up into the tree canopy, feeling dizzy. I wonder if I'm going to pass out.

"Okay, I'm looking and . . . I'm not seeing anything." There's a pause. "Rowan? Where do you think you saw—" Seth goes quiet then, but a moment later he's shouting, alarm in his voice this time.

I can't move. I close my eyes and place my hands tightly over my ears, not wanting to hear what he's shouting.

Because I know he's seeing what I did.

Someone *is* down there.

EDDIE, 1975.

<u>Your Body Is Beautiful, Inside and Out.</u>

Knowledge is power, and that means discovering the joys of your own precious body! Please refer to the copy of "Our Bodies, Ourselves," written by the Boston Women's Health Book Collective, which we have included in your welcome bag. You can also revisit the notes from the "Voyage to the Vulva and Beyond" session, which are found on the following page. I'd like to share what Betty Friedan wrote a couple of years ago in her <u>New York Times</u> article "Up from the kitchen floor": ". . . I like other women thought there was something wrong with me because I didn't have an orgasm waxing the kitchen floor."

Don't be afraid to seek out pleasure, and resist the notion that it isn't deserved. We are all worthy, my fellow Wild Women!

—Eddie C. xx

*From *Camp Callaway's Wild Women Handbook*, 1975

Y OUR GO," SAM SAID, DRAWING EDDIE'S AT-
tention back from the Frisbee game happening on the
expansive front lawn to the small table between them.
They were seated on the grand porch of the dining hall, playing a game of Connect Four, which one of last summer's guests
had left behind. Eddie picked up one of the red discs, pursed
her lips and tilted her head, then dropped the disc into the
third slot from the left. It rested in place in the row, on top of a
black disc.

"Hmm . . . interesting choice." Sam cupped his chin in his
hand, setting his elbow on the tabletop as he perused the game's
yellow plastic board, which was about a third of the way filled
with his black discs and Eddie's red ones. He dropped a black
disc in the row beside where Eddie had put her red one, then
said, "Connect Four."

"What?" Eddie sat up straighter, eyeing the rows, seeing
the four black discs running in a vertical line up the board.
"Damn. I missed that."

"Come on now, Eddie," Sam replied, chuckling. "I only beat you because you're somewhere else. What's up?"

She took a sip of her chocolate milk, leaning back in her chair. "I have a few things on my mind."

Sam glanced over at her, mirroring Eddie as he leaned back in his own chair. "Anything you want to talk about?"

"Yes, but not yet," she said, smiling at him. "All in good time."

Just then Eddie saw Rebecca, the guest with the bruises on her upper arms. She was sitting alone on the grass, watching the others play Frisbee.

Sam's eyes followed Eddie's, to where Rebecca sat. "She okay?"

"It seems not," Eddie replied. "She hasn't joined any of the sessions yet."

"She also hasn't eaten a meal with the group since she arrived." Sam gathered the discs, now ejected from the board, into a pile. "Jude took her a picnic box last night."

"I'm going to go talk to her." Eddie drained her glass of milk, then stood. "Thanks for the game."

"Thanks for letting me win," Sam said, laughing.

"You won that fair and square." Eddie started walking down the front steps of the dining hall. "But I'm already planning my comeback."

A few moments later, after catching and then throwing the Frisbee back into the game, Eddie walked over to where Rebecca sat. She was a petite woman, younger than Eddie, and had a four-leaf clover resting on each of her cross-legged knees.

"I've never found a four-leaf clover before," Rebecca said as Eddie sat down beside her. "And now I've found two. In this little patch of grass around me."

"You should press those," Eddie replied.

Rebecca nodded, gently fingering one of the clovers.

"Sam told me you haven't been in the dining hall since you've been here. Can you tell me why?"

The woman shrugged, her eyes still on the clovers. "I've not been hungry, I guess."

"I am *always* hungry," Eddie said, and Rebecca looked over at her. "Even when I'm sad."

There was a pause, and then Eddie asked, "Can you tell me why you're sad, Rebecca?"

"I don't know."

"I think you do." Eddie's voice was quiet but firm. "And you don't have to tell me, but I wish you would. Sometimes saying it out loud helps, even if it can't be easily fixed."

Rebecca stared at the women on the lawn, their laughter and shouts growing louder as the game's intensity ratcheted up. "I hate my life," she finally whispered.

"Hmm. I see. What specifically do you hate?"

At that Rebecca turned to Eddie. Blinked once, then twice, her mouth in a tight line. "Everything."

"You aren't wearing a wedding ring today." Eddie pointed to Rebecca's left hand, her ring finger bare. "Is that part of what you hate?"

"Yes." The woman's voice was strained. Barely controlled. She wrapped a hand around the opposite arm, covering the spot where Eddie had seen the bruising.

"Does your husband hurt you, Rebecca?" Eddie asked gently.

A resigned nod. Then, "All the time. In so many ways."

Eddie didn't say anything at first, having learned over the past few years when to speak and when to be silent. The things you could discover about a person if you stopped talking and waited for what really needed to be said.

"I'm not pretty enough. I'm too insecure. I'm too fat. I'm too emotional. I'm too busy with the kids. I'm a terrible cook. I'm too high-strung. I'm too demanding," Rebecca said, mimicking her husband's complaints. "How can I be both too insecure and also too demanding?"

Eddie nodded in silent acknowledgment.

"I left the kids with my parents," Rebecca continued. "And honestly, I wasn't sure I would go back. Not to him. And . . . maybe not to get the boys. They're safe. Better off without me." That last part came out so softly Eddie had to strain to hear her.

"What do you need from me, from us, Rebecca?"

Tears streamed down the woman's cheeks now, but she made no move to wipe them away. "A place to hide, I think. Or maybe you can teach me how to change?"

"But you are perfect just as you are. I can see it, clear as day," Eddie replied, stretching her long legs out in front of her, bathing the fine hairs on her shins in golden light. "I spent years trying to change things about myself, for all the wrong reasons. For example, I was quite vain as a younger woman, particularly about my figure. See, my body likes to be 'softer'— to carry a touch of padding here and here, especially." Eddie tapped her thighs and stomach, gave Rebecca a smile. "I used to be *so thin.* I could circle my wrist, thumb to first finger." Eddie tried to demonstrate it. There was about a half inch between her fingers now, and she shrugged. "I wasn't happy, though. I was hungry all the time, and the constant worry was dispiriting. Sometimes I still can't believe I used to be a woman who measured her worth by the size of her wrist. And not all that long ago, if I'm being truthful."

Rebecca wiped at her eyes then, sniffling beside Eddie. "I'm always on a diet."

"It's tedious, isn't it?" Eddie asked, and Rebecca agreed. "I used to do this egg and wine diet. Have you heard of it?" Rebecca shook her head, and Eddie chuckled. "I would say, 'Lucky you,' but I have a sense there isn't much you feel lucky about these days.

"Anyway, it was from this book called *Sex and the Single Girl*, by Helen Gurley Brown. And I wasn't single when I picked up a copy—I was a married mother, and in those days had no business reading a book about sex for the single woman—but I was struggling to get rid of a few pounds after the holidays and had friends swear the egg and wine diet from the book was revolutionary. I kept it hidden in my bathroom vanity, and would read it while I bathed at night. It promised you could lose five pounds in three days, and quite clearly stated this was a diet that men liked. A diet men liked!" Eddie laughed, big and loud. "As if men should have any say about what we do with our bodies."

"What was the diet?" Rebecca asked, itching at her nose. She had stopped crying now, but her eyes were red.

"Well, breakfast was one egg—any way you wanted, I liked mine soft boiled, without butter or seasonings—and a glass of white wine. Then for lunch you had *two* eggs and *two* glasses of white wine. Dinner was a steak, and the rest of that bottle of wine. Repeat for the next two days."

"So you ate eggs, steak, and a bottle of wine every day, for three days? And lost weight? That actually doesn't sound like the worst thing," Rebecca said.

Eddie laughed again. "Oh, I don't think I actually lost weight. I just got tired of eggs, and I got drunk. I never tolerated alcohol very well. But you know what was the worst part of doing that diet? No one else noticed. Not the effort, not how fuzzy-headed I was, not the ongoing hunger, not the sadness of depriving myself. I did that three-day diet once a month, for almost two years. And no one ever noticed anything different, not even me! I remained unchanged, and I don't just mean my waistline. You know why?"

"Because there wasn't anything needing change?" Rebecca spoke softly.

"I told you before that you are perfect and don't need to change for anyone. And that is the truth," Eddie said. "But that isn't the same thing as *being changed.*"

"I think I understand," Rebecca said, after a pause.

"Good. Now, will I see you at Judith's writing workshop later?" Eddie asked. "It can be incredibly cathartic. I always feel lighter afterward. Perhaps you'll come up with something for the Wishing Wall?"

Rebecca smiled, then nodded. "Looking forward to it."

"Same. My life is far better for having met you, Rebecca." Eddie stood then, brushing a few blades of errant grass from her shorts.

"Thank you, Eddie. For taking the time, for . . . believing me."

"That's how it works here," Eddie replied. "And you're most welcome."

EDDIE WAS GIDDY at the prospect of revealing her secret. She knew some wouldn't understand what she was doing or why—because it wasn't a small gesture. What she would hide in the beautiful bronzed jewelry box passed down from her mother was no tchotchke: It would change someone's life, which was precisely the point.

There were complexities for how this would unfold, especially because she wanted to keep it a surprise up until the last minute. Aren't the best adventures those that come with unexpected delights?

Her heart rate increased as blood pumped through her body—the speed of her walking becoming faster, the terrain more challenging. Eddie always felt clearheaded when she overexerted herself—like the struggle to take in enough oxygen allowed her brain to focus on the most important question, or issue, of the moment.

Today's exploratory early-morning hike did not let her down.

She stopped abruptly on the trail, her pulse pounding in her ears, only interrupted by the incessant buzz of hungry mosquitoes nearby. Suddenly, she heard *everything*—cicadas at work; birds chirping their songs; the softness of small animal feet scurrying across beds of moss, leaves, and fallen sticks; the stream's glugs as the water traveled over rocks and around earthen bends. The cacophony of the woods, in perfect harmony. And in that moment, she mentally checked off the last box on her to-do list: She knew exactly where to hide the treasure.

AFTER SHE RETURNED from her hike, Eddie joined the group of women waiting for her at the shooting range, near the back of the main camp property. She hadn't hunted anything in decades, and hadn't shot a gun for almost thirty years. Despite Eddie's being a vegetarian and vehemently anti–sport hunting, this particular workshop remained one of her favorites to lead.

The "Target Your Power" session was also a popular retreat offering. Eddie had found pointing a hunting rifle (empty of bullets, as none were ever on camp property) at a specific target helped her guests unlock whatever was holding them back. It also provided a visceral, physical reminder of what it felt like to harness one's power.

The retreat had only been running for two full days, but Eddie already felt connected to the group. She had made the time, like she always did, for each one of them: chatting during mealtimes or later in the evening in the wisdom tent. During these visits Eddie asked each woman three questions: one, where she was from; two, what was her favorite dessert; and three, what she hoped to take home with her from this camp experience. The first two questions were meant to relax and disarm so to better assure an honest answer to the final question. Then Eddie would move on to the next guest, but before she did, she would smile, rest a hand on the woman's shoulder or upper arm, and declare, "Also, you are beautiful, in case you didn't know that. And please know that's the least interesting thing about you."

"Hello, my friends," she began. She took off the bandanna around her neck and rubbed sweat from her hairline, pausing briefly to take a sip of water from her canteen. Eddie saw a few faces from her earlier hiking workshop among today's group of seven: Patricia, one of the road-trip-by-van couple, and Ingrid, the woman who longed to become a mother. Rebecca was there as well, and she and Eddie exchanged a warm smile.

"Who has shot a rifle before?" Eddie now glanced at the few hands up in the air, nodding. "Here at camp, safety comes first, so there are no bullets in these guns. We don't keep any here at camp. The 'shooting' we'll be doing is metaphorical, these rifles ornamental, but I promise it will be no less effective." The women glanced at one another, clearly unsure about the purpose of this particular workshop.

"But before we get started, I'd like to share a story."

EDITH WAS FIFTEEN and eating breakfast with her mother in the camp's grand dining room when her father walked in, a grin on his face. He was dressed for a day of hunting, in his shooting trousers and herringbone jacket, with his hat tucked under one arm. Walking over to Edith and her mother, he planted a kiss on Delilah's upturned cheek before crouching beside his daughter.

"What do you say you come with us today, Dee-Dee?"

Clearly her parents had already discussed this, because when Edith whipped around to see her mother's expression, she merely looked amused as she picked at her bowl of fruit salad.

"Are you serious, Father?" Edith had asked when she turned back to him. He was standing now, the grin still on his face as he nodded. "Are you coming, Mama?"

Delilah Callaway was quite the outdoorswoman, as well as a skilled shooter. "Not today, my love. Have fun with your father."

Edith, as an only child, did everything she could to please her parents. So, even though she felt a host of challenging emotions (fear about shooting at an animal, which she had never before done; worry about being ridiculed by the men in the party; desire to make her father happy; delight at being invited), she ran out of the dining hall that morning and back to the family's cabin to get ready, her half-eaten breakfast forgotten.

She rushed getting dressed, afraid her father might change his mind, and soon enough she was at George Callaway's side as they walked quietly through the woods heading toward the first clearing, the crunching of sticks and foliage underfoot.

They were a small army—eight men and one fifteen-year-old girl with bouncy waves tucked under her hat, whose only goal was to make her father smile again, as wide as he had that morning.

IT HAD BEEN a clean kill. No one was more shocked than Edith when the group realized she had taken down a ten-point buck so swiftly. She was fairly sure she had closed her eyes at the last second when she pulled the trigger.

Upon seeing the fallen buck—realizing then what she'd done, that she had taken this beautiful life—she had wished fervently that she had not accompanied her father that day. She should have stayed behind and eaten fruit salad with her mother, played a game at the bowling alley maybe, hiked to the creek to catch crayfish for fishing. She did not want this to be part of the fabric of who she was.

Edith didn't want to be responsible for death of any kind, and wondered if she'd ever forget the glassy-eyed buck, with its tongue lolling from its bleeding, frothing mouth as it lay dead on the ground. She would not, as it turned out.

But then she had seen the look of pride on her father's face, the cheers and high praise from the other men in the hunting party, and it had filled her with something that was both intoxicating and all-consuming. It was the feeling of acceptance and power—though it was the power of taking the creature's life, which was altogether different from what Eddie would seek years later.

A few days later young Edith had returned to the spot where she'd killed the buck and created a small memorial out of stones and nearby greenery. The only sign left from what had happened was a slight flattening of the underbrush where the deer had fallen—everything else, including the gut pile and the blood, was gone. Having become nourishment for other animals as well as the earth beneath her feet.

"I DON'T CONDONE hunting of any kind anymore," Eddie told the women. She picked up her rifle, feeling the smoothness of the barrel in her hand, the weight of it against her palm, the ghost of the kickback pressing into her shoulder.

Eddie felt powerful in a different way now when she held the rifle. It was the presence of *choice*: to live how she wanted, without limits imposed by others. The "rules" were hers to set, to follow, and to change. This workshop was about sharing that learning. To give these women a tool to eviscerate their fears and pain—even symbolically.

"We're only pointing our rifles at tins. No shots will be fired because we don't need bullets." She tapped the side of her head. "We have our imaginations."

Eddie then handed out an empty Quik chocolate powder tin to each of the women, along with a sticker and a marker. "Please write down whatever's holding you back—a fear, a painful memory, a worry—on this sticker and then put it on the tin. Give it a name or draw a picture. And please be specific."

She waited a moment, watching the women uncap their markers and begin writing. Eddie thought about what was written on her own tin can ("being alone"), sitting yards away from the group, and was happy to see the women engaged in the task, knowing this would be something they wouldn't soon forget.

"Now, everyone, grab your tin and put it on the bench beside mine. If you'd like to keep your message private, just face the sticker to the back." The women capped their markers, started walking their tins toward the target line.

"Great. Well done, everyone. Okay, come on back and stand in front of your tin. Then we'll take turns 'shooting,'" Eddie said. "It may feel silly at first, but we'll all shout 'BANG' as a group when each of us pulls the trigger. And as you pull your own trigger, imagine that fear—make it big, give it loads of space."

Eddie took position, demonstrating how to hold the rifle for those who never had.

"Time to trust the process," she said. "This is going to blow that insecurity or fear of yours to smithereens. Now, who's first?"

IT WAS THE middle of the night when Eddie shot up in bed. She had been screaming in her dream, and awoke violently with the echoes still reverberating through her mind. The room was dark, except for the faint glow of the burning beeswax candle beside the bed, which made everything smell like thick, warming honey.

Eddie had been having the same nightmare for years. It didn't happen every night, and there were stretches of time where the dream went dormant, but it was always waiting on the periphery, ready to show itself again. For a moment upon awakening, Eddie forgot where she was, and then a firm palm came to rest against her naked back.

"Shhhhhhh, you're okay. Take a deep breath," Samuel said, cupping the back of her neck and gently massaging it as she tried to calm her breathing and not cry. Her head hurt, and the curlers she wore to bed felt too tight against her scalp. She ran her fingers over the curlers, hoping to loosen the strands of hair, and then settled against Samuel's hand as she tried to anchor herself back to reality. He continued rubbing her back and massaging her neck until her breathing evened out and it felt less like galloping horses had filled her chest.

"The nightmare again?" he asked quietly. Eddie nodded, tears streaming down her cheeks.

Samuel spent most nights with Eddie, except when she was with Judith. While they had never placed any labels on their relationship, what she had with Samuel was precious and tender, and it sustained her. He had pulled her out of this nightmare many times before as her body thrashed, her legs running uselessly under the thin sheet or warm quilt, depending on the season.

In the dream Eddie was at camp, and it was a beautiful summer's day. Theo—only ten years old—had asked to pick raspberries for a pie. The thickets in and around the camp were bursting with berries that time of year, and there were more than enough for all the creatures who enjoyed the sweet, juicy red fruit. She and her son suited up for berry picking—DEET oil for the mosquitoes, long sleeves and pants to avoid the prickly canes, and washed-out ice-cream cartons to collect the fruit. Theo ate as many as he dropped into his carton, but Eddie didn't mind.

But then he stepped around a patch of raspberry cane, and out of her sight. She called for him, but there was no response. Eddie started running, but it seemed her feet wouldn't move and she was rooted in place. Then Theo came back around the corner, but he wasn't himself. His little arms were outstretched, his mouth open in a silent scream. Theo was covered in angry, buzzing hornets that were stinging him, crawling in his mouth and up his nose, covering his hair so it looked like it was black versus blond. And still, Eddie remained rooted in place. Unable to reach him. Unable to save him.

She could never fall back asleep afterward.

"Want to talk about it?" Samuel whispered near Eddie's ear, his breath warm and reassuring against her skin.

"Not really," Eddie said, leaning back against him and sinking into the soft, curly black hair on his chest, feeling it tickle her skin as she did. Samuel kissed her bare shoulder and then the delicate skin behind her ear, and she sighed contentedly. He wouldn't ask her again if she was okay, or if she wanted to talk. Samuel had his own horror stories from the war, as well as occasional drenching nightmares, both of which he didn't often discuss, nor did Eddie push him to share. They understood each other in a way that was sacred and rare. The loved each other to their cores.

Sometimes, after the nightmare, when she couldn't sleep, she would ruminate on her insecurities. Had she naively traded her extravagantly "easy" life for a quite complicated one, as Stewart had suggested? Why had she been so determined to forsake the comfort and straightforwardness of being Edith Hoffman? Why turn her life upside down when she could have merely written generous checks?

Was she really making a difference?

Maybe after her divorce, if she hadn't lost Theo, she could have appreciated the deliciousness of answering to no one but herself. Bought a van, like Patricia and Shirley, and traveled through the nooks and crannies of the country. Or maybe she would have joined her old friend Gin, flirting with men on weekends, attending weekday protests, all while wearing fashionable shoes. But after Theo, there was a wound in her that refused to heal over—an emptiness that festered with aloneness and lack of purpose. Resurrecting Camp Callaway had started the mending, and being loved well by her "family"—Samuel and Judith in particular—ensured it wouldn't split back open.

Eddie closed her eyes, quieting her mind as Samuel's arms wrapped around her, wondering if maybe this time she might be able to fall back asleep. But then she noticed something odd, and quickly sat up again. "Sam . . . do you smell that?"

He took a long sniff of the air, his body going tense behind her. "Something's burning."

She glanced at the candle, the flame lazily bobbing about, safely encased in a glass pickling jar. But that wasn't the cause of the smoke permeating the cabin with its acrid smell. Eddie jumped out of bed and threw on her tank top and shorts, slamming her feet into her unlaced hiking boots. Samuel was right behind her. Her heart pounded as she opened the cabin door, the smell of smoke stronger now—more than what would have been caused by a campfire. It was then she saw what caused the smoky smell, and heard the panicked shouts of others that filled the air.

The arched wooden "Camp Callaway" sign, each side held up by hewn-log pillars, was raging with fire. Great orange flames leapt into the dark sky, plumes of smoke billowing.

For a moment Eddie stood still, watching the sign and pillars burning, mesmerized and paralyzed. Then Samuel grabbed her hand and squeezed it hard enough that it shocked her back into action. She nodded at him, then took off as fast as she could toward the burning arch, shouting directions to the group of gathered women—"Stay back! Get the hoses! Grab buckets of water!"—as she ran.

"WHAT ARE YOU thinking, Eddie?"

The room was heavy with tension; everything and everyone

smelled of smoke. It was cloying, and nauseating, but no one had taken the time yet to bathe it away. Eddie and her closest confidants—Samuel, Florence, Judith, and Dot—had gathered in the great dining hall, and were clustered shoulder to shoulder around one of the round wooden tables by the front windows. It was late in the night or early in the morning, depending on how you looked at it. Either way, the sky was still black, but the stars were dimming, and a new day was nearly upon them. Their skin and clothes were covered in soot, damp due to the water they'd used to put the fire out, but luckily no one had been hurt. It made Eddie physically ill to even think about what might have happened, with all the guests they had on-site.

The dining room was majestic and ornate—wide wooden pillars sculpted into forest animals ran floor to ceiling, and the chairs set around the dining tables had deep green velvet seats. George and Delilah Callaway had lived large, and frequently hosted parties at the camp, unfussed by little Edith Jane participating in the hoopla. They had been loving parents, but they were also not traditional in how they raised their daughter— she had her first taste of champagne at the age of seven, when her mother gave her a small glass of it during one of the roaring parties. She had not cared for it, but had drunk it straight down regardless because she adored her mother and wanted to make her happy. Sometimes Edith fell asleep under the tables while her parents entertained late into the evening, only to be carried back to bed in her father's strong arms after everyone else had gone to their cabins for the night.

Now Eddie got up from the table and started to pace the room, walking between two wooden black bear sculptures. As she marched, she chewed her fingernails, which were nearly down to the quick. Again, Samuel asked, "Eddie, what are you thinking?"

The fire was long out, and the retreat guests were all back to their cabins. The crisis was over, but inside the dining hall emotions still ran high. The local fire chief, along with commenting how lucky they were for the significant rainfall the week prior (things weren't bone dry, the way they could get in the summer), had suggested what Eddie already felt to be true—it could have been an arson event, though an errant lightning strike couldn't entirely be ruled out. There had been reports of some thunder and lightning in the area, the chief had mentioned.

"It was Victor Valence. Or maybe one of his cronies," Eddie said, pacing faster now.

"Why do you think it was Vic V?" Samuel asked.

"Victor has been wanting to get rid of me for years! He can't stand what we're doing here. You all know it. He hates women, and he hates me the most."

"Yeah, he's a misogynistic ass, but I don't think he's near brave enough to pull this off, Eddie," Sam replied. He glanced around the table at the others. "Besides, I can't imagine him risking an out-of-control blaze. Not with his camp so close by."

Eddie stopped her anger march, staring at Samuel. "You don't get it, Sam. You're not a woman."

Samuel cleared his throat and looked at his hands, clasped on the table. Dot gave him a small, comforting smile. No one else moved, or spoke, until Judith—her tone pointed—said, "Eddie, come on. Sam's one of us."

"It's all right, Jude," Samuel said, rising from the table. "I'm going to make us some coffee before I start the breakfast prep."

If Eddie felt bad for her response to Samuel, she didn't immediately show it. Nor did she stop her muttering and fingernail biting, until Florence stood and blocked her pacing path.

"Let's take a breath." She set gentle hands on her friend's shoulders, holding her in place.

It was as though a trance were broken, and Eddie suddenly came back to herself. Her eyes widened and her lip quivered. "I should go talk to him," she said, glancing over Florence's shoulder toward the kitchen's door. "Apologize."

Florence steered Eddie back to her chair at the table. "Let's just pause for a moment first, okay?"

Dot reached out and held Eddie's hand as she sat down. "You all right, hon?"

"Yeah, I . . . Sorry. Sorry, everyone," Eddie said, her voice wobbly with emotion.

"We know," Judith said. She rubbed Eddie's arm, squeezing it so she'd meet her gaze. "But we are stronger together than apart. Right?"

Eddie nodded, looking bereft. These women, and Samuel, understood her the way no one else did, maybe ever had. Outside the camp's gate she was many things: formerly known as Edith Jane Callaway, runaway heiress; eccentric "wild woman" of the woods; zealous feminist; devoted mentor; loyal friend of her community. Here at camp, however, she was simply Eddie. Perhaps untamed at times, certainly single-minded on occasion, but unflinchingly generous, with a heart that knew her truth and was prepared to fight for it.

"It *might* have been Victor." Eddie was exhausted, bone-tired. She sighed heavily and rubbed at her eyes, then looked at the faces around the table. "You heard him the other day, Flo. That was a threat if I've ever been handed one."

"I think Sam's right, Eddie. Freddie Flintstone wouldn't risk anything happening to his precious camp," Florence replied.

"And how could he have started a fire without anyone

seeing him? Dot and I were in the lean-to nearest the gate. We didn't see anyone, or notice anything strange." Judith turned to Dot, who nodded. "At least until we smelled the smoke."

"It's true. There was no one else out there," Dot confirmed. "We would have heard something. Someone."

"If it wasn't Victor, then who? You heard the chief. Arson is most likely," Eddie retorted.

"He did say it could have been lightning, too," Judith replied, her voice low and soothing. Though when Eddie asked if anyone had heard thunder, the group shook their heads.

"We'd been smoking, Eddie," Dot said, shrugging. "We were pretty much in la la land at that point."

"Well, there's only one thing to do." Eddie clapped her hands against the tabletop, making everyone jump. "I'm going over there to ask Victor to his face."

"Now?" Florence asked. "It's four o'clock in the morning, Eddie."

"So what?" Eddie started pulling out her curlers, dropping pins on the table. *Ping. Ping. Ping.* The curls bounced up as they were released. "Am I going to screw with his beauty sleep?"

"At least have some sustenance first," Samuel said, having rejoined the group. In his good hand he held a tray with a carafe of coffee, a pitcher of milk, a tin of Quik chocolate powder, and half a pineapple upside-down cake. He set the tray down and squeezed Eddie's shoulder until she looked at him.

Then, more softly, he added, "There's nothing *anyone* can do while it's still dark."

As Judith and Dot got plates and silverware for the cake, Florence poured coffee into the mugs on the table. Eddie chose cold milk instead, and gave Samuel an appreciative look as she added two heaping teaspoons of the Quik chocolate into her mug. The powder sat like a mini mountain on the milk's surface.

"I'm sorry for what I said, Sam. I was out of line," Eddie said, making eye contact with him. He shook his head gently and smiled, his message silent but clear: *No harm done.* She let out a long breath and allowed her shoulders to drop a couple of inches. Then Eddie picked up the knife from the tray and cut the cake into even squares.

She served everyone a piece, and was about to take a forkful when she swallowed hard, tears forming. Eddie set her fork down—she couldn't eat anything right now, not even cake. "What if we hadn't been able to put it out? I can't even think about that without wanting to throw up."

The idea of a fire engulfing the camp, burning it to the ground, hurting (or worse) the guests and her friends, the flames reaching past the camp's perimeter to the woods beyond, where it wouldn't be so easily stopped . . . it was unthinkable. She shuddered, let the tears fall without wiping them away.

"But we *did* put it out. And we'll fix the sign. All of us, together," Samuel replied as the others nodded in unison. "Look, everyone is exhausted. It's late. Or early? I don't even know anymore. But what I do know is that you have nothing to apologize for." Sam sipped his milky coffee, holding Eddie's gaze over his mug. In that glance she saw nothing but the pure love he held for her, and she nearly collapsed from the relief of it. To be loved with the same stamina and patience that you love . . . that is a gift not to take for granted.

"Dear friends to the end," Eddie said to the group in front of her, holding up her glass of chocolate milk. It was her anchoring affirmation for her inner circle. The sort of statement that could be viewed as trite, or clichéd, but carried deep meaning for those who called Camp Callaway home.

"Dear friends to the end," they repeated, clinking mugs and sharing smiles around the circle.

They drank the strong, fragrant coffee in silence—Samuel made the best coffee—and Eddie had a second glass of chocolate milk, and then the sun rose above the trees and it was dawn.

Pop Your Pain

This is the at-home version of "Target Your Power."

Fill a balloon with air, then carefully—in dark-colored marker—write the source of your pain (a person, a loss, a place) on its surface. I have learned that while it is one of the hardest acts, there is great peace in exposing your darkest corners. Even if only to yourself.

Take a pin or some sharp instrument, and once you acknowledge your pain, embracing it and surrounding it with understanding and love (take your time, as we can't rush awareness), say "Pop!" as you pop the balloon. Repeat as many times as needed.

—Eddie C. xx

*From *Camp Callaway's Wild Women Handbook, 1975*

ROWAN, 2021.

THEY ARE DEFINITELY BONES, SETH SAYS ("Human, too"), with tatters of fabric ("Nylon shorts, I think?") clinging to what's left of the skeleton. One weather-beaten hiking boot, its leather cracked and absent a lace. Remnants of what appears to be a yellow windbreaker, the zipper still intact. One of the femurs is broken clean through. There's also a pink enameled smiley face pin that looks just like the one the crow brought me pinned to the jacket. And a plastic water bottle partially buried under debris—the shape more rectangular than cylindrical, like a liquor bottle, with a red stopper and forest green screw lid. Seth guesses the skeleton is female, based on the clothes, and that she has been there for a long, long time. He takes a few photos, but I don't want to see them.

I have no doubt we've found Eddie Callaway.

"We'll call the police as soon as we get back in cell range," Seth says. "But . . . we can't leave this." He points to the box from the tree hollow, and I shake my head.

"I'm not saying we'll keep it." He tugs again on the small

lock that holds the lid closed, but it still won't budge. "I just need to find out what's inside."

"No. We need to leave it here. With the . . ."

I'm about to say "body," but it feels wrong to call our discovery that. Now that I know who she is. "*With her.*"

Goose bumps rise on my skin, and I glance back at the embankment. "It doesn't belong to us."

"It doesn't *not* belong to us, Rowan. It has obviously been out here for a while, and we have no idea *who* it belonged to. Besides, we don't even know if it has anything to do with . . . what's down there." Seth's jaw clenches, and I feel sick again. "I'm not leaving it here. It might be valuable."

"So, you just want to take it and open it and then what?" I am close to tears. "Then what, Seth?"

He shrugs, tucking the box under his arm and tightening his hold. As though I might try to wrench it from his grip. "Cross that bridge when we get it open."

WE DON'T SPEAK again until we're back inside the cabin. And then not until after Seth has answered the ringing landline, which is trilling before we even open the front door.

"Hey, thanks for calling back. Yeah, she's better today," Seth says. He watches as I change out of my now-filthy clothes and into a pair of leggings and an oversized sweatshirt, listening to whoever is on the phone. My feet and hands are chilled, and I want to take a shower. But I'll wait until we've called the police.

"Thanks . . . yeah . . . we really appreciate it." Seth glances my way again, gives a smile that I don't return. I've tucked away my anger and hurt at his betrayal *for now*—I can only prioritize one emotional crisis at a time—but in its place is a foggy numbness. Smiling back suggests I'm okay, and I could not be further from okay.

"That sounds great. See you then." Seth hangs up the phone. "We're having dinner with Jess and Aidan. Tomorrow night, around seven."

I pause, only one sock on. "How are you making dinner plans right now? We haven't even called the police yet."

Whereas Seth's mood and color improved the farther we got from the embankment, the tension inside me has continued to build. It's like I'm filled with live wires—the electricity snapping and coursing unfettered. The need to get help, to tell someone what we've discovered deep in the woods, is overwhelming—it's almost physical, the urge I have to pick up the phone and dial the number.

So that's what I do. But I don't know the number for the local police, and there's no phone book I can see. "I guess we just call 9-1-1?"

"Rowan. Wait."

Ignoring him, I punch the 9 then the 1, and then I feel a hand on my shoulder, squeezing. It's my sore shoulder, but I don't flinch.

"Wait . . . ," Seth says.

I turn to face him. "For what?"

My mind flashes to Clara's email, despite my best efforts not to think about it. The reality that Seth tried to sabotage my career, for reasons beyond me, makes me want to cry. The fact that we just found parts of a skeleton—perhaps belonging to a woman who has been missing for over four decades—and Seth is more focused on the box from the tree, and dinner plans, makes me want to scream.

Eyes slightly downcast, I press the 1 again and hold the handset tight to my ear, raising my eyes back to Seth's. I watch his face change, his jaw tighten.

"Uh, yes. Hi," I start once the call is picked up. "I need to report something. I think we found a body."

. . .

HOURS LATER, SETH and I sit in silence in the back of the police cruiser on the side of the dark, gravel road a few miles from our cabin, waiting while officers and paramedics hike on foot with bright lights and search and rescue dogs to the spot where we found the bones. There are so many flashing lights around us—a half dozen vehicles pulled over on the side of the road— that the sky is alight with a kaleidoscope of white, red, and blue.

"Yes, they appear to be human remains," the officer who drove us says, once word the skeleton has been found crackles across the radio. "No, we can't be sure who they belong to. Not yet. But they've been out here a long damn time."

"Is there anything else either of you could tell me? Anything?" the officer—her name tag reads "P. Blackburn"—asks. I can't remember her first name, though she told us when she picked up us. "It could be helpful."

"No, ma'am," Seth replies to Officer Blackburn, who is now crouched beside the open back door of the cruiser, the flashlight in her hand pointed to the ground to avoid blinding us. "Like I said, we were hiking. My fiancée slipped and fell, and when I went down to check on her, we saw . . . the bones. Do you want to see the pictures again? If that's helpful?"

Seth clears his throat and pulls out his phone, opening his photo album. I press my lips together and stare into my lap.

OFFICER BLACKBURN—I remember her first name is Paige—drops us back at the cabin, leaving us with her card and a request to call her anytime "if anything comes to mind."

Inside the cabin we've left a lamp on, and Seth and I sit on the couch—side by side, but not touching. The lamp casts strange shadows throughout the small room. It's past midnight, but I'm wired—struggling with my sense of time.

We've been arguing since the officer left—about me calling 9-1-1 so quickly ("What could we possibly be waiting for?"), about Seth hiding that ever-important email from me, about whether we should just pack up and go home in the morning. But mostly we argue about the box, which remains locked, resting on the coffee table in front of us.

Seth assures me he'll hand it over to the police, *eventually*, and won't take anything from it—"if there's anything even in there to take," he adds. He promises that after we unlock it, we'll report it. But not, of course, before we film the whole thing for our channel.

"If that really is Eddie Callaway down there, and this is in any way connected to her, well, they won't be able to turn away, Rowan. It will be that damn compelling. Besides, we have a *responsibility* to share our experience, don't we?"

According to Seth, we've done our part by reporting the bones. No one needs to know we found the box. Not yet. After, we can say we stumbled upon it during a hike in the woods. Or at Camp Callaway, when we were innocently exploring and shooting some B-roll shots (of *private property*, I remind him). Seth is unconcerned, annoyingly so.

"Why were you in my email in the first place, Seth?" My voice is hoarse by now.

There's a pause. Then a guilty look, which morphs into one that is more resigned. "You were in the shower. We'd gone for a run, remember?" I did. Seth finally wore me down, suggesting a run to get us in shape for our upcoming hikes. "Your phone was on the bed, right beside me. It pinged and . . . I glanced at the screen. That sound is Pavlovian, you know?"

I don't respond. He reaches for me, and when I get up to move away from him, he sighs.

"Something just came over me, Rowan. I wasn't thinking! I don't know, maybe I wanted to punish you, a bit. For that night."

"That live stream *boosted* subscribers, Seth. Isn't that exactly what you wanted?" My voice rises.

"Look, I know you don't care about the channel the way I do," Seth says, his tone measured. "But when I'm working on our content, I feel . . . like I'm making something that people will want to watch. *Want more of.* Even if it's just good entertainment, it feels . . . relevant, you know?" I don't, because I don't feel that way at all.

"That doesn't happen when I write," he continues. "There's no audience. No way to engage."

"You haven't found your audience yet, but you will." While I'm furious with him still, my feelings about his talent are unchanged.

"Will I? I can't even finish this one manuscript, Rowan. And what I *have* written isn't good enough. Besides, it just feels like work. And the channel, it's fun, right? We can make money doing it. More than I'll probably ever make writing novels. So I wanted to ride this out, with you. At least for a couple of years."

"*A couple of years?*" It hits me that we have a quite different version of what our life looks like a couple of years from now. Married. Me, scriptwriting professionally. Seth's novel published, his sophomore project in the works. YouTube a distant memory. "You thought I'd do this for a couple of years more? I don't even want to do it now!"

We stare at each other. Neither of us moves.

Seth breaks first. "I hid that email because I need you to be here with me. To do this with me. We both know the channel performs better when you're on camera. The subscribers like you, they always talk about that in the comments. You're so *relatable.*"

"I have no clue why."

Seth frowns. "You're a good and honest person, Rowan.

People can see that. They want someone they can connect with."

I feel trapped inside the tiny cabin that has been swallowed up by the big, dark woods now that night has fallen. I should have been explicit with Seth about my conflicted feelings on YouTube—the fear that it would poach my creativity, not to mention my time, from my screenplays. That I wanted . . . *more*, even if this was enough for him.

"I'm sorry, okay? I shouldn't have . . . I'm sorry." Seth shakes his head. "What else can I say? I need you, Rowan."

"I'm sorry, too." For what precisely I don't say, and he doesn't ask.

I CAN'T SLEEP, again. *When was the last time I slept well?* Seth manages to drift off, somewhere around four in the morning, but I stay on the couch. I run my fingertips around the edges of the smiley face button; I read Judith's poem, and the Wild Woman handbook in its entirety. Then I go back to the handbook's opening letter, and the "Future You" letter-writing exercise, after which I open my notebook, inspired to write my own letter. But nothing comes, and the blank page remains blank. Maybe it's as Eddie said in her letter to the Wild Women of Camp Callaway: Dwelling on the past is an enormous burden. We must learn from it and move forward, carrying with us only the most precious tidbits we'll need for what lies ahead.

Perhaps I'm not quite ready to learn from my past.

Either way, Eddie's voice is beginning to feel familiar— there's comfort in her words, her drawings, her stories. I imagine

I'm one of her 1975 "Wild Women," being handed the book after a magical retreat in the woods. I drink three cups of coffee and do five sun salutations on the porch, at sunrise, wondering what advice Eddie Callaway might impart to me.

THE BODY IS all over the local news by the next day, and we quietly watch the young reporter, wearing a red rain jacket with the news station's logo on it, deliver the story in somber tones on the cabin's small television. We're referred to as "a couple out hiking when they came upon the discovery." Seth tries a few times to open the rusted lock—groaning with increasing frustration each time it resists. There's a small shed that contains a chain saw and a hacksaw, along with a series of hammerheads with no handles. Overkill for the small lock, and Seth won't risk damaging the box.

It rains nearly all day, which I blame for my dull headache. At one point Seth suggests we drive into town so I can reply to Clara.

"It's too late," I say.

"How do you know?"

I shrug. "You know how this works, Seth. I missed the window."

At this he sighs. "So, you're not even going to try?"

It occurs to me he's desperate to believe he hasn't completely blown my chances with Clara. That would go far in soothing his guilt, I'm sure.

"Like I said, it's too late," I reply.

"Okay, fine, Rowan. Be difficult for the sake of being difficult." He shuts his laptop lid harder than it deserves, but I don't engage. I simply don't have the energy.

Seth says he's going for a walk (in the pouring rain), and I manage to fall asleep for a couple of hours. Then I sit on the porch, one of the wool blankets wrapped around my shoulders, waiting for the crow to visit. But the bird never comes. Perhaps it took shelter somewhere else to avoid the teeming rain. The rows of peanuts remain untouched.

The rain eventually stops, and the skies have brightened by the time we leave for Jess and Aidan's, the forest emanating that cloying, if not refreshing, scent of wet earth and droplet-soaked greenery. Getting into the car, I inhale sharply as I reach for the seat belt. My shoulder remains tender, and hot flashes of pain radiate through the joint with the movement.

"Here, let me," Seth says, carefully reaching for my seat belt and then buckling it.

"Thanks." I stare straight ahead, waiting for him to start the car. It's getting muggy inside, and I want to put my window down.

But he doesn't start the car. Instead, he sets his hands on the steering wheel, his knuckles whitening. "How long are you going to stay pissed off, Rowan?"

"I don't know."

"*You don't know?*"

I look over at him. Then, after a moment, repeat, "I don't know."

Seth murmurs "Screw this" and finally starts the car. As he puts it in reverse, I put down my window. Hearing a familiar call, I turn toward the cabin to see the crow land on the railing, taking a peanut into its beak. The lone white feather crisp and bright.

AFTER JESS REMOVES Seth's stitches, a much less dramatic affair than putting them in (Seth doesn't ask me to film

221

it), we settle in for dinner. Aidan has prepared wild mushroom risotto, with fungi foraged that morning, along with steamed greens and garlic, and homemade bread with fresh goat's cheese. Everything is either from their homestead or local farmers, and it's all delicious, even if I don't have much of an appetite.

We avoid talking about the skeleton. Jess and Aidan let us steer the conversation, and so we keep it light. But I'm quiet, in part because I'm exhausted, but mostly because I feel disconnected.

Jess, noticing my mood, suggests after dinner that she and I go outside for some air. Aidan and Seth offer to clean up, and so Jess and I settle into rocking chairs on the yurt's front porch.

The sky is midnight black now, but the stars' brilliance smatters the darkness. I still haven't gotten used to the way the stars illuminate the entire sky out here, with no competing city lights. Jess sets a match to the citronella torches, then hands me a soft knitted blanket, which I place over my lap. She pulls something small, white, and tube-shaped out of her pocket.

"Dessert," she says.

I laugh. "I'm in."

I'm a very occasional marijuana smoker, but tonight I'm happy for anything that might take the edge off. Jess lights the joint, then takes a drag. Holding her breath, she hands it to me.

The cigarette paper crackles as it burns, and I hold the smoke in my lungs until they feel they might burst. In a rush I release my breath, and rest my head back against the rocking chair.

"So how's our leucistic crow?" Jess asks.

I take another puff, then pass it to Jess. After I exhale, I say, "It brought me something."

"Oh yeah?"

I take the yellow smiley pin from my jean jacket pocket.

"That crow likes you," Jess says, holding the pin up to the light from the torch. "It's a gift, for the peanuts. It looks vintage, too. Wonder where it came from?"

I don't say anything about the nearly identical pin we found with the skeleton. Maybe because I don't want to be ridiculed for suggesting the crow brought me that smiley face pin on purpose: a gift, but also a clue. However, it's silly for me to worry. Jess isn't one for ridicule. Maybe I just want to keep it secret.

We share the joint back and forth for the next couple of minutes, both of us quiet in a companionable silence. I hear Seth and Aidan inside, the clatter of dishes and the deep tones of men's voices. I wonder what they're talking about.

"Thank you. I needed this." I sigh contentedly through pleasantly tingling lips.

"You bet." Jess drops the nub of the joint into a clay ashtray that appears homemade. "So, do you want to talk about it?"

I turn my head toward her. "I'm not sure you want to hear about it."

"Try me."

I pause, briefly. "I think the bones we found might be Eddie Callaway's."

"And I think you're probably right," Jess replies.

I tear up, hearing this. Then a lightness settles over me, like I've just taken off a very heavy backpack. It's the release of being believed.

"It never made sense to me that she would leave the camp the way she did," Jess continues. "Why would she abandon everything she worked so hard to build, without any trace or explanation?"

"I don't think she would have." I let the tears that have been threatening all day come.

"I'm sorry this happened, Rowan." Jess reaches over and holds my hand.

"I can't stop seeing her, like that." My breath hitches, my nose runs. "And then thinking about what it would have been like for her, in those last moments. All alone like that. She must have been so scared."

"No one should have to die alone." The way she says it makes me realize she has personal experience with this. I don't say anything, giving her the space to tell her story if she chooses to. Which she does.

"When I was in my late teens, I volunteered at a hospice. All my friends did placements at animal shelters, children's camps, the local newspaper. I would sit with the hospice clients when their families took breaks so they were never by themselves." Jess smiles, but it's small, sad.

"Maybe an odd placement for a teenager, but my dad died when I was young—he spent the last two weeks of his life in hospice—and I thought it was the most wonderful, beautiful place to be, at the end."

"I'm sorry about your dad," I say.

"It was a long time ago, but thank you."

I'm even more taken by Jess. She's a woman who seems to know precisely what she wants, and has set up her life to ensure she gets it. But she also has this vulnerable side. A past that lives inside her like a wound that leaves an indelible mark, which I know a little something about. Yet it does not define her. I'm thankful she shares this other side of herself, because it suddenly helps me understand how moving beyond something is not the same thing as forgetting about it. I think again about the letter I tried to write that morning, about Eddie's words on learning and letting go.

"What am I supposed to do now?" I ask, knowing my question is convoluted and not for her to answer.

"Whatever you want." Jess shrugs. "I don't mean that to sound flippant, Rowan, but I've found it's never as complicated as you tell yourself it is."

I nod, though I'm not sure I agree. It sure feels complicated. Impossibly so.

"WHAT DID YOU and Jess talk about?" Seth asks on the drive home.

"This and that," I reply. I stare out the window, still soft-minded from the joint.

"I didn't say anything about the box. To Aidan," he adds.

"That's fine. Whatever you want."

Seth turns toward me. "Wow, you're high."

"No kidding." Then I chuckle lightly. I'm feeling good. My shoulder doesn't even hurt anymore.

"That probably wasn't the smartest idea," Seth says, irritation clouding his words. "You're not exactly in the best frame of mind."

"Who are you, my mother?" I cross my arms over my chest and lean back, eyes closed. The car speeds up, Seth's frustration giving him a lead foot.

"I didn't say anything about the box, Seth. *Relax.*"

Of course, telling someone to relax typically has the opposite effect. Seth grumbles that he doesn't need to *do* anything, including *relax*, and I try to stay awake.

WE GET BACK to the cabin, and while I just desperately want to sleep, Seth wants to *talk*. About the box. He reiterates that keeping it is not the plan. "I only want to see what's inside."

I comment how it might look suspicious: The couple who found human remains on a hike later finds a treasure box on another? Seth brushes off my argument and concerns, tells me I'm overthinking everything.

"Suspicious how? We've done nothing wrong, Rowan."

I'm still buzzed, so it takes me a while longer to get revved up, but when he brings up the YouTube channel again—" . . . we'll film what's inside, and then report it . . ."—I snap.

"Do you really think being a YouTuber is a legit career path, like long term? How many fifty-year-old couples do you see making stupid, pointless videos?" I shout at him. The cabin's interior is so small a whisper would suffice, so my voice is painfully loud.

Seth is stunned for one brief moment. Then he shouts back. Accuses me of changing my tune and being "a creative snob." He moans about how unfair this all is. All he wants is for us to do this together. *Of course* he doesn't picture being a YouTuber for the rest of his life, but why not squeeze everything out of it that we can while it's a viable money-making option?

I have grossly misinterpreted Seth's ambition. That much I understand now. It's clear he doesn't have a plan beyond growing the YouTube channel (his manuscript on the back burner, as it can't bring him the same quick fame and adoration he craves), while I have very clear plans that have nothing to do with TheWrightStory. We are *not* a team; we are two people who don't want the same things, standing at a fork in our road.

I finally see what being apart from him, from this dichotomy, would mean—and with that comes a feeling that takes me by surprise: *calmness*. However, it's quickly followed by the opposite sense—one of panic, and of being unmoored. We've been partners long enough that I'm not sure who I am without him.

Unaware of my churning thoughts, Seth continues yammering about the channel. "Whatever's inside this box could get us past a million subscribers, like overnight! Imagine that, Rowan. *A million subscribers.*"

"Look. If this really *is* the mysterious Callaway treasure," Seth continues, putting on his "let's all calm down here for a minute" voice, "it was put out there in the woods to be found. And we found it. So . . . I know what I said about turning it in, but why *shouldn't* we keep it?"

"Actually, I found it, Seth."

He stares at me. His eyes narrowing. "It's only out of that tree because of me, Rowan."

"I never should have told you. Never should have shown you where—"

"Well, you did," Seth retorts. We glare at each other for a moment; then he says, "I'm going to bed."

I stay where I am, watching him take off his shorts and T-shirt before getting under the covers. He turns out the bedside table lamp, the room going dark—only a slight illumination from the full moon streaming through the windows.

I think of all the nights Eddie lay alone under that rock, by this very moonlight. Later, when I can't sleep, I'll add it up: sixteen thousand seven hundred and ninety nights, give or take.

"I'm sorry it took so long, Eddie," I whisper, staring at the number on my phone's calculator. Then, finally, I sleep.

EDDIE, 1975.

"The Crow and the Pitcher," Aesop's Fable

A Crow, half dead with thirst, came upon a Pitcher which had once been full of water; but when the Crow put its beak into the mouth of the Pitcher he found that only very little water was left in it, and that he could not reach far enough down to get at it. He tried, and he tried, but at last had to give up in despair. Then a thought came to him, and he took a pebble and dropped it into the Pitcher. Then he took another pebble and dropped it into the Pitcher. Then he took another pebble and dropped that into the Pitcher. Then he took another pebble and dropped that into the Pitcher. Then he took another pebble and dropped that into the Pitcher. Then he took another pebble and dropped that into the Pitcher. At last, at last, he saw the water mount up near him, and after casting in a few more pebbles he was able to quench his thirst and save his life.

Little by little does the trick.

Be as resilient as the crow. You are the only one who can fill your own pitcher.

—Eddie C. xx

*From *Camp Callaway's Wild Women Handbook*, 1975

ONCE A WEEK EDDIE WENT INTO TOWN TO pick up supplies and run camp errands. Today's trip included a stop at Hopper's Diner for a few dozen pies she'd ordered. Carole Hopper, the owner, made the *best* pies, and Eddie liked to support the woman and her restaurant. Plus, it gave Samuel a baking break during hotter weeks, as the camp's kitchen could get roasting.

She drove her truck—an old pickup that was as reliable as it was sturdy—down the dusty, pothole-filled gravel road, one tanned arm resting on the rolled-down window. One of her favorites came on the radio, and she cranked the volume.

"Help me . . . I think I'm falling . . . ," she crooned along to Joni Mitchell's hit from the year before, her foot stepping firmly on the gas pedal. She hummed along to the melody, but her voice faded and her foot came off the gas as the truck approached a familiar spot on the road. Eddie pulled over, dust swirling into the truck's cabin. She chewed her fingernail, staring down the driveway across from her.

She had promised she would let it be. That had been the

group's agreement when dawn broke earlier that morning; they would leave the incident to the fire marshal's office. No one had been hurt, and yes, the camp's entrance sign was damaged, but the rest of the crew was already at work to restore it.

Eddie knew she should keep driving. ("Don't poke the bear," her dad always used to say, "because the bear will poke back!") Turn Joni up and carry on. But now that she was here, at this driveway . . . *how could she not go and say her piece?* The words she needed to say sat uncomfortably in her throat, like a piece of dry toast that didn't want to make its way down.

Just then a "caw-caw" filled the air, and Eddie followed the birdcall to an ink-black crow perched on the log fencing that ran down either side of the driveway.

"Hey, friend!" Eddie reached into the truck's glove box for the bag of peanuts. She tossed a handful of the nuts out her truck window, and they flew in a high arc before landing near the fence post where the crow rested. It cawed and then jumped down, taking one of the peanuts in its beak before looking back at Eddie.

"You're welcome," she said, watching the crow fly away, knowing it would come back later for the rest.

With another glance at the driveway, Eddie made her choice. She turned off the truck and got out, closing the door behind her. Eddie wanted to approach on foot; it would offer her the element of surprise.

The wooden gate at the end of the driveway was locked, but she easily climbed it and hopped over, landing heavily on the other side. A sharp stab of pain exploded in her ankle as it rolled, and she cursed, waiting for the searing pain to subside. As numbness took over the agony, she knew the ankle was swelling, and Eddie felt stupid for not having worn her hiking boots. But she'd been in a rush and had slipped on her sandals instead. She'd ask Dot for some salve later.

Eddie had no real strategy, and now that she was inside Victor Valence's camp compound—uninvited and having jumped the fence, so also trespassing—she felt less confident about her decision. Pushing ahead, she limped up the gravel walkway to the front lawn, where she recognized the Valences' oldest boy playing catch with a younger child whom Eddie didn't know.

The children stopped, and Victor's son tossed the baseball from one gloved hand to the other, watching her approach.

"Hey there," Eddie said. "Is your dad around?"

"William!" Victor Valence shouted at his son, who quickly turned at his dad's booming voice. "Off you go. Take your cousin with you. Your mother said it's time to wash up for lunch."

The boys took off at a run, though the sloppy and gangly kind of running young kids do, and Eddie felt a wave of longing.

"What do you want?" Victor was clearly displeased to see her.

She squared her shoulders, shifted her weight more to her left side to give her throbbing ankle a rest. "Why did you do it?"

"Do what?" Victor asked. Eddie noticed he had a sunburn, his nose peeling. She also saw he had a few bandages wrapped around his fingers.

"What happened there?" She pointed to his hands.

"You're trespassing" was his only reply.

"*Why did you do it*, Victor?"

He gave her a blank look, and she wondered if maybe she was wrong after all—maybe Victor really had nothing to do with the fire.

"I don't have time for games, Callaway," he finally said.

"We have guests arriving soon. And not that it's any of your business, but I got a few splinters. From my boat."

Victor's business was construction, but his hobby was boat-building. It was reasonable to believe that those bandages covered precisely what he said they did—but at the same time, Eddie couldn't help but imagine how lighting Camp Callaway's sign on fire could have resulted in similar injuries; how Victor, in the dark and in his haste, got clumsy, the matches or torch catching too fast to avoid burning his fingers . . .

Eddie shook her head, then slowed her breathing, hoping to calm her heart, which was jackrabbiting inside her chest. "I believe you started that fire, Victor. But you won't scare me off. Fire or otherwise, okay? So *back off.*"

Victor Valence's eyebrows knitted together. "Fire? What are you talking about?"

"Give me a break," Eddie huffed. "You've been trying to run me out of town and shut down my camp for years now."

"I have no clue what this fire shit is about, but I had nothing to do with it."

Eddie observed Victor for a long moment. Thinking about what the others might say if they knew where she was and what she was doing. She decided to push the tiniest bit more, just to test the waters. "I don't believe you."

Exasperated, Victor threw his hands in the air, then pointed back down the driveway. "You're crazy, Callaway. Get the hell off my property!"

She took a step closer to Victor and held his gaze. "You cannot scare me, Victor. I have as much right as you do to use my property how I see fit. I've been here longer than you, and I bet I'll be here long after you, too. Camp Callaway is my home, and no one—you included—can change that."

Then Eddie turned and walked away. She knew Victor was watching her, so she clenched her teeth against the pain in her ankle—refusing to limp—and didn't wipe at her watering eyes until she was at the gate and out of sight.

Her breath hitched with the pain in her ankle, and she allowed herself a few moments of reprieve before climbing back over the gate, being more cautious this time about her landing. Once again, she heard the crow before she saw it, its familiar song filling the air.

"Hey, friend. Whatcha doing on there?"

The black bird was perched on Eddie's side mirror of the truck, watching her. Maybe it had been trying to get to the peanuts she had left on the passenger seat. Crows were intelligent birds—more intelligent and intuitive than some humans (like perhaps Victor).

Eddie limped to her vehicle slowly, not wanting to scare the bird. "There, there, just let me in and I'll get you some peanuts, okay?"

She moved to the passenger side, carefully opening the door. The crow stayed on the mirror, watching Eddie. Peanut bag in hand, Eddie came back around the truck and scattered two handfuls of the nuts at the base of a nearby tree, then slowly backed away. The crow watched until Eddie was a good distance from the tree, then gave another "caw-caw" before flying over to where Eddie had left the peanuts.

"I probably shouldn't have done that," Eddie said to the crow, which was nudging its beak among the piles of peanuts. She glanced at her ankle, noting the swelling. "You're lucky. You get to just *be* a bird. That's all anyone can ask of you."

Looking at Victor's camp sign at the mouth of the driveway, Eddie sighed. She probably should have listened to her friends and let it be. Yet she refused to be intimidated. With that in mind, she unpinned the smiley face button from her shorts—Eddie was never without the enameled pins, having ordered dozens to hand out during her retreats. Then she took a pencil from the glove box, wrote a sentence on a blank page in her supplies notebook, and ripped it out.

She limped back to the gate, and holding the pin firmly between her fingers, she stuck it through the top of the paper and then into the wood just beneath the gate's lock. Eddie pushed hard to ensure the pin was deeply embedded into the wood's pulpy fibers, and it held the paper firmly, though the bottom of the page fluttered with the slight breeze.

"There," she said, tilting her head to look at her handiwork. The yellow smiley face pin was bright against the wooden slats—it would be hard to miss.

"You can tell Victor I left him a love note," Eddie said to the crow, once she made it back to her truck. The bird seemed to have little fear as it picked at a peanut shell, barely acknowledging her presence. Then Eddie got in her truck, rolled her windows down as far as they would go, and started driving toward town.

"WHAT HAPPENED?" FLORENCE asked as Eddie walked gingerly up the stairs to the main lodge, carrying two paper bags.

"Turned my ankle. I'm fine."

Florence took the bags from Eddie's arms, glancing at her injured leg as she did. They headed inside the dining hall. "Seems pretty swollen, Eddie. Make sure Dot takes a look."

"I will," Eddie said, limping after Florence, wishing again she had been more careful.

Samuel came out from the kitchen. "Did they have the pineapple?" Then, noticing Eddie favoring her ankle, he asked, "What did you do?"

"Minor sprain. Like I told Flo, I'm fine."

He pulled out a chair and gestured for Eddie to sit down.

"Not you, too," Eddie grumbled, but she dutifully sat.

Samuel crouched in front of her and ran his hand down her lower leg and over the ankle bone, which had swollen to twice its normal size. It looked as though Eddie were smuggling a golf ball under her skin, which was now also mottled with red and blue bruising. "I wore sandals instead of my hikers. I stepped off a curb weird at the diner."

"This happened in town?" Samuel asked.

"You know how clumsy I can be." Samuel and Flo exchanged a look. Eddie was definitely not clumsy.

"I was distracted, excited about the pies. Guess I wasn't paying enough attention to my feet." She shrugged, feeling bad for the fib, but also not prepared to admit the truth.

"I'll get you some ice." Samuel pulled out another chair and gently placed her foot on it. Eddie grimaced. "Were you able to get your 'top secret' errand done?"

"Yes!" Eddie grinned. "And *no*, I will not tell you what it was. So don't ask. You know I want it to be a surprise for everyone. Even you two."

"I like surprises," Samuel said.

"Happy to wait," Florence added.

"Hey, Sam, before I forget," Eddie said. "If there are any empty Quik tins lying around, could you set them aside for me?"

"You bet," Sam replied, before heading back to the kitchen to get ice for her ankle.

Florence started back toward the truck to get the rest of Eddie's things, and help Samuel carry in the pies that were stacked in the flatbed.

"Flo, there's a paper bag inside the glove box. Can you grab it? Just . . . don't look inside it, okay?"

Florence nodded, saying only, "You bet."

Eddie smiled at her friend, the pain in her ankle momentarily forgotten as a thrill moved through her, thinking about what was in the glove box. Tomorrow would be the start of something truly extraordinary.

WHILE NEARLY EVERY piece of her plan was sorted, there remained one element Eddie hadn't decided upon: the perfect hiding spots for the Quik tins. Not impossible to discover with a pointed clue, but also not so easy to find as to steal the deep sense of satisfaction from whomever the lucky woman—or group of women, if they decided to work together—was who uncovered them.

After icing her ankle and allowing Dot to do some massage on it to move the swelling along, Eddie had retreated to her cabin for a quick rest before dinner. She'd eschewed company, claiming the need for a solid nap after losing sleep the previous night, because of the fire. But really what Eddie needed was to put the final touches on her plan.

She had to wait only a bit longer, as hard as it was. After breakfast tomorrow Eddie would gather the guests on the lawn in front of the dining hall, or in the barns if the weather or bugs were uncooperative, and tell them (along with her friends, who were equally unaware) about this epic adventure she had crafted.

Eddie's cabin had plenty of hand-stitched pillows scattered on the floor for when she invited her closest confidants over for brainstorming sessions, or when they gathered to celebrate the end of a successful retreat. The small couch was sometimes used for naps when too much grass had been consumed by the camp's skeleton crew (Florence, Samuel, Judith, and Eddie), which happened more frequently during the camp's restful, quieter off-season.

Now she sat propped up in her bed, her ankle on soft pillows, taking stock of what she had left to do before dinner. Glancing at her bookshelf, her eyes tracked over some of her greatest treasures, including first editions from her father's library and a beloved bronzed jewelry box that had been her mother's. The box was mostly empty (though not for long), the only item in it Theo's watch. Eddie hadn't wound it once since it had been taken off his wrist at the hospital. Its face was cracked, but no matter; she wasn't interested in fixing it, wishing instead for it to remain the way it had been.

Turning her attention back to the empty Quik tin beside her, she pried off the lid. A faint scent of chocolate mingled with the smell of Dot's salve, which had peppermint and camphor in it and made the skin on her ankle tingle. It felt similar to having a slight itch, but Eddie resisted scratching and focused on what had to go inside the tin instead.

Reaching across the patchwork quilt—a thank-you gift from a former retreat attendee—Eddie's fingers found the paper's sharp edge in the soft folds and pulled it toward her. She unfolded the paper, and her lips moved soundlessly as she read the words she'd typed out. She flipped it over, rereading the poem, happy with how it had turned out. Then she refolded the page and popped it into the empty tin with the yellow label, along with a small evergreen bough, the sharp scent of the green needles filling her nose.

THERE WASN'T TIME to properly hide the tins now—that would happen in the very early morning, before she left on her hike. That way she could move about camp more easily, without her secret being discovered prematurely. One of the tins would be placed at the shooting range, where it could hide among the many others used for the target practice workshop.

She remained unsure about the perfect spot for the second tin. Maybe it could go somewhere in the bowling alley. Yes, she liked that idea.

She slid off the bed, being cautious to take less weight on her bad ankle, and tucked the tins under her arms. The paint had dried, the "Look Inside" message she'd brushed onto the side of each tin easy to read. Eddie set the tins on the shelf, beside the jewelry box but hidden by a row of books. Judith was staying over tonight, and Eddie didn't want to ruin the surprise by having her see the clues ahead of time.

Eddie was in the kitchen, having decided at the last minute to add a third tin (she had printed an extra page, in case one of the others ripped, and figured three clue tins were better than two), when there was a knock at the door. Her hands stilled momentarily; then she quickly folded the final typed page, dropping it into the Quik tin with a piece of evergreen.

"Just a second!" she shouted out, giving the lid three swift taps with the hammer to seal it. She set the paint and brushes under the sink. Then, looking for a temporary hiding spot for the tin, Eddie's eyes went to the pantry only a foot away. The door was tall and narrow, but the shelves were surprisingly deep and there was a dark nook on one side where the tin could hide in the shadows. Eddie could have easily left the tin out on the countertop—*not* finding Quik powder in Eddie's cabin would have been strange. However, she didn't want to take a chance, especially with the freshly painted message on its side.

So she quickly slid the tin into the dark nook, and noticed she'd accidentally smudged the black paint. "Shoot," she fumed, frustrated with her rushing.

Eddie looked around for something to wipe the paint off her finger. An extra handbook sat on the edge of the kitchen countertop. It would have to do. She pressed and rolled her paint-damp fingertip against the handbook's back cover, leaving an oblong black fingerprint on its surface. Then she tucked the handbook in beside the tin and closed the pantry door firmly. She would take both out later, when it was time to hide the tins.

"Come on in," she shouted to whoever had knocked, running her hands under the kitchen faucet at the same time, trying to scrub off the last bit of paint.

It was Judith, coming to get her for dinner. "Thought you could maybe use a hand?" Then she glanced at Eddie's leg. "How's the ankle?"

"So much better. Dot's a miracle worker," Eddie replied. "Give me a minute, okay?"

"Take your time." Judith sat on the couch, chitchatting while watching Eddie apply her lipstick. Judith had just come from her creative writing workshop, and was impressed with this group's creative energy.

Then, with coral-painted lips, her stomach so full of excited butterflies she wasn't sure she'd be able to eat, Eddie took Judith's arm and walked over to the dining hall to join the others. Her fingertip carried only a hint of the black paint, but she tucked her hand into her shorts anyway, not wanting to give anyone a reason to ask about it.

This was a secret she was dying to keep.

ROWAN, 2021.

BY NOON THE FOLLOWING DAY WE STILL haven't heard anything further about the bones I found. I'm agitated, and I can't stop replaying the scene in my mind or thinking about Eddie Callaway. Though the authorities have yet to confirm it was Eddie at the bottom of that embankment, I have little doubt. If it looks like a duck, swims like a duck, and quacks like a duck, then it probably is a duck, as my dad likes to say.

Most specifically, I can't stop thinking about exactly how she ended up under the rock ledge some forty-six years ago. Was it foul play? Or some terrible accident? Did she fall like I did, minus my luck? As a storyteller, I'm wired to fill in plot holes, and so want to understand what happened. No, it's stronger than that: I *need* to know what happened.

Restless and impatient, I flip through the handbook again, looking for answers I know aren't in there. I press my pointer finger against the black smudge on the handbook's back cover, wondering if it's Eddie's fingerprint I'm touching.

The jewelry box remains locked, and Seth's preoccupation with changing that is getting to me. That, and everything else he's doing: slurping the milk off the spoon with every mouthful of cereal; tapping out a song streaming through his headset with his fingers against the tabletop; murmuring to himself as he works on the lock, the sounds of sandpaper against metal distracting, grating. I crave solitude to think—the absence of . . . I'm not sure, exactly. All I know is that right now the cabin is too small for the both of us.

He doesn't hear me when I say I'm leaving, engrossed with the sandpaper and lock, his headphones on. I wave my hands impatiently in front of him, and he moves one earcup to the side. "What's up?"

"I'm going to town."

"Okay," he says, letting the earcup snap back into place, but then adds, "Oh, wait. Can you pick up a small screwdriver? A flathead one. And maybe a hammer with a handle?"

"No," I reply. I slide my phone into my purse. Then I bend to tie my sneakers. My shoulder tightens with the movement, but the two ibuprofen I washed down with my coffee have gotten rid of the dull ache.

"What do you mean, 'no'?" Seth removes the earphones now, resting the headband around his neck.

"I told you. I want no part in this, Seth."

He leans back, hands over his face, and groans in frustration. "Rowan, I know what I said last night, but I promise you we'll report it, okay? Like I've already told you, *only a hundred times or so now . . .*" I ignore the sarcasm. "Aren't you even a little bit curious?"

Of course I am. But I can't separate the box from Eddie's body—I am convinced that one belongs to the other. Forcing the box open feels like disrespecting the woman who locked it all those years ago. I know Seth won't understand, will tell me (again) that I'm overthinking everything. So all I say is "See you later," before stepping onto the porch.

I hear Seth mutter "Whatever . . ." with exasperation, which I ignore. Then I make my way to the car, setting my fingers against the yellow smiley face pin now attached to my canvas purse.

I FIND A table at Hopper's Diner and wave back to Glenda, who noted my arrival and is just finishing up with another customer.

"Happy to see you again, Rowan," she says, smiling warmly. "Coffee?"

"Yes, please," I reply. She nods and pours me a cup from the carafe that always seems to be in her hand. "Just you today, hon?"

"Just me." I push away thoughts of the last time Seth was here alone. Of the email.

"Well, what can I get you?"

I glance at the menu, though I already know what I'm ordering. "I heard I have to try your cheeseburger."

"I'm biased, but I would agree," Glenda says. "Fries on the side?"

I nod, thanking her.

"Coming right up." Glenda takes a few creamers from her apron's pocket, setting them on the table beside my purse. "Oh my word. I haven't seen one of those in *years*. Where on earth did you find it?"

"It was a gift, actually," I begin. "From a crow that has befriended the cabin where I'm staying. Or I guess befriended me? Though I know how that sounds." I laugh, then glance at the pin. Stop laughing when I think of the pink version we found with Eddie.

"Lucky you," Glenda replies. "That one is in great shape. Okay, give me a few and I'll be back with that burger."

While I wait for the cheeseburger, I type out the email I've already composed in my mind to Clara. I apologize, explain that her note ended up in my spam and that I'm in the woods with limited access to Wi-Fi. I close the message with a request: Is there any chance she and Robbie would still be willing to take a meeting?

Soon Glenda's back with my lunch. The cheeseburger is thick and juicy, the melted cheddar dripping to the plate below, and the pickled onions add the perfect amount of acid and texture. It's a culinary masterpiece—Jess was right.

When Glenda comes back to check in on me, she's carrying something postcard-sized in her hand. "After you were in last time, asking about Eddie Callaway and her camp, I remembered that I had something you might be interested in."

I set my nearly finished burger down. "Oh yeah?"

"I meant to give it to your beau. Seth, right?"

I nod.

"It got so darn busy that morning that I forgot all about it! But then that pin on your purse there . . . Did you know that was Eddie's signature, those pins?"

"I didn't know that." My voice is faint. Thinking again about the pink pin. Eddie's bones.

"She always wore one, and handed them out to the visitors who came to her camp, and here in town, too. But I haven't seen one for ages. *Ages.* Anyway, I found this, in one of my old photo albums."

Glenda hands me a photograph. It has that yellowish look to it that older photographs do, all the colors faded and less vibrant. The photo was taken outside the diner, the "Hopper's Diner" sign framing the top of the picture. In it stand two smiling women with stacks of white boxes in front of them. When I hold the photo closer, I can see they are pie boxes—the top ones with lids open to reveal the baked goods inside.

"That's my aunt Carole, with Eddie. The day she came to pick up all those pies she ordered for the camp."

She doesn't have to tell me which one is her aunt and which one is Eddie Callaway—I know instantly. In part it's because of the outfits—Aunt Carole (Glenda looks a lot like her) is in simple black slacks and a white short-sleeve top, an apron over her clothes, while Eddie wears patchwork denim jeans, the bottoms flared and bell-shaped; a beige tank top with no bra underneath; and sandals. She's taller than Carole, by maybe four inches, and her long curly hair is held back by a red bandanna. Eddie is grinning, one arm over Carole's shoulders. My heart feels like it's in my throat, seeing her.

"Thank you. This is amazing," I say. "I couldn't find a picture of her when I was searching online."

"She was pretty elusive when it came to media stuff. Liked to keep to herself. My aunt told me it was because she didn't want to become the 'story.'" Glenda used air quotes here. "She said she didn't want to take attention away from the camp itself, or bring the gossip hounds to town.

"But Eddie posed for this picture to help the restaurant out. She was a big fan of our pies," Glenda says, smiling. "Apparently it was supposed to run alongside an article in the local paper, but it was never published. She disappeared a day or so after that was taken."

I flip the photograph over. There's a date, written in black-inked cursive—*July 5, 1975. Carole Hopper and Eddie Callaway.*

"I'm guessing you heard about what they found, over by the old camp?"

"I did hear." I keep my eyes on the photograph to avoid eye contact. I swallow repeatedly, trying to keep myself from crying.

"A damn shame if it does turn out to be Eddie," Glenda says. "I always hoped she'd left for some great adventure."

"Me, too," I reply softly. "Thanks again for letting me take a look at this."

I go to hand the photograph back to Glenda, and she shakes her head.

"Oh, you can keep it, hon. Maybe it can help you with whatever you're working on."

"Thank you, Glenda. I'll treasure this. Truly."

"Good luck to you, Rowan. And *thank you*—I've enjoyed this trip down memory lane."

After saying goodbye to Glenda, who insists my lunch is "on the house," I leave enough money to cover the bill, plus a large tip. Then I remove the smiley pin from my bag and set it on top of the stack of bills.

EDDIE, 1975.

S HE STOOD IN THE CAMP'S MAIN KITCHEN, having just finished a slice of pineapple upside-down cake (a perfectly acceptable breakfast food, she believed, because it had fruit in it). Eddie washed her dish and fork, then packed a few of Samuel's seedy granola bars for the morning hike she couldn't miss, even though it had been raining for hours and the trails would be wet and mucky. She was just cinching her bag when she heard her name being shouted in the main dining hall.

It was six a.m. The only male voice Eddie typically heard at camp was Samuel's, and he didn't start on breakfast until closer to 6:30 a.m. But when her name was called out once again, more urgently this time, she knew precisely who was waiting for her in the other room.

With one deep, calming breath, she left the backpack on the kitchen's prep counter and pushed through the doors into the dining room.

"It's a touch early for a social call, Victor," she said, stopping a few feet away from the man standing by the dining hall's main entrance, lit only by the outdoor lights that streamed about a foot inside the room. Impatience filled her tone, despite her best efforts. "So, who did you catch in your boathouse this time?"

When he didn't answer, Eddie said, "I thought we weren't playing games anymore. Honestly, Victor . . ." She sighed. "Why are you here?"

But Victor remained silent, holding one arm behind his body in a way that looked awkward, though Eddie didn't think too much of it. Then he threw something at her with his other arm. Victor did not have an athletic build, but he apparently had a decent arm and aim, and the tossed item hit her square in her chest. She kept her expression neutral, even as shock burst inside her as the enamel pin, paper still attached, hit her body and then dropped to the ground at her feet.

Eddie glanced down at the yellow smiley face pin, and the piece of notebook paper (on which she had scribbled "Fuck You"), then crouched to pick it up. "Thanks. Must have dropped this last time I visited you."

She turned back to the kitchen doors, the pin and paper she had stuck into Victor's wooden gate a day earlier now clutched in her hand, and worked to control her breathing. Eddie hated that he made her nervous, and certainly didn't want to give him the benefit of seeing his effect on her. *Do not give him the satisfaction . . . Do not give him the satisfaction . . .*

But then she stopped, statue still, when she heard the click of a shotgun's safety being unlocked. Eddie hadn't seen the gun, but now realized that must have been what he was holding behind his back. Her heart beat furiously inside her chest, and it took everything she had to turn around to face Victor Valence.

Never in her life had someone pointed a gun at her. Having grown up with hunting enthusiasts, she'd had it drilled into her from the time she was a young child: "You never point a gun at anything—not a target, not an animal, and especially not a person, Edith—unless you intend to use it," her father had told her repeatedly.

Resisting putting her hands up in the air in surrender, Eddie swallowed back the fear-generated bile that threatened to breach her throat.

He wasn't going to shoot her.

The rational part of her brain—which she could barely access as survival-instinct adrenaline flooded her system—told her Victor merely intended to scare her. He had been pushed to his brink; she knew it because it was her doing.

"Vic V, please put the gun down." Her voice was resolute and strong. She used his preferred name for the first time, hoping it might shake him out of this furious trance he was in.

"This is no way to handle a disagreement," she said. "Look, I've thought about it some more and realize you would never have started that fire. I'm sorry for what I said. It was wrong of me. I got a bit carried away yesterday. No harm done."

She took a small step toward Victor, slowly, and did what she understood would work. It was time to perform again. Eddie made her face go slack, rolled her shoulders forward to appear meek, and smiled gently without showing teeth. All of it to let him know she was not a threat, even though that was clear, as she was unarmed and he was the one pointing a shotgun at her.

Victor blinked rapidly, as though trying to remove a speck of dust from his eyes. The trance appeared broken—a slight look of confusion came over his face, replacing the rage-filled one that had been there moments before. He seemed to relax, his fingers softening their grip on the gun, which he began to lower from his shoulder.

Eddie stayed still, kept her smile in place, her voice low and soft. "There . . . see? We don't have to—"

But she didn't get the rest of her sentence out because out of nowhere someone tackled Victor to the ground. It happened so fast, so efficiently, that Eddie had barely registered what was going on.

"She won't listen, man! She just won't listen!" Victor was saying, trapped under Samuel's body. Samuel had the man on his stomach, straddling his back, Victor's own arms pinned under his body so he was helpless to fight back.

"Stop fighting me, Vic. Stay put, you hear me?" Samuel barked at Victor, holding him down. He looked over at Eddie, his eyes wide with concern. "Are you okay?"

She opened her mouth to speak, but nothing came out. Shocked by how only five minutes earlier she had been wrapping up granola bars, thinking about the bulky item that was nestled inside her backpack, Victor Valence the furthest thing from her mind.

"Eddie! Are you hurt?" Samuel gave her a searching look. Victor had stopped struggling and lay limply on the ground, but his breathing remained fast. Samuel stayed where he was, ensuring Victor couldn't get up yet. Eddie could see his biceps and sinewy forearm muscles twitching as he held Victor's shoulders to the ground.

"I'm fine, Sam. I'm okay." Then she strode over to the gun and clicked the safety before opening the chamber, planning to take the shotgun shells out. But the chamber was empty. She glanced at Victor, who had turned his head toward her, still on his stomach and trapped under Samuel's strong body.

"Let him up."

Samuel shook his head, seemed to tighten his grip on Victor's shoulders. "Not yet, Eddie."

"Samuel, let him up. Please."

He took a long moment to consider her request, then released his grip and got off the man, but he stood nearby, ensuring he remained between Eddie and Victor. She was grateful to Samuel, but didn't need him to protect her. "Why don't you go into the kitchen? I know you have plenty to do before breakfast."

"No way, Eddie. I'm not leaving." Samuel's voice, normally steady, broke slightly. He was shaken, too.

But no one was more shaken than Victor, which became clear when he finally dragged himself off the dining room floor. A dark stain had bloomed at the crotch of his trousers. Eddie locked eyes with her fellow camp owner, handing him back his gun. "Please don't come back here unless you've been invited."

Victor took the gun from Eddie with shaking hands, even as Samuel twitched in response to her handing it over—Samuel might have made peace with his time in Vietnam, the nightmare of being taken a prisoner of war along with a group of fellow reporters, half of whom never came home, but the body, and those uncontrollable instincts, never forget prior traumas. Without needing to be asked twice, Victor ran out of the dining hall door, and Eddie saw him moving quickly across the rain-doused front lawn. Dawn's light was starting to come up over the trees now, but the camp remained in slumber.

All was quiet in the dining hall for one brief moment, and then Eddie started laughing. It began slowly, more a giggle than anything else, and grew from there until she could barely catch her breath. Initially Samuel had simply watched her, a confused look on his face, before he, too, started laughing. He ran a hand over his face, laughing hard but silently, so only the movement of his shoulders up and down gave him away.

Eddie threw herself into Samuel's arms then, and the two stopped laughing nearly instantly. He held her tightly against his chest, and she stayed like that until her breathing returned to normal.

Samuel pulled back to look at her, but his thumbs rubbed gentle circles on Eddie's hips as he continued to hold her. "Promise me something."

"I'll do my best," she replied.

"If you ever need me, call for me, okay?" Then Samuel softly whistled their secret birdcall, and Eddie whistled it back.

She hoisted her backpack up, and he helped her do up the straps. Then she leaned forward to kiss him before saying, "See you soon."

THE RAIN HAD stopped by the time Eddie left the dining hall, only a half hour behind schedule, which was impressive considering what she'd already been through that morning. Samuel hadn't wanted to let her go, worried about her running into Victor again in case he hadn't yet left the property. He'd offered to hike with her, which was unrealistic because Samuel had to get the food ready for the breakfast crush that would happen within the next hour. Besides, they both knew Eddie never invited anyone on her morning hike.

The trail's path was damp and slick, though the deeper into the woods she got, the easier it was to traverse, and her footing became more assured. Her ankle still throbbed, but it was tightly wrapped and Dot's salve had done wonders for the swelling. She picked up her pace, hoping to make up time she'd lost, no thanks to Victor's unexpected visit. *Victor.* A flutter of anger, and remnants of fear, filled her belly, but she pushed the feelings aside.

When Eddie shed her former life and moved to the camp permanently, she had promised herself three things: One, she would never again shave; two, she would dedicate the rest of her life to improving the lives of other women; and three, she would only hold on to anger just long enough to learn from it. What had she learned this morning from Victor Valence? That everyone has a breaking point, and that no one can predict what another's line in the sand would be, so you should do your best to not push people to (and beyond) that edge.

Eddie believed in taking responsibility for her actions, and she knew she bore blame for Victor showing up with his empty shotgun that morning. But no matter. It was over, she had apologized, and she expected Victor had learned his own lesson: that he would have to live with Eddie and her "proclivities" because she wasn't leaving. Yes, Samuel had been the one to bring Victor to the ground, but it had been over before that happened, and both she and Victor knew it.

Eventually, her muscles straining and her breath labored, Eddie came to the familiar fork in the path—where the large, triangular-shaped rock rested—and she made her choice (to the right), ducking under a newly fallen branch as she did. Droplets of water trickled under the collar of her shirt, and the coolness was refreshing. She appreciated a hot summer's day, perfect for sunbathing on the dock, but there was nothing she loved more than the forest after a drenching rainfall. The aromatic smells, the sights of perky trees and plants, their roots' thirst quenched, the green leaves glistening with prisms of water.

She took in a long, cleansing breath through her nose and then smiled, knowing she was close.

Samuel's Pineapple Upside-Down Cake

Time to have your cake and eat it, too.

—Eddie C. xx

Set oven to 350 degrees.

Cake batter:
Sift together . . .
1 1/2 cups flour
1 cup sugar
2 teaspoons baking powder
1/2 teaspoon salt

Add . . .
1/3 cup soft shortening
2/3 cup milk
1 teaspoon vanilla

Beat 2 minutes.

Add 1 egg, beat 2 more minutes.

Melt 1/3 cup butter in heavy 10-inch skillet or 9-inch square pan. Sprinkle 1/2 cup brown sugar evenly over butter. Arrange drained pineapple rings (crushed may be used if well drained) in attractive pattern on the butter-sugar coating. Decorate with pecan halves and cherries, if desired.

Pour batter over fruit and sugar. Bake 40 to 50 minutes, or until toothpick in center comes out clean. Immediately turn upside down on serving plate. Leave pan over cake a few minutes. Brown sugar mixture will run down over cake. Serve warm with whipped cream.

16

*From *Camp Callaway's Wild Women Handbook,* 1975

ROWAN, 2021.

I'M SITTING ON A BENCH OUTSIDE THE DINER, Glenda's photograph carefully tucked inside my purse, eating an ice cream—black raspberry, in a waffle cone, and delicious. I'm too full from the burger for ice cream, but I'm procrastinating returning to the cabin. Avoiding Seth, mostly.

A phone rings nearby, and I realize it's mine. With some difficulty, due to the quickly melting ice cream, I pull my phone out of my pocket. I consider letting it go to voicemail, but then decide to answer. With a flutter of hope, I think maybe it's Clara, calling about my email. Or perhaps the police, with an update.

"Hello?" Tucking the phone under my chin, I reach for the napkins beside me. The ice cream drips down the sides of the golden-brown waffle cone, pink and sticky. It's hot again today.

"Hello, is this Rowan?" I don't recognize the voice.

"Speaking."

"Oh, hello, Rowan. I'm glad to reach you—I've been trying for a couple of days, but there wasn't an answer, and, well, I didn't want to leave a message."

"Of course. How can I help you?" I'm mildly curious, but also distracted by my liquefying ice cream.

"I received your email," she begins, and I scan through my recently sent emails in my mind. When I don't reply, she adds, "It's Judith. Judith Swann."

I've been leaning back against the bench, but now I sit up. My back straight as a pin. The ice-cream cone drops to the sidewalk below. "Ms. Swann, hi! I'm . . . so glad you called."

"And I'm so glad you emailed! But please call me Judith." She has a lovely lilt to her voice—infused with warmth. "I haven't heard Eddie's name in so long. Too long."

"I'm sure," I say. I'm still trying to gather myself. I never expected to hear from Judith Swann.

"Um, so, like I said in my note, I, well, *we*—my fiancé and I—found your poem at Camp Callaway. We're in the park for research—Seth is an author, and his book is set somewhere similar, though it's dystopian with some apocalyptic themes, so not exactly the same, and we came across the camp and then the tin, with the poem inside . . ."

I pause, quite aware I'm rambling. Feeling anxious about the inevitability of telling her what was at the bottom of the embankment.

"We found the old Quik tin. With your poem inside. And please let me say, I'm sorry we were poking around. We didn't see the harm in exploring a bit, but it's private property—your private property, I've since learned. We shouldn't have gone in."

At this Judith laughs. "Don't you worry about that. I am quite certain you aren't the first, nor the last, to do so. Besides, Eddie's vision for the camp was all about exploration and adventure, so she'd be pleased you took a peek around. And I'm delighted you found that tin, and my old poem."

"It's beautiful, the poem," I say.

"Thank you," Judith replies—easily, without disclaimer. Even though it was written long before she became the famous poet she is now, I can tell she's proud of her work. As she should be.

"I can take credit for the words, but Eddie's the one who shaped them into an evergreen tree," she continues, referencing the picture I sent along with the email. "It has been a long time, but I do know it wasn't more than regular stanzas handwritten into a notebook. Eddie must have done that after I gave it to her. Ah, I miss that clever woman."

All the moisture leaves my mouth. I lick my lips—they're sticky and sweet. "The thing is, Judith . . . the poem is not all we found."

"No?"

I stare down at the fallen cone, the deeply hued pink ice cream now a small puddle at my feet. I think about the photo of a grinning Eddie, inside my purse. My stomach gurgles unpleasantly. "This is going to be hard to tell you . . . hard to hear . . ."

"I assure you I can handle it, Rowan. I am the mother of two sons and four grandbabies—all boys, can you even imagine? I've spent most of my life surrounded by women, and now the amount of testosterone in my daily life, well, let's just say I'm prepared for anything."

I laugh lightly, though I remain hesitant to tell Judith about the other discovery.

As though sensing I'm not quite ready, she continues. "As much as your note made me miss Eddie, I had to smile, thinking about the Quik tin. Chocolate milk was Eddie's favorite thing. She drank that ghastly stuff at every meal, sometimes even before breakfast." She goes momentarily quiet, and I press the phone closer to my ear.

"Eddie had such a big heart—a do-gooder to her core. Not

many know this, but she felt terrible guilt about her wealth. It's unimaginable, really, to have the kind of money she did. A different sort of burden. That was one of the reasons she started the retreats and invited women free of charge. An attempt to 'balance the scales,'" Judith says.

"She sounds like an incredible woman," I reply.

"Hmm. That she was. I know feminists like Eddie and me—the 'second-wave dinosaurs' . . . ," Judith begins. "Well, we're not viewed through such positive eyes these days. In some cases with good reason! It was all well intentioned, I believe, but still inequitable. However, progress *was* made, despite the ease with which it is sometimes discounted." Another brief pause, an intake of breath. "Eddie was a trailblazer, and she deserves to be remembered as such."

I tell Judith that's how I see her, too.

"I used to say we were 'twin flames,' me and Eddie," Judith adds. "If she had never left that morning, gone missing . . . I don't know. Maybe this is exactly where I would have ended up, in this wonderful life I have. But I can't say for sure. She inspired me while she was alive, but even more so after she was gone."

I understand precisely what she means. Which I tell her, before telling her everything else.

WE TALK FOR nearly an hour. I learn more about the final twenty-four hours of Eddie Callaway's life before she disappeared. She went into the woods that early July morning with a backpack, a canteen of water, and a determination to see her latest—and maybe her greatest, if you asked her—idea through. Samuel Harrison, a friend whom Judith referred to as Eddie's "great love," had been the last person to see her alive. Judith says she's sorry Sam himself died (of leukemia, nine years after

Eddie went missing) before Eddie was found—she believes their dear friend's disappearance affected him the most, and he never quite recovered from her loss.

"I hope wherever Eddie and Sam are, they're together. Eating pineapple upside-down cake and reminiscing. *Laughing.* It makes me happy to imagine that," she says, her voice strained with the pain of loss.

But while Sam was the last to see Eddie that morning, she and Judith had spent the night before together. Eddie, according to Judith, was energized and couldn't sleep. Excited and buzzing, Eddie wouldn't share precisely what she had planned, only saying she would tell Judith everything after she returned from her morning hike. Though she let it slip that it involved a treasure hunt of sorts, and that the final step of it was being put into place in the morning.

"What sort of treasure?" Judith had asked.

"The kind that can buy freedom and at least a cupful of happiness," Eddie replied. She grinned as she said this, then told Judith not to ask any more questions, lest she ruin the surprise.

Judith hadn't pushed, and shortly afterward she fell asleep. She never saw Eddie again.

In Eddie's will, Camp Callaway was left to Judith and Sam. "We tried, for a time, to hold on to Eddie's vision for the camp," Judith says. There's sadness in her tone, and she pauses momentarily.

"We were Eddie's crew of misfits, I like to say, our backgrounds as diverse as our talents, some of us decades apart. But we were greater than the sum of our parts. 'Dear friends to the end' was our mantra. And Eddie was our North Star."

The bulk of the Callaway fortune ultimately went to charitable endeavors, Judith tells me, including a sizable sum gifted to Florence to start a school in her hometown (one of her dreams) and an endowment to Dot's former hospital, which the ex-nurse decided to name the Theodore Hoffman Center for Pediatrics.

"She left more than enough to keep the camp running for decades," Judith says. However, in the end and without Eddie, no one could muster the energy to do so. "It was as though the heart and soul of the place disappeared along with her."

After Eddie was declared dead, in 1982, Samuel, Florence, and Judith decided to hold a memorial at the camp. A camp fund had been paying for maintenance and care of the property, but no one had stayed there since the fall of 1975, when the search was finally called off.

"We invited everyone back—all the crew, anyone who had ever attended a retreat—for one more weekend. It was August of 1983. The camp was packed, people sharing single beds, sleeping on floors, in tents, even on the docks in sleeping bags . . ." She pauses, lost in the nostalgia. "The place was so full of life and energy. Eddie would have loved it."

Tears prick at my eyes as I imagine the scene. Maybe they welcomed that first morning back at camp with Eddie's sun salutation ritual, finding earthworms to tickle or a tree to hug afterward. Perhaps they enjoyed meals of nettle pasta and pineapple upside-down cake, and wrote letters to themselves detailing the futures they hoped to manifest.

I feel this strange, deep connection to Eddie Callaway, considering I only heard of her for the first time a couple of weeks ago, and she died nearly two decades before I was even born. I don't mention to Judith that I've recently begun dreaming about Eddie, or that I can't shake her from my waking thoughts either.

"That's actually how I met my wife, Margaret," Judith continues. "She'd been one of the first guests at Camp Callaway. In 1972, the summer before I arrived. I never would have met

Marge if Eddie hadn't gone missing, if she . . ." I hear rustling, a sniff. She clears her throat.

"I like to think Eddie orchestrated the whole thing from wherever she is so I could experience love again. I had no plans to settle down with anyone. Which would have been just fine with me. It's lovely to be loved, but I never minded being alone, really."

I wonder what that feels like. To be comfortable with only your own company.

Those who knew Eddie best always maintained something terrible must have happened to her. There was no other explanation, as far as they were concerned. Samuel thought maybe Eddie's neighbor, another camp owner named Victor Valence, had somehow been involved. Apparently Eddie had believed Victor the arsonist of a small fire at Camp Callaway that summer (later proven to be the result of a lightning strike during a "dry thunderstorm"). He had shown up to Camp Callaway early on the morning Eddie disappeared, and Samuel had walked in on Victor pointing a shotgun at Eddie in the dining hall. But it hadn't been loaded, and Victor later claimed when questioned that he'd only meant to scare Eddie. Between his alibis (his wife, plus his cousin and other family who were staying with them) and a lack of other evidence, no charges were ever brought against Victor, or anyone else, for that matter.

Judith's also adamant that rumors of a midlife crisis and perhaps a tragic, self-destructive decision (as some have suggested) were *hogwash*. "Eddie was passionate about the camp and her mission there, and deeply valued her life," Judith explains.

"I always knew, in the deepest part of me, that Eddie didn't run away," she says. "It wasn't her style—she was resolute about her purpose. Absolutely steadfast. She dedicated those last few years to trying to help women change their own lives, but she never *expected* anyone to change. That was her greatest strength—seeing people for who they were, and offering them a door, without judgment, to walk through if they were so inclined."

Despite the search parties combing the woods around the camp (made more difficult, Judith explains, by heavy rains, which unfortunately diminish scent and other evidence), they also never found anything else Eddie took with her that day. Judith, Samuel, Florence, and Dot had repeatedly told the authorities and search parties to look for her backpack, especially. It would have stood out, because it was bright red and covered in Eddie's favorite statement pins (including the smiley face ones) and sewn-on patches. You couldn't have missed it out among the trees, the grasses, the dark earth. It was fairly bulky and weighted down, Samuel told the search team, having helped her put it on that morning. "He said whatever was inside was about the size of a shoebox."

I tell Judith what we found in the tree's hollow, explaining the mystery of what Eddie had tucked away in her backpack. Judith asks if I opened the jewelry box.

"It's locked," I say. "I'm happy to ship it to you, if you send me your address? You should have it, Judith." I don't care what Seth might say about this.

"Oh, I don't believe that's true," Judith replies. "Please open it, if you can, and keep whatever goodies Eddie tucked away in there. I need neither freedom nor a 'cupful of happiness.' I've had plenty of both."

I tell her that's very generous, but that keeping the box doesn't feel right to me.

"Whyever not?" Judith exclaims. "Eddie hid a treasure in the woods for someone to discover and benefit from . . . so, why can't that be you, Rowan?"

EDDIE, 1975.

Cookie Cutter Birdseed Feeders

Empty one package of gelatin into two tablespoons of cold water. Let rest for a minute or so. Add two cups of birdseed to gelatin, and stir to combine.

Choose your cookie cutters, and set out on a piece of waxed paper. Fill each with the birdseed mixture, packing it in well. Make a hole at the top for the string (you can use a stick, a screwdriver, a large nail), and then let the birdseed harden. This may take a few hours, or a day. Tie a piece of bird-friendly twine (it can be used later for a nest) through the hole, and your bird feeder is ready to hang.

Find yourself in nature as often as you can. It will be your greatest teacher, your most loyal confidant, and the sacred landscape for your evolving self.

Please remember to leave nature as you found it, but also leave these edible gifts for the birds!

—Eddie C. xx

*From *Camp Callaway's Wild Women Handbook*, 1975

U P UNTIL THEO STARTED HIGH SCHOOL, HE and Edith had spent as much time at Camp Callaway as they could. It was their escape from city life, as well as Theo's classroom and playroom during long summer stretches, and the place where Edith felt restored.

She and Theo—often it was just the two of them, as Stewart was needed at the hospital—would walk the trails around camp for hours, discovering which birds preferred which snacks. They would hang homemade cookie cutter birdseed feeders on tree branches as they hiked, and bring peanuts to scatter for the crows. Theo also collected handfuls of snails from damp rocks and green ferns as they walked the trail, which he'd leave for the ovenbird that nested near the base of a very special tree. Their favorite tree of all the trees.

It was a "quaking aspen"—so called because when even the slightest breeze hit the flat-stemmed leaves, the tree appeared to quake . . . or *dance*, as Edith preferred to say. In the summer this tree put out the most spectacular canopy of leaves, which filtered the sunlight and created a cool spot to rest when the sun was high. In many ways this tree looked like its cousins in the great forest near Camp Callaway—nothing noteworthy, when compared to the others. That was, until you followed the thin-barked trunk up to the sky, to the thing that set this particular tree apart.

About seven feet up the trunk was something that appeared to be a large knot. Theo noticed it first. But it was deceiving, like an optical illusion, because it was an inward notch. A nook in the trunk that was large enough that you could fit two hands inside (if you could reach it).

Edith and Theo discussed how that notch came to be. She suggested it likely came as a result of a lost tree limb, and over time the hole grew larger as animals and other critters dug it out further, finding great value in its shelter. Theo, who was only six at the time, suspected it was more mystical. He figured it had been a forest gnome that created the hole in the trunk, as a dwelling for when it needed rest from helping save animals in the woods. Edith solemnly agreed, telling Theo her grandfather, his namesake, had shared tall tales of forest gnomes and the role they played in the health and safety of these woods. Her son had embraced the stories with gusto, and Edith vowed to never change his mind.

AS EDDIE MADE her way down the last stretch of familiar "path"—a narrow track that wove through the trees, which would be hard to recognize as leading anywhere unless you had hiked it before—she sped up. The weight of her backpack tugged at her shoulders, the sharp edges of what was hidden inside pressing uncomfortably through her thin yellow jacket. Eddie was getting warm, glad she had worn her quick-dry nylon shorts today even if the grasses left stinging whip marks on her shins as she hiked.

Eddie came to the tree once a week, and she never stayed

long. But it was where she felt Theo the most. Here she could speak freely with him, even though there was never a reply.

Removing her pack and jacket, she fluttered her shirt away from her body to help dry the sticky sweat that coated her back. Taking out her canteen, she had a long drink of water, followed by one of Sam's delicious granola bars, which she chewed slowly and thoughtfully.

Soon, she heard a familiar birdsong and put a hand over her eyes to shield the rays of sun that peeked through the canopy above.

"Well, hello there, Jack Frost!" Eddie said to the black crow with the white feathers in a nearby branch. She unzipped another pocket of her pack. "You're far from home, but I'm happy to see you." Tossing a handful of peanuts to the side, she watched as the crow swooped down from the branch to the coveted treats below.

Replenished from her own snack, Eddie stood, hands on hips, and looked up to the nook in the great tree before her. She heard the squeaky-wheel call of a nuthatch, then the rowdy song of the blue jay. And for a moment she closed her eyes, bringing to mind an image of her sweet boy in front of this very tree. Little Theo, who had regaled her with made-up stories about the dancing tree's gnome, his chubby fingers flying about as he gesticulated enthusiastically.

"Morning, my love," she said, opening her eyes. She saw the shimmer of him by the tree trunk, and held on to the vision as best she could. "Today's the day. I hope you don't mind what I'm about to do. I can't imagine you would—you were always one for adventure."

Her voice caught, her breath tight in her throat. But she focused on the mirage of her son, then carried on.

"I had another run-in with Victor this morning. He pointed his shotgun at me! In *my* dining hall." Eddie felt a wave of adrenaline move through her gut as she remembered the feeling of staring into that barrel.

"You would have gone over there and beat the hell out of him, I'm sure." She chuckled, now imagining her son as the strapping eighteen-year-old he had been when she last saw him. Their tree was taller and grander than when she and Theo first discovered it, and she couldn't help but picture an adult Theo standing beside it. Knowing he would have been tall enough to reach into the nook without a boost. It was the oldest she'd ever allowed herself to imagine Theo (would he be married? have his own children now?), and it nearly caused her to crumple in grief to the ground.

Shaking it off, Eddie refocused on young Theo—the boy she knew best. She had much to do (others needed her), and so reminded herself to be mindful of where she allowed her thoughts to wander. "I miss you, Theo. I know I say that every damn day, but it's no less true today than it was yesterday."

She missed other things, too: She missed the way Theo smiled, one side slightly higher than the other, and how there had been a time when he was so generous with his smiles for her; she missed her parents because they had been anchors for her in this life—she'd enjoyed a beautiful simplicity in being their daughter, Edith Jane Callaway; and if she were being totally honest, she also missed the bathtub at her home in Suffolk County, which had been luxuriously deep, made of smooth white porcelain.

It was silly to miss a bathtub alongside missing her only child, but she still did.

ONCE FINISHED WITH the snack and the task, Eddie put the waxed paper from the granola bars into her pack and cinched the shoulder straps snug. The backpack was much lighter now.

She tied her jacket around her waist as she evaluated her work, taking a step back for perspective. It had been trickier than she'd imagined, getting the box into the nook. She'd used a nearby fallen tree trunk, rolling and dragging it over as close to the base of the tree as she could. Eddie guessed it would give her about another foot or so of height. She was slick with sweat and breathless from the effort, and looked forward to a quick dip in the lake when she returned to camp.

Though it was challenging to keep her balance on the log, it had allowed her to reach high enough (standing on her tip-toes, and stretching her arms and fingers almost to the point of pain) to tuck the bronzed box into the notched hole. Thank goodness she was tall.

It was a near-perfect fit. Only a glimmer of bronze could be seen if you stood from the right spot, and if you didn't look up the tree, you would never know it was there. She was excited, her belly filling with so many flutters it almost made her feel ill. Then she dragged the fallen tree about a dozen or so paces back, sweating and grunting as she did, wanting to set the scene back to its original state.

She decided to take a look at the box from a different angle, to make sure it was at least partially visible but not overtly so. Eddie stood again on the log, eyes trained on the majestic tree trunk. *Yes, perfect.* But as she stepped off the log, she misjudged her footing—landing awkwardly on her bad ankle.

It turned inside her hiking boot, and she stumbled, trying to regain her balance. But she instead tripped over the fallen trunk she had only moments before dragged into place—in a most unfortunate position, it turned out, as it was too near the edge of the embankment. Her eyes were still on the nook and the box as she tumbled backward over the trunk and the earth's edge, disbelieving her poor judgment even as she fell.

The embankment was steep, with an almost cliff-like drop.

As she tumbled down, the exposed roots and rocks bruising and slicing her skin, she suddenly felt a deep pain erupt in her legs that made her scream. When her body finally came to rest, she was curled in a heap at the bottom. Everything felt out of sync, both inside her body and with the environment around her. It reminded her of when she would roll down the grassy hill at her childhood home, her brain always scattered for a few minutes afterward due to the speed her body took on as she flipped over and over.

Now, shaking her head to try and clear the fog, Eddie had three distinct and terrifying thoughts.

She was badly hurt.

She hadn't told anyone where she was going.

She was the only one alive who knew about this place.

ROWAN, 2021.

H OW WAS TOWN?" SETH ASKS WHEN I AR-
rive back at the cabin.

"Fine." I set my phone down. I say nothing about my call with Judith. Nor do I show him the photograph.

"Did you . . . send an email? To Clara?" Seth's tone is cautious, unsure what to anticipate as it's clear I'm in no better a mood—at least toward him—than when I left. But I suspect neither of us has much of an appetite for an argument, and so I keep my tone measured, my answer brief.

"Yes," I reply. I wonder, though, if Clara has read my email yet and what might come of that. I feel a small bubble of excitement, however dampened by the heaviness of the week's events, though I keep my expectations in line. I have to be prepared for it to be too late.

Seth merely sighs, then gets up from the couch where he was working on his laptop—I catch a glimpse of the screen and see thumbnails, which means he's editing and not working on his book, the entire reason we came out here. A sharp, now-predictable stab of frustration fills me, but then I remind myself of something Judith shared about Eddie. How the greatest lesson she learned from Camp Callaway's leader was to avoid letting your expectations of others, and any subsequent disappointment, compromise your own journey.

Seth is going to do what he's going to do, and I can't change a thing about it. While I'll never understand it, the YouTube channel means more to him than his novel, his MFA, his writing potential. And it is clear to me now that it's also more important to him (whether as a result of jealousy or fear of losing my support and participation) than seeing me succeed with my screenwriting.

"The police called," he says, pouring a glass of orange juice from the fridge. He says it so nonchalantly it takes me a moment to realize the significance.

I stop what I'm doing—putting on a pair of socks because I'm thinking of calling Jess to see if she wants to take a hike—and stare at him. My heart hammers in my chest. "What did they say?"

He takes a long gulp of juice, and I want to shout at him to hurry up and tell me. "Not much. They wanted to clarify a few things about the report, and . . ." He pauses, seeing the look on my face. "Are you okay?"

"Yes." But I don't feel it. My legs are wobbly, and I sit down right on the floor. "What else?"

"They, uh, said the skeleton is female. Like we thought," Seth replies. "But they haven't identified it."

"*Her*." I hold Seth's gaze. "It's Eddie Callaway. We both know it is."

Seth places his glass down on the tabletop. "Rowan, we know nothing."

"So, what . . . we find a skeleton with vintage clothing and a mysterious box, basically within a few feet of one another, and we know Eddie Callaway went missing after hiking into the woods to bury a treasure? And you're telling me they aren't related?" I give a short, mirthless laugh. "Give me a break, Seth. Obviously your MFA didn't teach you enough about plot."

He sighs again, rubs at his eyes. "Rowan, stop."

"Stop what?" I ask, my voice rising. "Did you tell the police about the box, Seth?"

"I will. *We will.*"

"It's evidence! And it might be helpful. We don't know what's in there. We have to report it." My throat goes tight. I know Judith believes I have as much right to the contents of the box as anyone, but it doesn't feel that simple to me. "It's Eddie's. It was never ours to take."

He shoots me a look I can't interpret. "It *was* Eddie Callaway's, *maybe.*"

"*It was not ours to take.*"

Again, I have the urge to get the box to Judith—as quickly as possible. It's the last piece of Eddie Callaway that exists, and she should have it.

"You are exhausting," Seth replies, his back to me now. His voice has no energy to it, but his words cut me deeply. "New York State law says it's ours to keep, Rowan. *We found it.* And who am I to break the law?"

I feel like I don't know him anymore, and I tell him so.

"I could say the same about you," he replies.

I'm still sitting on the floor, and wrap my arms around my bent knees. I don't feel well all of a sudden, guilt and dismay and worry needling at my guts, mixing with the creamy-sweet ice cream. But Seth doesn't notice my physical discomfort.

And when he turns back toward me, I see something I don't understand. The hint of a smile, which he quickly tries to hide.

"What?" I ask.

"I did it," he says.

"Did what?"

"I opened the box."

Silence hangs between us for a long moment. I'm sure Seth hears my heartbeat, as it's pounding excruciatingly hard inside my chest.

"You opened the box?" I scramble to my feet.

Seth nods. "I sanded off most of the rust, and then it was just a matter of getting something into the lock itself. I found an old metal nail file under the bathroom sink. It worked perfectly."

"What's inside?" I'm finding it hard to breathe, and put a hand to my chest.

"You'll see." It's then I notice the small rusted lock lying open on the table, though the box's lid remains closed.

I take a step toward the kitchen table, then another one, my eyes never leaving the box, as though it has me under its spell.

"I already did some filming, but maybe we can do more now that you're here? Then, I promise you, we will tell the police about it. I have it all figured out, what we'll say."

I don't respond, though I'm unnerved that Seth has already planned out the next inevitable half-truth to offer the police. I'm mesmerized by the box, and reach out toward the lid. My fingers quiver as they touch the bronze patina, then slowly—so slowly—I lift the lid.

I'm not sure what I expect to find inside. But the first thing I see is a square envelope, with the words "You just changed your life!" written on its front in black ink, in sweeping cursive.

I glance up at Seth. "Did you open this, too?"

He nods.

"Is it Eddie Callaway's?" I ask breathlessly.

Again, he nods, and has the decency to look somewhat somber.

I pick up the envelope, which is in excellent shape and appears as though it were placed inside the bronzed box not long ago, even though it has been decades. Opening the flap, which wasn't sealed but rather tucked inside, I tug out the stiff notecard. It's a soft peach color, and has the initials "E.J.C." on the top-left corner in gold foil. I read the sparse, handwritten note out loud, the cursive loopy yet precise.

Well done, fellow Goddess! You have solved the puzzle, and this is only the beginning. May what you find here help you to be your true, authentic self and live without compromise. My only purpose is to change lives for the better, and today that means your life, my dearest Wild Woman. Be brave, be bold, take up space, and never stop seeking your truth.

With deep love and admiration, Eddie Callaway xx

Peering into the box, I see what was under the letter. A fabric bag with the words "THIS BAG IS PROPERTY OF AND SHOULD BE RETURNED TO FEDERAL RESERVE BANK OF NEW YORK" printed in dark ink on its gray-white surface.

"What's in the bag?" I'm light-headed now, my breathing shallow.

Seth's expression turns serious. "Bundles of hundred-dollar bills. A lot of them."

"Oh my god." I touch the fabric bag, lifting it out of the box. Then I notice the only other item in the box, which is quite familiar to me now. I gently grasp it between my fingers.

It's another smiley face enamel pin, shiny, bubble gum pink, and in pristine condition. Like Eddie Callaway just dropped it into the box this morning.

I begin to cry.

EDDIE, 1975.

T HE PAIN WAS UNLIKE ANYTHING EDDIE HAD
ever experienced—deep in her bones, like they had
been shattered to dust—and it pushed everything else
from her mind. She tried yelling for help, but she knew it was
likely futile. This spot was miles from camp, and not on any
marked trails, so you were more likely to stumble upon it (as
she first had, all those years ago with Theo) rather than find it
on purpose.

As evening fell, the temperature dropped along with the
daylight. It became cold, and the tips of Eddie's fingers, which
she was grateful to see still moved when she asked them to,
tingled uncomfortably. It was chillier than she thought it should
be in July, but the rational side of her brain understood the shivering had more to do with shock and pain than cold.

Best she could tell, she had broken at least one leg. It wasn't
hard to figure out, because when she managed to tilt her head
to the side to see her left leg, everything below her knee was
pointed in the wrong direction. Her foot facing inward, her
knee jutting in the opposite direction. And with the insidious

pain in her right thigh, it seemed that leg might not have fared much better. Eddie had started to cry then, understanding there would be no way for her to get herself out of this mess. She needed help. Gathering strength, she began to shout again. As loudly as she could, in between the waves of pain that left her breathless. There was no response, only the familiar sounds of the daytime forest that did little to soothe her fear. Then, remembering her promise to Sam, she drew her breath and pursed her lips, singing out the birdcall the two had made up as children: a whistle, then two short notes, ending with a long, high-pitched trill. She whistled it again and again, until she was hoarse, but the call was never returned.

Night fell—the hours passing unbearably slowly in this strange and slowed-down world she currently found herself in. Eddie had managed to get her jacket back on and shift her body under a rocky overhang so she was somewhat out of the elements. It took hours, it felt, to move that couple of feet, and she lost consciousness a few times from the pain. But with great focus—her survival instincts as strong as her determination— she wriggled until her body was firmly pressed up against the embankment's dirt and rock wall. She managed to sleep a little, dreaming the earth wall beside her was first Judith and then Samuel.

No one came that night, nor the following day. Eddie knew her friends had to be looking for her—that she would be missed by now. She had told Sam to expect her back in a few hours, and to save her some breakfast. That had been yesterday morning (she was pretty sure—she decided then to stick small twigs into the dirt beside her to measure the passing days), so Sam and the others had to already be in the woods, searching.

But no one came by that second nightfall, and she cried when she stuck a second twig into the dirt beside the first one.

Though she tried to ration her one remaining granola bar and water (she sucked rainwater from a nearby pile of leaves, in order to save the water in her canteen), as the day turned black for a second time, she was again alone.

Eddie knew she should have told Samuel specifically where she was headed after she left him in the dining hall. If only she had answered Judith's questions while they lay in bed instead of being so coy. Only a few hours after the camp's breakfast she had planned to announce the treasure hunt and give the retreat guests clues for how to find it. Her secret spot might not have been secret much longer! If she had done the wise thing and told someone—anyone—what she had been up to, they would have known where to look.

But it never even crossed her mind, something going wrong. She'd expected that day's morning hike to go just like all the others she'd taken over the years. Except this hike would have been different in one significant way: Rather than simply carrying her nostalgia along with a lighter pack back to camp, this time she also would have been bringing home the most wonderful adventure for any woman prepared to undertake it.

The disappointment of that now-ruined plan hurt nearly as much as her broken leg did. However, there was little time for self-pity. Eddie Callaway was in the fight of her life, but this time her foe was her beloved woods.

As it got darker yet again and the forest grew louder, Eddie shut her eyes tightly, gathering images in her mind of her friends; of her warm, quilted bed; of a cold glass of chocolate milk; of Jude braiding her hair with gentle, grass-relaxed fingers; of Sam's strong arms encircling her wrecked body, making it whole again. In her fitful dreams she held baby Theo, swaddled in soft blue muslin, and kissed his rosy cheeks over and over, murmuring the sweet nothings mothers do.

Yes, someone would come tomorrow, she was sure. Sam or Florence or Judith would find a hint of her route, or maybe solve the clues in the Quik tins and know where she had gone. It was then she remembered the third tin—still in her pantry, hastily tucked out of sight. In her hurry to hide the tins and leave camp this morning before anyone woke up, she'd forgotten the third tin. She felt crushing regret for not leaving that one out in plain sight, where someone might find it, open it, understand by reading the note what she had planned.

Yes, she would fervently hope that those tins weren't hidden *too* well. That someone would happen upon one, and soon. Then the crew would set out, determined not to leave the forest until Eddie was found. Near the dancing tree with the notch in its majestic trunk, they would finally hear her weakening cries for help. This soothed her, knowing if they came—*when they came*—she wouldn't have to put a third twig into the dirt beside her.

When Theo arrived as dawn was breaking on her third day missing, in the form she last saw him, on the cusp of being a man, he crouched beside her and gently wiped the dirt from her face where her tears—back when she could still make tears—had created dirty rivulets on her skin. He said, "It's all right, Mom, I'm here," while gently setting sweet red raspberries between her parched lips, and she smiled with the calm of knowing she was saved at last.

<u>What Wild Women Do</u>

MAKE OURSELVES BIGGER and louder than may be initially comfortable.

TAKE UP SPACE rather than becoming smaller to fit something narrow and unyielding.

SHOW EMOTION, be it anger, sadness, hurt, joy—we are human, and therefore have earned our feelings.

ARE FEMININE when it suits us, because we want to be, but never because someone else asks it of us.

RESPECT OURSELVES, because not everyone else will.

SEEK PEACE without shrinking from chaos, which can be a catalyst for change.

ENJOY LIFE on our terms, as we only get one to live.

TRUST OTHER WOMEN and be trustworthy to our sisters in return.

BE BOLD in every space of life, from the bedroom to the boardroom, and take a seat at the table.

<u>This is what Wild Women do.</u>

—Eddie C. xx

*From *Camp Callaway's Wild Women Handbook*, 1975

ROWAN, 2021.

AUGUST.

AT THE FIRST HINT OF LIGHT, I RISE FROM the couch where I've been resting. I'm fully dressed, including my hikers, and have only one thing left to do before I leave the cabin. Quietly, I move over to the kitchen table where Seth's laptop and phone rest—both charging for the night. Glancing over at the bed, I can tell by his breathing that he remains deeply asleep. I have nearly changed my mind about my plan a dozen times—and almost do again, watching him. Without a doubt, our visions for what comes next will not align. But each time I waver, I remember Eddie's note inside the box.

May what you find here help you to be your true, authentic self and live without compromise.

With quick fingers I type Seth's password into his phone. He shared his passwords ages ago, back when I would sometimes help with the YouTube editing. If I feel any guilt about what I'm doing, I don't let it bubble close enough to the surface to stop me. This is the only way. I know Seth will struggle to understand, and will probably never forgive me. However, I'm not sure I'm ready to forgive him either, and what that means for us, or our future . . . I'm not sure. But that's a worry for another day.

Once I get his phone open, I tab into his video files, knowing that because of the lack of Wi-Fi and cell service, he won't have uploaded the more recent videos to the cloud. The copies on his phone and laptop are the only ones.

In rapid succession I delete all of the videos he's filmed relating to the box—there are more than anticipated, and I grow nervous he might wake up before I finish. Double-checking to ensure I've deleted them all, I shift over to his laptop to scrub it as well.

NEW YORK STATE has a "finders keepers" policy when it comes to buried treasure—it is the finder's lucky day, as long as the original owner can't be found (or is deceased) and you didn't trespass. Initially it seemed we *would* have to turn the box over, as we found it on what we believed to be Camp Callaway private property. However, Judith had gifted most of Camp Callaway's acreage back to the state in the 1990s, to create more space for the public to enjoy, so Eddie Callaway's final resting spot—and her hidden treasure—was no longer on private property. Also, Judith told me Eddie had no living next of kin (her ex-husband passed away in 1992 and, most sadly, their only child, a son named Theo, died in 1969 at the age of eighteen, in a car accident), meaning no one would contest the discovery of the treasure trove.

It makes me emotional, thinking about Eddie's family tree ending so abruptly—which also makes me realize how crucial it is to live your life while you have it to live. Obvious? Perhaps. This is a truth that has likely been niggling at me ever since that car ran into me and my mom, but it has taken this most recent experience for it to fully resonate.

Living your life means more than going through the motions.

It's damn tempting; the idea of all that money is unbearably intoxicating. While I do believe the adage that money can't buy happiness, I suspect it certainly helps make it more accessible. But no matter which way I spin it, keeping the treasure feels wrong in the part of me no one else gets to see—the part you should always listen to. Was it fair to make the decision for Seth as well? To be so proprietary about the discovery and what happens next? Maybe not. However, I'm the one who found it. It's *my* discovery, not his.

If I had simply unearthed the treasure box, and not also Eddie Callaway's body, perhaps I'd feel differently. It's hard to explain, but it's like I didn't so much stumble upon her by accident as I was led to where she lay, waiting for the right person to arrive. The person who wouldn't circumvent her intentions, and would instead help her see them through. Since the discovery— and when I manage to sleep—my dreams are filled with a living Eddie Callaway leading me silently on a path through the woods. It's one that I don't recognize, but it's familiar nonetheless. She's fuzzy in my mind, like the way someone looks from a distance—the whole of the person intact, but the distinguishing details less so. Except for the red bandanna. That is in Technicolor.

We never speak, yet I know that I must follow her, and it feels urgent that I do so. Then she turns around and smiles at me, pointing up to the sky, where the crow with the white wing feather rests in a tree with a yawning-wide hollow in its trunk. The certainty I feel at this moment in the dream is difficult to describe, and it doesn't leave me when I wake up.

So, no. Keeping any part of what Eddie hid in the woods is not an option. She needs this from me, and I'm prepared, and willing, to give it to her.

IT'S TIME. I set Eddie's notecard letter back into the box, on top of the fabric currency bag and the stacks of bills that would have made our—my—life easier without question, and then close the lid firmly. The lock clicks into itself again, and within a minute the box and its hidden treasure is once more intact.

With one last look at the old bronzed jewelry box, I slide it inside a canvas shopping bag. It doesn't quite fit, but it's easier for me to carry the clunky box this way versus just in my arms. I hold my breath as I open the cabin door, car keys in hand, praying for the screen not to creak and groan, the way it always does. Somehow, I'm granted this wish and so leave the cabin soundlessly, Seth still snoring quietly in bed. The mist is heavy, the early-morning light barely strong enough to filter through. I drive carefully, my fog lights on, feeling jittery and impatient as I meander toward my destination. I will have to hike eventually, alone, but thanks to Jess, I'm comfortable with the route and know this time I won't get lost.

YESTERDAY AFTERNOON, AFTER Seth showed me the contents of the box, I called Jess while he was in the shower. Asking if she wanted to go for a hike, and then leaving Seth a note that I was taking a walk to clear my head. I had a plan in mind, but it was rough around the edges and I needed help.

Maybe I shouldn't have trusted Jess—or anyone—with such a weighty secret, but my options were limited. Plus, despite my only knowing her for a short time, Jess has never given me any reason not to trust her implicitly. She is, as my dad likes to say, "a good egg."

Jess and I walked for a while, chatting about inconsequential things, and then, when we stopped for a water break, I told her about my plans for the box. I also shared my conversation with Judith, along with Eddie Callaway's letter (I had written down her words in my own notebook), Glenda's photograph, and, finally, the bag of money. Jess never questioned my plan, or suggested I maybe take a little more time to contemplate the repercussions of what I was doing—both for myself and for my relationship.

She did ask, "Why not *you*, Rowan?" Why couldn't I be the benefactor of Eddie Callaway's generosity, echoing what Judith had said. I was, after all, the one to find the treasure. But I told her it didn't sit well with me. That I knew, deep in my gut where your best instincts live, that I wasn't meant to keep the box.

"Maybe I was meant to find it," I said, "precisely because I wouldn't keep it. I think I'm supposed to help Eddie Callaway finish what she started."

At that Jess nodded. Then, aside from assuring me she would keep this a secret—even from Aidan, because, as she said, it wasn't hers to share—the only other question she asked was "How can I help?"

I needed her expertise about the woods. About a spot where the box could rest, until found by someone traipsing through the forest, seeking a "great adventure"—like Eddie Callaway had always imagined.

It was perfect, the spot Jess brought me to. And Judith's poem, with her permission, when I called to tell her my plan, could continue to be relevant to the hunt . . . That had been important to me, when finding the next hiding place. Because I had an idea that went beyond secretly re-hiding the treasure somewhere in these woods.

Jess showed me how to nestle the box deep into the moss, making sure it was secure—though not invisible—when the time was right. Then we made the long hike back to the car, talking little. The only sounds around us the birds singing their songs, and our breathing, which had become heavier as we made our way over rocks and fallen trees, the path under our feet barely visible with the overgrowth. It was probably my imagination, but I felt a comforting presence surround me as I walked through those woods with Jess, and it made me smile.

It's never as complicated as you tell yourself it is.

I PARK THE car, pulling the straps of the bulky canvas bag over my shoulder as I get out. Then I start walking.

I wrote down the landmarks Jess showed me, then committed them to memory and burned the piece of paper, along with the three pages underneath it in my notebook, because they had fine lines of memory from where I pressed down with my pen. I don't want any clues left behind.

The box nests easily in the spot I've chosen, and I secure clumps of moss around it to camouflage it even more. And just like that, it's hidden once again.

I have no idea what really happened to Eddie Callaway that fateful day in the forest, and know it is likely the mystery will never be fully solved. But her story doesn't have to end that way, at the bottom of an embankment, her entire vibrancy— her *life*—reduced to bones discovered purely by accident. And now—thanks to a dear friend, a beautiful mother tree I can barely wrap my arms around because of its impressive girth, and a few handfuls of soft, bright green moss—it won't be.

MY MOM AND I take a long walk, at my request, the night I arrive home from the Adirondacks, only a few days after I re-hid Eddie's treasure (and told Seth what I'd done).

"Did you know there are trees called mother trees?" I say as we set out after dinner.

"Is that right?" my mom replies, looking over at me.

I nod. "My friend Jess showed me, on one of our hikes. She's an ornithologist, and lives off the grid in the woods with her partner, Aidan." A wistful pull comes over me, and I realize how much I already miss Jess.

"An ornithologist? I think it would be lovely to spend all your time with birds," my mom says. I instantly know she would love Jess as much as I do, and hope they get to meet one day. "So, what makes them mother trees?"

"Well, they're the really big ones, the ones that have been growing for decades and are now at the top of the canopy—getting all the sunlight. Somehow these trees know their kin. Like, each mother tree is aware of which saplings are hers, and it makes sure those saplings get nourishment. Through the roots, thanks to some wild underground network of fungi, these mother trees communicate to and nourish their baby trees. Isn't that unbelievable?"

"It's fascinating. But I'm not surprised in the slightest." She smiles at me. "I am a mother tree, after all, with three perfect saplings."

"Hey, Mom . . . I'm sorry I've been such a pain in the ass

these past few months, like before we left for the cabin," I say after we've walked a block in silence.

"You have been a bit of a jerk, it's true. Your dad and I agree." She gives me a pointed look then, and I laugh. It feels good.

"I know, and I'm truly sorry."

"Apology accepted, kiddo."

"I'm not sure things are going to work out with Seth." Sadness and relief swirl through me in equal measure. It has been a long, difficult week. We drove back to Ann Arbor together—the most uncomfortable road trip I've ever taken, the two of us trapped in the car with nothing but hurt and anger between us—but have barely spoken a word since. I, for one, have no idea how to move forward, and I suspect he feels the same.

"Hmm. And how do you feel about that?"

"I'm okay." And I am, I realize as I say it.

"I'm glad. All I want is for you to be happy, honey."

"I know." I stop then. "Mom, why don't you ever ask me about my screenwriting stuff?"

"What do you mean? I ask all the time how it's going."

"That's not what I meant." I kick a few small pebbles on the sidewalk, and they dance ahead of me. "I sort of feel like . . ." I take a deep breath—I'm nervous. Worried about how what I say next will land on my mother.

"When you lost your leg, it seemed like you also lost some of your, I don't know . . . adventurous spirit? Your drive? And then it felt like you expected *me* to be more cautious, too. Or something." I shake my head, frustrated with how it's coming out—not at all like I planned. "I'm not explaining myself well. I'm tired."

I expected, when I ran through this scenario in my mind, that my mom might get defensive. Even angry. Definitely emotional. But to my great surprise, she laughs. Throws her head back as we stand there, no longer walking, and *laughs*.

"Oh, Rowan. You are such a delight to me." She reaches out with the hand not on her cane and sets it against my cheek. It's warm and smells faintly of garlic, thanks to Dad's infamous roast chicken, which he made for my welcome-home dinner.

"And my dearest one, you aren't wrong." My mom begins walking again, and it takes me a few moments to regroup and catch up.

"I'm confused. What's happening?" I reply.

"Honey, if there's one thing I hoped to teach you and your sisters, it's to speak your minds. To express what's inside you, for better or worse. *That's* why you are such a delight to me. That and a hundred other reasons."

I link arms with her, being sure to stay on her non-cane side.

"Rowan, losing my leg was by far the worst thing that had— *has*—ever happened to me. It was traumatic and terrifying, and I am not the same person I was before, and not just in the physical sense. But when they say things could have been much worse? It's true. Something could have happened to *you*."

I look down at my arm linked through my mom's, at my scar.

A moment later my mom stops again. She points at a nearby evergreen tree, about thirteen or fourteen feet tall. "Do you know what that is?"

I shrug. "A tree?"

"Ha-ha, smart girl." She puts her arm around my shoulders, tugging me close. "I should have made you come back here so long ago, Rowan. I'm sorry that I didn't."

I glance over at the tree again. And then look around. Suddenly, it's as though I'm seeing the landscape with different eyes, and everything slows down.

I notice the pale yellow house with the large front porch, and the familiarity of it hits me like a punch to my stomach. It's the porch the man sprinted from (he and his wife were enjoying the weather with after-dinner glasses of sherry that evening) right after the car slammed into me and my mom. He was the first person on the scene, his wife right behind him calling 9-1-1 as she ran to us in her socked feet. The wife stayed with me, her husband with my mom. I can't even remember their names now—I'm not sure I ever knew them.

I'm a touch breathless, and my mom rubs my back.

"But the tree . . . it was split in half! It can't be the same tree?"

"It isn't, honey. Your dad had the city plant a new one. This is *that* tree. Look how much it has grown!" She kisses my cheek then. "Just like you, Rowan."

"Why do we never talk about what happened?" I whisper this, drawing my teary eyes away from the tree and back to my mom's.

"At first I didn't want to. That's the truth." She shrugs. "But also I guess I figured we didn't need to? Because it's part of our fabric, Rowan. The stuff that makes us who we are, and, well, we're bonded because of what happened here, in a way I'll never be connected to your sisters, or your dad. I imagined you felt what I felt. But I shouldn't have assumed. I should have given you the space for your own experience."

"You're doing it now," I reply, laying my head on her shoulder. "Thanks, Mom."

"It is both a beautiful and heartbreaking thing to be bonded to another person through a tragedy. Like an awful club that you wouldn't wish its membership on anyone."

I nod at that, marveling at the truth of it. I think about Eddie Callaway, how maybe the reason I was so compelled to help her, decades after her death, was because we, too, are bonded. My finding her in the woods is *our* shared experience.

"But that bond also means you're never alone with it, either," she adds.

"Hmm, I can see that, too," I murmur.

"I am so proud of you, honey. Not just for everything you've been through recently," she begins. I confided in my parents about the box, finding Eddie Callaway's skeleton (dental records have since confirmed her identity), and my decision to return the treasure to the woods.

"I am impressed with your heart, your conscience, *and* your ambition. Trust me, I will be first in line for any film you make. Always and forever the president of the Rowan Fairfax Fan Club, my love."

"Thank you, Mom." I hug her fiercely, only letting go when she does first.

"I can't wait to get fan club T-shirts made!" She winks, and I laugh heartily.

Arm in arm, with a last glance at the evergreen tree, we begin walking home.

SEPTEMBER.

AFTER SETH AND I RETURN TO OUR APART-
ment in Ann Arbor, we don't know how to be with
each other. Initially there is a truce: He doesn't mention anything about the money or the videos I deleted, and I
never bring up Clara's email or how epically he has hurt me.
But there is this indelible grimy film covering us, like a cloudy
piece of cellophane. We try, once, to talk it all out. But it's too
heated, too accusatory to be productive, and soon there's nothing left to say. So I leave, and move temporarily home with my
parents. Seth packs his things, takes the engagement ring back
after I insist (along with the car), and sets off for a buddy's couch
in New York City.

Last I heard, through a mutual friend, Seth lives in Brook-
lyn with a few other guys in an old brownstone. I admit I occasionally check in on his YouTube channel, which still carries
the name TheWrightStory, and is nearing 800,000 subscribers.
I'm happy for him, though it might be more relief at not being
a part of that life anymore.

At times I still can't believe how quickly things fell apart between us, or how easy it was to go our separate ways in the end. For some it takes a long time to acknowledge the reality right in front of them. Maybe I would have been one of those slow-to-see-the-truth people, too, if not for the woods, the crow that befriended me, and the pin-backed button that belonged to someone else from sometime else.

OCTOBER.

I 'M SO GLAD WE'RE DOING THIS. FINALLY!"
Clara says, after the compulsory long hug when we meet
at the restaurant. I've been back in LA for just over a
month. Having gone straight from my childhood home to film
school, where I shared an apartment with two other girls, then
to being with Seth . . . I hadn't ever lived on my own before.
Now I rent a tiny but charming one-bedroom apartment within
walking distance of the beach. I'm happy, and am settling effortlessly into this West Coast life again.

Turns out being alone suits me just fine.

"And now that you're back here permanently, we can make
it a regular thing," Clara adds.

"I would love that," I reply, opening my notebook. We're
drinking a bottle of crisp rosé and sharing a plate of oysters during our "working lunch," and I enjoy feeling the California
sunshine again after being away for nearly a year.

I recently heard from Jess and Aidan, who are preparing the
homestead for the upcoming winter. She called to thank me
for sending Aidan a Bob Ross Chia Pet for his birthday ("It's

already sprouting!"), and for her care package (a bird-themed needlepoint kit and a handmade coupon for a steak burger with cheese at LA's Apple Pan diner, hoping to convince her to visit soon).

Clara and I spend the first hour of our lunch date getting caught up on our personal lives. She loves her job, the SoCal weather—she was raised in Alaska, but left as soon as she could for sunny shores—and recently decided to take a year off of dating because she found Californians a touch too "precious." I joke that she might prefer life in the Adirondacks, where "rugged" is an often-seen trait.

"I LOVE YOUR tattoo," Clara says, and I look to my right arm and the new artwork that adorns it. The piece is fine-lined and stretches delicately halfway up my forearm, incorporating my scar. I love it, too—because it reminds me about who I am . . . or at least who I'm trying to become. Less afraid and more resilient, my own roots anchored with newfound strength.

"Thanks." I run a finger over the design, feeling the ridge of my now-hidden scar under the tree trunk's striations, the black-inked evergreen boughs deeply hued against my skin. It has almost entirely healed. I haven't told Clara what happened in the woods yet, or why this particular tattoo is so meaningful. I'm saving that for the working part of our lunch, because it's relevant to the idea I want to share with her.

"So, are you ready to talk shop?" I ask, clicking my pen open and setting its tip against the blank page. A tiny dot of ink blooms, and I stare at it for a moment. Gathering my courage. Yes, Clara is a friend, and so in many ways this is a soft pitch. Even if she hates the idea, I know she'll let me down easy. Still, my nerves hum like a nest of busy bees.

"Ready . . . just as soon as I top up our glasses." Clara picks up the bottle of wine from the chilling bucket, tiny droplets of ice water landing on the glossy wood table. "Okay, the floor is yours. Go for it, Rowan."

"So, I know we were discussing something else. The script I pitched you earlier this year, about the prophecy-after-lightning-strike woman?"

Clara nods, sipping her refreshed wine.

"I'd like to put a pin in that one because I have another script in mind, and it's a stronger concept. The hook is undeniable with this one."

"*Tell me more*," Clara says, resting her chin in her hand. I have her full attention now.

"Something fairly unbelievable happened to me while I was away this summer. I haven't talked about it, and hardly anyone knows, but I have been writing about it." I've been doing nothing *but* writing for weeks, actually. "I promise that you and Robbie will want this script before I take it anywhere else."

I pause briefly to take a sip of my wine, allowing the moment to build.

I have rehearsed this dozens of times, to the point where I have it so fine-tuned it flows out of me naturally, as though I'm telling it for the first time. This is important for the pitch because I need Clara to feel the energy, excitement, and possibility—the pull of both tragedy and optimism. It must appear effortless; no story deserves more to be told.

"Right after I found out what Seth did to your email, I took off—I ran out of the cabin—because I felt like I was suffocating, you know?"

Clara mutters, "That bastard." I see now that she's one of *those* women—the sort of friend who always takes your side and has your back. No matter if you might be partially to blame, or whether you deserve that level of unflinching support, she'll offer it freely and without question.

"So I took off, not clear on where I was going except deeper into the woods—the only place I could escape to out there."

Clara nods, her eyes not leaving mine. I don't blink.

"But it turns out I wasn't alone that day, in the forest. And what happened next—what I *found*—changed me . . . probably forever."

"What did you find?" Clara takes another sip of wine, but seems rapt.

"An old jewelry box, hidden in a tree hollow, full of hundred-dollar bills. And then, only feet away from that . . . a body."

Clara's mouth opens in shock, and I push on, even though no matter how many times I have rehearsed this part, I still have trouble controlling my emotions. My hands tingle, goose bumps erupting across my skin. I'm nearly certain if I turn to my right, Eddie Callaway herself will be seated there—grinning, chin in hand, red bandanna taming her wild curls as she waits for her story to be told. A slight nod of her head to let me know she's ready whenever I am.

"But it's about so much more than a buried treasure and a skeleton, Clara," I continue. "It's about a woman who tried to change the world, in her own way and on her own terms, before she disappeared without a trace in 1975. So, let me tell you about Eddie Callaway . . ."

DECEMBER.

A COUPLE OF WEEKS AFTER MY LUNCH WITH Clara—with whom I'm now working on a script about Camp Callaway, and Eddie's life more specifically—I hit send on my story about the treasure, which includes a call for people to go find it. I purposely chose an independent magazine focused on hiking and other outdoorsy endeavors, but it didn't take long for the major news media to pick up the story. Judith's poem was included, too. We've stayed in touch, Judith and I, and I've booked a plane ticket to visit her and Marge in Florida in a few weeks. They're going to take me on a riverboat tour of the Everglades to see the alligators, and blow my mind (according to Judith) with Marge's key lime pie. I can't wait.

Judith has been a staunch supporter of my plan for the treasure since the moment I shared it with her. "I believe Eddie would be delighted with what you're doing, Rowan. Just delighted!"

After that call, where for almost two hours we discussed my idea, and she shared more stories about Eddie and the camp, she sent me an email I cherish. I've pinned it to the top of my inbox, and read it every morning.

Dearest Rowan,

I so enjoyed our talk. Thank you for sharing your wonderful idea with me! I can't help but think that if Eddie had done the same, and shared at least a few details of her plan with us, perhaps we would have had the clues to find her. However, I've lived long enough to know nothing good comes from marinating in regret. Instead, I'm choosing to look to the future, as Eddie would have wisely advised. Please know you are never alone in this next adventure, as you're now part of my personal "crew of misfits"!

Your friend,
Jude xo

Once news of a real hidden treasure in the Adirondack Park comes out, linked to the enigmatic Eddie Callaway, who disappeared in 1975, I'm inundated with interview requests—some paid, others simply offering significant platforms—all of which I turn down. The treasure box contains life-changing money—bundled stacks of bills, totaling $100,000 in cash—and so generates plenty of interest.

Yet soon enough the flurry of excitement turns to criticism, and I'm accused of fabricating the story. Of lying about the treasure, because I'm an "aspiring" screenwriter, a "media whore" looking for my fifteen minutes—even though I have photos of the box and its contents, which I released with the story. That physical proof doesn't convince everyone I'm not just making it all up, for reasons critics enjoy speculating about (all too boring to give an iota of energy to defending). Seth doesn't come forward to claim his role. I keep him anonymous, only sharing my side of the story, and we have no contact after the story publishes.

I've been back to the Adirondacks once since Seth and I left, just before moving to California. I rented the same cabin, just for a few days. It was strange returning, alone this time, as there were endless reminders of Seth and our time together, both good and bad.

But it was nice to see the crow, which remembered me, much to my delight. It would "caw-caw" from the porch railing if I was late with the morning peanuts. Before I left, I bought bags of peanuts in town, and tacked a note to the cupboard with a mention of the white-feather crow for future visitors. I also spent some time with Jess and Aidan and had breakfast at Glenda's diner, happy to see everyone doing well.

While I didn't return to the treasure's new hiding spot, I did hike to where I found Eddie. I sat on the edge of the embankment, with my legs dangling. From there I gave Eddie updates about the script, about my plans for the treasure hunt, about becoming fast friends with Judith. I thanked her for helping me find the untamed part of myself, my own "wild woman," who seems to be blossoming—now that I've gotten out of her way. I imagined what Eddie would say about all this, if she could.

Of course there's no way to guarantee only women will go hunting for the Callaway treasure, despite that having been of great importance to Eddie. But I like to think she would see how being more inclusive now makes sense—that we all deserve the thrill of an adventure, no matter our gender, race, age, or creed. I believe Eddie would be pleased to have so many people enjoying the woods she adored. Yes, the treasure is the point for most, but the by-products of the hunt can be wonderful. Connecting to nature, stepping away from the incessant noise of screens and modern life. Discovering truths about yourself you haven't yet been able to see and finding strength where you believed there was none.

Wasn't that the point all along?

So far, it appears that Jess and I chose the box's resting spot well. It has only been a couple of months, but the treasure remains hidden and undiscovered. Impervious to even the most dedicated and motivated hunters, of which there have been many (even now, with snow blanketing the forest). Apparently, according to Jess, Glenda's diner has been a hot spot for the treasure hunters to gather, most of whom I expect are enjoying both her homemade pies and friendly nature. Nestled in its bed of moss, the box tucked so cleverly out of sight in the notch of another tree, it might be another forty years—maybe longer, even—until the next lucky person arrives at the right place, at the right time.

Maybe this person meets a curious crow with a white wing feather that brings a clue in exchange for a peanut or two. Maybe, during a long, meandering morning hike, this individual casts their eyes to a seemingly insignificant spot among the trees . . . just as a sunbeam finding a path through the leaves illuminates the box's aqua-green patina, shining like a beacon against the trunk's rugged brown bark. And then, if that day comes, *when that day comes*, Eddie Callaway's wild woman legacy will finally be carried out of the woods.

"Better late than never," Eddie would probably say.

Look Up

Look Up
Into the arms
Of wooden branches
Encircling me.
In the meanders of this fullness
I look toward the light,
the sun that powers each of us where
all is warm and safe.
I close my eyes and hear whispers
of love? of peace? of belonging?
The undulating rustling of wind through pines.
Look down where roots are formed, through earth
To water that is sucked up as in straws toward the core
Giving life to that trunk, those branches, soft needles
To nurture in plenty. And here we are between sun and water
That nourish us, that flourish us. Yet we pay no heed
We desecrate this precious gift that's been given.
We pollute the waters and block the sun. Where is
our gratitude for this life we live in union,
with the forest, the planet?
Look Up. I am here.
I give thanks
In the quiet
meditation.
Looking
Inward

—Jude, 1975

Poem found in a Quik chocolate milk powder tin, discovered in an abandoned Camp Callaway cabin in 2021

ACKNOWLEDGMENTS

I turned fifty right around the time I was finishing up edits on this book. At times I can't believe I've only been writing novels for ten years . . . other times it's as though I've never done anything else. Each book has taught me something, but I've learned more from writing Rowan's and Eddie's stories than any of the others. Maybe it's because I relate to Rowan's ambition, to her desire to create something tangible "with legs" (and a heart) in a world perpetually driven by viral trends, 24/7 news cycles, and flavors of the moment. Or perhaps it's because I am on the cusp of the third act of my life, when women—too easily dismissed at every age—become nearly invisible, even as they brim with experience and wisdom (and clear humility about what they still *don't* know). In this way I identify most with Eddie, and include in that familiarity her insecurities, her curiosities, and her desire to understand. I write stories about women seeking and achieving agency, and this book is no exception. It is also a love letter of sorts to my 1970s hippie childhood, and the forests of my youth, in which I spent many hours exploring. In this story, birds have a leading role, inspired by a newfound obsession that began suddenly and joyously when I was forty-eight years old. I have come to see that turning into a birder is simply part of aging well, and I am here for it—and for whatever surprises come next. Now, words of gratitude for everyone who played a role in this book becoming a book. While I may sit alone with a story for a long time, its physical manifestation requires many advocates. Thank you to the best crew an author can have, including:

My editors, Maya Ziv and Lara Hinchberger, who have been fervent caretakers for this story from the beginning. I know they feel Eddie and Rowan as keenly as I do.

Those responsible for the behind-the-curtain magic, especially Lexy Cassola, Lauren Morrow, Amanda Walker, Stephanie Cooper, Nicole Jarvis, Christopher Lin, Mary Beth Constant, LeeAnn Pemberton, Gaelyn Galbreath, Ashley Tucker, Tiffany Estreicher, Sarah Oberrender, Susan Schwartz, Ryan Richardson, John Parsley, Christine Ball, Ruta Liormonas, Dan French, Bonnie Maitland, Nicole Winstanley, Kristin Cochrane, and Kathleen Carter.

Carolyn Forde and the team at Transatlantic Literary Agency. Carolyn, I feel confident I could text you at midnight with a note that reads, "We ride at dawn," and you'd be there on time, ready for an adventure. I couldn't do this without you.

My mom, Judith Woodburn-Schoenfeld, for the beautiful concrete poem she wrote for me, which is the same one that lives on the page as the character Jude's poem. I am a voracious reader and writer, among other things, because of you. My feminist dad, Bob Woodburn, for showing me what it means to be a seeker, and to be curious about this one, great life. Thank you both for taking me and Jenna to Camp Sagamore, which over forty years later became the inspiration for Camp Callaway and this story.

My dear friends and fellow authors, Ashley Audrain (thank you for Theo's bowling rhyme), Nicole Blades, Mary Kubica, Colleen Oakley, Amy E. Reichert, Jennifer Robson, Fiona Davis, Bryn Turnbull, Heather Marshall, and Heidi Sopinka for reading versions—early and later—of this book. Thanks also for your kind words, and for helping me keep my chin up.

Elan Mastai for questions about life as a screenwriter, and insights about the hierarchy that exists in that industry. David Peterson for a lively conversation about backyard vegetable gardening—maybe one day my black-thumbed self will grow something off the page. Taylor Jenkins Reid for sharing what it's like to be married to a fellow creative, and for a meaningful friendship that exists almost entirely through our message inbox.

Adam and Addie. You are the embodiment of my own Camp Callaway—a place I cherish, full of endless possibilities. Glad we get to do this wild life together.

Books I found useful as I was writing, in no particular order: *Women Who Run with the Wolves* (Clarissa Pinkola Estés, 1992); *Save the Cat! Writes a Novel* (Jessica Brody, 2018); *My Life on the Road* (Gloria Steinem, 2015); *The Feminine Mystique* (Betty Friedan, 1963); *Tidal Wave: How Women Changed America at Century's End* (Sara M. Evans, 2003); *Braiding Sweetgrass* (Robin Wall Kimmerer, 2013); *Great Camp Sagamore, The Vanderbilts' Adirondack Retreat* (Beverly Bridger, 2012); *Feminism Is for Everybody* (bell hooks, 2000); *The New York Times Natural Foods Cookbook* (Jean Hewitt, 1971); *Better Homes & Gardens Dessert Cook Book* (1967 edition), whose pineapple upside-down cake inspired Sam's recipe.

ABOUT THE AUTHOR

© NATALIE D'SOUZA

Karma Brown is the author of five novels: the #1 international bestseller *Recipe for a Perfect Wife, Come Away with Me* (a *Globe and Mail* Best Book of 2015), *Globe and Mail* and *Toronto Star* bestsellers *The Choices We Make* and *In This Moment,* and *The Life Lucy Knew.* She is also the author of the bestseller *The 4% Fix: How One Hour Can Change Your Life* and co-authored two holiday rom-coms under the pen name Maggie Knox. An award-winning journalist, Karma has been published in *SELF, Redbook,* and *Today's Parent,* among others. She lives just outside Toronto with her husband, teenage daughter, and a Labradoodle named Fred.